DESTINY OF THE DELBHANA

A MATRIARCHIES OF MUIRIN NOVEL

MEYARI MCFARLAND

MDR PUBLISHING

SPECIAL OFFER

The rainbow has infinite shades, just as this collection covers the spectrum of fictional possibilities.

From contemporary romances like *The Shores of Twilight Bay* to dark fantasy like *A Lone Red Tree* and out to SF futures in *Child of Spring, Iridescent* covers the gamut of time, space and genre.

Meyari McFarland shows her mastery in this first omnibus collection of her short fiction. Twenty-five amazing stories, all with queer characters going on adventures, solving mysteries, and falling in love are here in the first Rainbow Collection.

And now you can get this massive collection of short queer fiction, all of it with the happy endings you love, *for free!*

Sign up here for your free copy of Iridescent now!

CONTENTS

OTHER MATRIARCHIES OF MUIRIN STORIES:

In Reading Order:

The City of the Ladies
Fight Smarter
Hide and Seek
Stormy Arrival
Repair and Rebuild
Storm Over Archaelaos
Facing the Storm
Tea and Knives
Luck of the Dana
Homecoming
Delicate Introduction
Following the Beacon
Coming Together
The Solace of Her Clan
Running Before the Storm
Fighting the Morrigan's Hand
The Silk of the Guardian
Secrets in the Prayers
Fitting In

D2D ISBN: 978-1-64309-094-8

Cover image

ID 67864137 © Hsiu Chuan Yu | Dreamstime.com

ID 1504082 © Masta4650 | Dreamstime.com

ID 12236541 © 350jb | Dreamstime.com

This book is also available in TPB format from all major retailers.

❀ Created with Vellum

This collection is dedicated to my husband, yet again.

1. BUFFET PLOTTING

Raelin hummed as she strolled through the Dana ballroom towards the buffet table. The spring evening had turned humid rather than frigid so the windows had all been thrown open to the street. Sea salt mixed with the smell of the port, drowning out the smell of the huge bouquets of flowers that Father had arranged at every window.

At least there was a slight breeze. Otherwise they'd all be sweating through their clothes. Raelin dodged a dancing couple, the Delbhana woman in her scarlet and black smiling nastily as her poor dance partner nearly smacked into Raelin's bad shoulder. Rude of her to make him attempt to hurt Raelin but that was the Delbhana.

If it weren't Daire's wedding, not a single Delbhana would be there. For any other event, Mother wouldn't dream of inviting Delbhana. Every single other noble, certainly, but not Lady Etain or her vicious daughter Siobhan. Or any of the cousins that were left in the city.

None of the sane ones, the ones who cared about business more than politics, were left. Most of them were probably dead since the old Queen was dying and Siobhan was now officially a princess and heir to the throne.

Danica had disappeared a few months ago. Sinead, well, everyone believed Sinead was dead. Raelin kept her scowl firmly off her face for that one. She knew perfectly well where Sinead was, having smuggled her out of Aingeal and off to Atalya at the other end of the world.

Still, it was a problem that all the moderates in the Delbhana were being driven out, killed or beaten into submission. Dangerous for the Delbhana, worse for the country with Siobhan destined to be the queen after the old Queen died of her cancer, and worst still for the Dana.

She tried very hard not to frown about that as she dodged a pair of her older Aunts and Uncles dancing as vigorously as they possibly could, feet and elbows flying as they whirled at the Delbhana couple who'd almost run into Raelin. Maybe should intervene there. But probably not. Aunt Ita and her husband Uncle Murray were full adults in their fifties. They could handle themselves if it turned into a brawl in the middle of the ballroom.

Mother had warned everyone not to pick fights but Aunt Ita was anything but levelheaded. Uncle Murray wasn't much better. The two of them were almost as bad as Anwyn about picking fights. Raelin wasn't surprised when the Delbhana couple fled the dance floor rather than get close to Aunt Ita and Uncle Murray. Just made them grin wider and dance like they were twelve as they continued around the ballroom.

Oh well, as long as they were having fun.

It wasn't every day Dana Daire, youngest brother of Dana Laoise, married. After a full year engagement with what seemed like plots to stop the wedding every single day, they were due a good time. Though maybe not quite this much of a celebration.

His marriage to Ruadh Caitlin promised to be the event of the year. Instead of one wedding feast with both families and their friends present, Daire's wedding was turning into a week-long celebration of the Dana and Ruadh Clans' power and generosity. Tonight was the first feast, the first party, and every single one of Raelin's siblings, aunts and uncles was there. They'd all been called back from across the globe to be there for the wedding even though Raelin would much rather be up in Atalya making sure the Sinead was all right.

Even Anwyn, who glowered at the Delbhana from the spot she'd put herself near the punch bowl, was home. She glowered at Raelin, too, as Raelin walked over. Annie's eyes skipped over the dramatic scarring marring Raelin's cheek, took in the formal coat and pants and high-gloss boots that Raelin had shoved her feet into, and then snorted.

Annie was just as formally dressed but she'd managed to rumple her cravat and her pants were wrinkled like she'd been hauling bales of silk off a ship. Where Raelin had put serious effort into smoothing down her horribly curly hair, Annie's hair was a wild mass of curls that made her look like her head was on fire.

Matched her temper at least.

"You could go talk to people," Raelin suggested as she carefully poured herself a glass of punch. The damage that scarred her cheek extended down her shoulder, arm and side. Her arm was still weak and her control wasn't the best but she managed not to drop the glass or spill the punch so it was good enough. Half a glass was better than none and it didn't look like Anwyn was going to offer to pour for Raelin.

"I'm not talking to anyone," Anwyn declared so ferociously that Raelin rolled her eyes. "Siobhan's here. I'm staying right here. If I do anything, Siobhan'll turn it into a huge fight and it'll mess up Daire's wedding. I won't do that."

"I'm not saying you're wrong," Raelin said, turning to study the crowded ballroom, "but you are paranoid."

"Justified," Anwyn replied.

She truly wasn't wrong. Ever since Anwyn was seven, she'd been at war with Delbhana Siobhan, then heir to the Delbhana Clan and now destined to be the next Queen of Aingeal. They'd fought each other long before that, truthfully. Putting the two of them in the same room was like mixing oil and a lit torch. But after Anwyn accepted Siobhan's dare to go out to the City of the Ladies on the river, it had gotten so much worse.

For everyone. The Delbhana, terrified of the Ladies' power, had banned everything related to them. Then they'd banned the old religion, as much as they could. Eliminating the worship of the Goddesses Chin, Tahira and Ragna was more or less impossible, but they'd done their best.

Everyone associated with the old ways was fined. Taxed. Harassed and pestered until they changed their ways. If you tried to keep the old ways, you risked imprisonment anymore. All the Clans objected. Well, most of them. The Delbhana had their hangers-on and allies. They seemed clear to sail straight through this storm.

The Dana? Not so much. But then no one in the Dana had ever shirked at work or backed down from a fight, even with it was in their better interest. So Annie deciding that she'd stay in a corner rather than properly celebrate Daire's wedding was saying a lot. Even Anwyn's fierce determination was getting worn down by the Delbhana onslaught.

Raelin looked at Siobhan, off on the exact opposite side of the ballroom. She stood, bright and smiling in her flaming red jacket, pristine white shirt and tight black pants, and snarled a 'smile' in their direction. Prince Toryn stood by her side, lips pinched and brows drawn together in a scowl that was directed fully at Siobhan. Not that Siobhan noticed. She'd never cared what anyone thought of her.

Other than Anwyn.

Siobhan stared at Anwyn like she was staring into the eyes of the Morrigan herself and daring the Morrigan to reach her claw-like hands out to claim her soul. Would be nice if the Morrigan would. Raelin sipped her punch, nodding approvingly at the mix of spices and good rum. Father had done a great job with this batch. Not too strong, good flavor.

"How can you just stand there, drinking punch?" Anwyn hissed at Raelin.

"Father did a good job with it," Raelin said. She shrugged at Anwyn's disgusted snort. "Well, he did. You're doing a lovely job scaring everyone away from the punch bowl, Annie. Someone should appreciate it."

Anwyn froze, mouth half-open for a snappish retort. She looked around, realized that there was a good three yards between her and the nearest guests, and then groaned. Dramatically. While blushing as bright as their red hair.

"I didn't mean to scare people off the buffet," Anwyn complained. She pouted at Raelin as if she was six instead of seventeen.

"No, I'm sure you didn't," Raelin said, sipping the punch again to keep from grinning outright. "Come on. I'll chaperone you. Not even Siobhan is going to pick a fight with crippled old me."

"You're only nineteen," Anwyn said. She huffed when Raelin batted her eyes in an innocent look that only Aravel, Raelin's twin, could have carried off. "You're two years older than me, Rae. Stop acting like you're Great-Uncle Jarmon's age."

"No one's his age," Raelin said, getting an amused snort out of Anwyn.

She prodded Anwyn into getting a cup of punch and then into refilling Raelin's glass for her. Then they set off around the ballroom together, Anwyn watching Siobhan who watched her right back and Raelin smiling and making polite small talk to all the guests they encountered. Who did their best to ignore Anwyn and Siobhan circling each other like sharks going after the same kill, tentacles out and violent reds and purples flashing over their skins.

"I'm surprised that it's not a proper dinner," commented Lady Fiora from the Ruadh Clan. "I had thought that Laoise had decided to have the dinner and then celebrate for the rest of the week."

She'd chosen a lovely formal coat in a striking dark green that complemented her coloring perfectly. The embroidery on it, all gold and silver, had to add another ten pounds to the outfit. A year's wages for Raelin on the Tourmaline Dreams, sitting on her lapels and cuffs. Such extravagance.

"Well, after the courtship Uncle Daire and Caitlin had," Raelin said, moving so that she blocked Anwyn from going off by herself, "they're entitled to a bit more than the normal wedding, I suppose. Years of pining for each other and a full year since the engagement. Took that long to get everyone on their side and ours into the city for the wedding. Also, you know Mother. Any chance to rub our wealth in Lady Etain's face is a good chance."

Lady Fiora grinned suddenly. "Very true. I was actually quite surprised to see both of you here. The gossip was that neither of you would be allowed back into the city for any reason. You, especially, Raelin. Punching a Delbhana in the face is generally not the best idea."

"Not like I've got the strength in my right arm to do any damage anymore," Raelin said as she shrugged and moved again, along with Lady Fiora, locking Anwyn into a corner between them and one of the chairs of the old uncles along the wall. Anwyn glowered at them but stopped trying to escape from the small talk. Not that she tried to join in. Of course not. She was seventeen, after all. Sulking was more important.

"Mother tried to insist that we were needed out at sea but Great-Uncle Jarmon refused to hear it," Raelin said even though it was the other way around. "We were all recalled. Everyone in the direct family line is here right now. I think that this is the first time in a generation that all of our ships are in port at once. Our dock is scarily crowded right now. But we'll be heading back out in a week after Daire's safely married to Caitlin."

They all looked across the room to where Daire was leaning against Caitlin's side, the two of them looking as incandescently happy as any true love match couple could. Which they were. There were treaty things in the background, negotiations that kept the Ruadh from being true contracted allies to the Dana, but the two of them looked as happy as it was possible to be.

From the way Lady Fiora smiled, she was pleased with her cousin's match. They weren't close relatives, second or third cousins twice removed, but she'd done well for Caitlin once everyone accepted that she'd marry no one other than Daire. The price for her to join the Dana promised to be truly earth-shaking, not that Mother had revealed it yet.

The big issue was that Caitlin was joining the Dana. Not Daire joining the Ruadh. If it'd been the other way around, they probably would've been married in days instead of years.

Lady Fiora chuckled, shaking her head at them. "Your family does manage to make good marriages. It's a wonder. Pity you're so stingy about allowing your men to marry out. It didn't used to be that way. Old Lady Mab was saying just yesterday that in her day Dana men were highly sought after."

Instead of answering, Raelin nodded slowly. She sipped her punch, scanning the ballroom. Women clustered around Raelin's twin brother, Aravel. He looked utterly delighted by the attention as long as you didn't know him. Raelin could see how tense he was, the way he giggled and flirted in a completely brainless fashion that promised absolutely nothing while still enthralling the women talking to him.

Anwyn's brother Cadfael had on the widest kilt, buoyed out by dozens of petticoats, that Raelin had ever seen. He danced, sharp and sour-faced, with a Griogal woman who had to lean over a bit to be able to hold his hand as they spun around each other. She spent more time staring at her feet so that she didn't step on the fortune's worth of lace and ribbon decorating his kilt and petticoats.

Caddie's lace 'armor' kept women at bay. It didn't stop the hungry way the guests watched him. Andros, all of eleven and still in little boy's short kilts, was tucked tight against Father's side. He wouldn't look at the teenaged woman trying to flirt with him.

Same was true all over the ballroom. The guests, all

different clans including Delbhana, flirted and seduced, trying to get the Dana men to their side. Raelin hummed as she lowered the now-empty cup. Something was up. Another plot and this time Raelin didn't have her source of information inside the Delbhana to rely on.

Not that it was going to stop her from figuring it out. One way or the other.

2. HIDDEN CURRENTS

Anwyn's head throbbed as she stood in the corner with Lady Fiora and Raelin. Neither of them were being honest. Raelin was doing the social thing, chatting and smiling and making nice while fishing for information. Lady Fiora radiated fear even as she smiled and laughed at Raelin's little joke about stubborn men making up their own minds.

All the while, Siobhan stalked around the far side of the room, thinking of murder.

Damn her to the Morrigan's hands, how could no one else see what she was? All she cared about was hurting people. Men in particular. Prince Toryn, all but chained to her side by Siobhan's firm grip on his waist, had several spots that throbbed with pain. He didn't show it. Temper, annoyance at Siobhan, but the pain?

No.

That didn't show at all, even when Siobhan dug her fingers into what had to be a cracked rib on his left side. Prince Toryn lifted his chin, smiled nastily at Siobhan, and controlled the wince that Anwyn could feel from across the room.

"I do wonder what changed," Lady Fiora said to Raelin, all but screaming a warning that couldn't, wouldn't slip past her lips.

Raelin shrugged, suddenly highly aware of where every single man in the ballroom was. "I'd say that society changed, actually. In Lady Mab's day, men were educated much like women. They held jobs. Opened shops. Held their own property and had full legal status in the world. Now, well. It's not the same. I'm not surprised that our men have no desire to leave our Clan when they know they'll lose their money, their freedom and their rights."

Lady Fiora jerked. Very slightly but enough that Anwyn saw it. So did Raelin. She nodded to Lady Fiora whose shoulders dropped and breathing eased.

Message received and understood.

Oh, great. Siobhan and the Delbhana were plotting to get the boys again? Why? They'd failed every single time they'd tried. Gavin wasn't going to let that happen.

Anwyn scanned the ballroom and found Gavin standing with his wife Mari by his side. They were by the buffet table, smiling fixedly at Murphy Elva who sneered right back at them. Elva didn't try and walk past them to get at Eoghania and her husband Sean but she clearly wanted to.

Gavin wasn't aware of the plot. Mother wasn't either. She was too busy arguing animatedly with old Lady Mab about something. Silk prices by the feel of it. No, silk from Chinwendu and whether it could be dyed by the new pigments that the Delbhana had brought in from the north.

No one was aware of this new plot. Anwyn moved to slip away again only to be blocked by both Lady Fiora and Raelin. Again.

"I don't have to stay by your side, Rae," Anwyn snapped at her.

"Mmm, no," Raelin said with a little smirk that twisted the nasty patch of scars on her cheek. "But I think it's probably better to keep you solidly away from the buffet table right now."

"I didn't want to go to the buffet table," Anwyn complained. "Siobhan's over there. I wanted to go grumble at Mother."

"Princess Siobhan," Lady Fiora corrected. She held up a hand when Anwyn huffed at her. "I know, I know. The two of you have history. That doesn't excuse failing to use her title."

Anwyn snorted at that. "Like I care about what Siobhan thinks."

She crossed her arms over her chest and glowered at Lady Fiora. Instead of an apology or even a smile, Lady Fiora frowned at her. With fear in her heart. It radiated out of her, like she'd suddenly turned into a torch whose flames were fear.

"It's not a matter of whether you think Princess Siobhan wants you to say it or not," Lady Fiora said so sternly that Raelin snapped to attention and Anwyn winced. "She is the princess. She is heir to the throne. And until there is a new dynasty, may the Goddesses grant that it is a long run in the future, her position demands respect."

No matter what Anwyn or Lady Fiora thought of the person holding the position. The fear was tainted with disgust at Siobhan, with horror at what Siobhan would do to Aingeal when the old Queen died. Couldn't blame Lady Fiora for that. Siobhan was one of the Morrigan's devils made human, no doubt about that.

"...You ask a lot," Anwyn said, doing her best pout at

Lady Fiora. "I'm not going to forget her trying to kick my ribs in, you know."

"Annie," Raelin said. The gently scolding tone was honest, true to the core, and three times as painful because of it. "No one expects that. But you still need to use the title. And not in a sarcastic tone of voice, either. If Caddie can do it, so can you."

Anwyn groaned at that, rolling her eyes so dramatically that both Lady Fiora and Raelin lit with amusement at her. Yeah, sometimes being visibly a teenager was a great way to distract people. Annoying most of the time but sometimes it was useful.

Siobhan spiked with fury across the room, all of it aimed at Anwyn. Seriously, how the heck had she figured out that they were talking about her? Oh, no, it was just that someone else commented about Anwyn and thus Siobhan got angry. Didn't take much at all for her to do that. She was as volatile as the southern seas and twice as dangerous as rainbow sharks in spring off the point of Minoo.

"Fine," Anwyn said, arms crossed over her chest and teenager pout firmly in place. "I'll be polite. When I say her name, I'll use her title."

Raelin stared at Anwyn for just long enough that Anwyn's cheeks went red. "You're not going to use her name anymore, are you?"

Lady Fiora burst out laughing. She slapped Anwyn's back hard enough to rock Anwyn then walked off towards the buffet table, still snickering. Thankfully, Raelin let her go. Weird part was that she promptly stopped to talk to one of the cousins. One of the male cousins.

But not like she was interested in him.

Well, she acted like she was interested but the emotions coming off her were all weird and reluctant. Anwyn grumbled, nudging Raelin's bad elbow gently. Got her a frown from Raelin and then a slow nod towards Mother who was still arguing with old Lady Mab like they weren't ever going to stop.

"Plotting," Anwyn murmured.

"I noticed," Raelin said. "Any idea what?"

"Mmm, seems like getting the Dana men," Anwyn said, quiet enough that no one would hear but not a whisper because that was painfully noticeable in a party like this. "Lady Fiora doesn't want to do it. Most of the other women, yeah, they do. Must be something the Delbhana set up because their allies are doing most of the really determined flirting."

Always amused Anwyn that Raelin saw things that Anwyn sensed, but without the gift of the Ladies. She'd nodded, her heart already clear that it was a plot to steal the men, even though she only had her eyes and ears to go on. Yet again, the gift of the Ladies was more trouble than it was worth.

Not that Anwyn would ever try to give it back. She was who she was and it was and would always be a part of her.

Even when Siobhan made Anwyn's life miserable over it.

"It has to work on spider silk," old Lady Mab exclaimed as they got to Mother's side. Father shook his head, smiled at Raelin, frowned at Anwyn and then snorted as Mother threw up her hands in disgust.

"No, it doesn't 'have to' work," Mother half-shouted with a huge grin and nothing but delight coming off her. "Spider silk is picky. Those pigments are picky. Some of them work. Some don't. You can't assume that you're gonna get a perfect result from every single color, no matter what the Delbhana say."

"A quick word, Mother?" Raelin asked.

Politely. Quietly. In that 'no, this isn't a request' way that only Raelin had. Nobody else in the clan had the ability to draw Mother's sails up that sharply, tacking her so hard that she all but went keel-up in mid-sentence.

"Ah, sure?" Mother said, blinking at Raelin.

Rae passed her empty glass to Anwyn, pulled Mother off into the hallway and left Anwyn to huff at their backs. Old Lady Mab chuckled, nodding towards Anwyn.

"Gonna punch her when she gets back?" Lady Mab asked. And then grinned at Anwyn's glare.

"No, I'm not going to punch Raelin," Anwyn said. "Her right arm's no good for hitting with anymore but that left is still like the thunder of the Goddesses landing right on your head. Nobody picks a fight with Rae. Anyway, you're not looking for a boy to marry off to one of your great-granddaughters? Seems like everyone's looking to get married tonight. I mean, there's more flirting going on than Daire and Caitlin managed over all the years for their relationship so far."

Lady Mab jerked. Hard. Two spots of color flared on her cheeks as pure panic swept across her. Father saw it. Scanned the room. Glowered and then huffed at Anwyn as if she'd done something wrong.

Except that no, he didn't think she'd done anything wrong. Just that she'd been too blunt about it. As if anyone would ever believe Anwyn being polite and political about things.

"My girls don't need a Dana man," Lady Mab declared.

"Well, they do fight about as much as we do," Anwyn said with a little nod like that made sense. "No reason to make it worse by breeding brawling into brawling. Better to breed some common sense into the brawling line."

"I just wish that we could find someone with enough common sense to match you, Annie," Father said. He said it loud enough that the people not officially listening in but actually listening in grinned. Heads turned away so that Anwyn wouldn't see and get angry at them.

"Oh, Father," Anwyn said, deliberately as disappointed in him as possible because Lady Mab started cackling. "You'd have to find someone as even-tempered as Rae and as stubborn as Caddie. I just don't think that exists."

Made both of them stare and then Father was cackling along with Lady Mab. The people around them snickered, laughed, giggled, too. Good. Anwyn put on a scowl, well aware of the laughter and, more importantly, aware that Siobhan focused on Anwyn instead of on Raelin and Mother coming back into the ballroom with way too serious of faces.

The laughter swelled, then ebbed, as Cadfael swept up on the arm of his thoroughly intimidated lady. Anwyn didn't recognize her. One of the minor Delbhana, red coat, blond hair, pale face that was even paler because Cadfael dropped her arm like she was coated with fire ants.

"You don't have any punch?" Cadfael snapped at Anwyn.

"Nope, drank all of this," Anwyn said. She snorted as the Delbhana woman escaped post-haste. You'd've thought that she'd been caught in a riptide. "One of them was Raelin's. She dumped it on me. And no, I'm not getting you any punch, Caddie. That Delbhana is over by the buffet table so I'm not going."

Caddie looked, blinked, and then turned back to Anwyn with a purely disgusted expression. "Just say her name, Annie. Goodness, you are so ridiculous. Prince Toryn looks like he could do with a break. I should go talk to him."

"Go right ahead," Anwyn said. She shoved the glasses into his hands, much to his disgust. "I'm staying here."

Raelin shook her head and reclaimed both of the cups even though her right hand didn't look like it had a proper grip on the cup's delicate little handle. "I'll go with you, Caddie. It's good punch. I was hoping for more."

"At least one of my sisters knows her responsibilities," Caddie said with a little sniff of disapproval that was mostly for show. He felt of nothing more than the desire to escape the party and go back upstairs to his embroidery.

"I know my responsibilities," Anwyn declared so firmly that she got looks from everyone, Caddie included. "Don't pick a fight. Don't let anyone pick a fight with me. And please, for the love of the Goddesses, don't pick a fight."

Even Cadfael laughed at that one. He and Raelin headed off across the ballroom together, Caddie clinging to Rae's arm as if she'd protect him from the women schooling around him like sharks. It wouldn't work. Anwyn could feel it. Something was up and none of their men were safe.

3. PUNCH CONSIDERATIONS

"You do realize that they're trying to steal us again, don't you?" Cadfael murmured as they made their way across the ballroom.

He sailed across the floor like their biggest ship, skirt billowing around him with such aggressive flare that people parted before him with frightened looks. It was an interesting sensation, escorting Caddie at a party. Raelin usually avoided the sorts of parties that Caddie went to. She preferred to be at sea, first and always, and the politics that Caddie got dragged into as a matter of course made her head hurt. Her stomach, too.

"Certainly," Raelin replied. "Lady Fiora was all but screaming about it. Pretty sure Annie figured it out, too."

"One would hope," Cadfael said with a disapproving little sniff that made Raelin grin and Siobhan, who was at the punch bowl now, glower. "Oh, good, do pour us some, Princess Siobhan."

"One would think you could do that yourself," Siobhan said as snappishly as Cadfael while glaring at Prince Toryn who just raised his chin. "But then there are those kilts of yours. Can you even get close to the buffet table?"

"Of course not," Cadfael said before raising his chin just like Prince Toryn just had. "How else am I supposed to keep handsy women at bay? This much lace and ribbon is the best armor a man my size has. Prince Toryn at least could punch a woman and knock her down. All you'd have to do is put your hand on my forehead and I'd be doomed."

Prince Toryn started snickering. He raised one hand to cover his grin, taking the cup of punch Siobhan shoved at him with the other. Raelin rolled her eyes and gave her two cups to Siobhan who filled them with poor grace. At least until she sipped the punch and then she smiled.

"Much better than expected," Siobhan said, filling her cup a second time.

"Father does make an excellent punch," Raelin agreed. She turned to Cadfael who sipped his punch with slit-eyed approval. Or maybe that was slit-eyed wariness as he watched all the women in the room. "If you wanted someone to protect you while you got punch you should have asked Annie."

"And get blood from the fist fights all over my new kilt?" Cadfael asked with complete outrage that didn't look at all forced. "Absolutely not. I'm surprised Mother hasn't tethered Annie to her side. She looks ready to bash skulls and slit throats and all she's doing is standing there in the corner. All night. What sort of wedding celebration is it when all you do is stand around?"

Raelin nodded at that. Seen from the other side of the room, Anwyn did look like her own personal thunderstorm had stationed itself over her head. There was still a several yard clearing around her as people avoided talking to or acknowledging her. She had to wonder if Anwyn realized that her very attitude was what made people act so hostilely to her.

Other than Siobhan, of course, who glowered at Anwyn as if she wanted to be the first person to punch her.

"You promised not to fight at the party," Prince Toryn hissed at Siobhan.

"No, really?" Cadfael asked. He stared at Prince Toryn and then at Siobhan whose cheeks went flaming red. "Goodness, I'm shocked. I'm going to lose that bet with Aravel. Darn it."

Siobhan's mouth opened, then shut. She stared at Cadfael, then looked to Raelin while blinking rapidly. Raelin shrugged.

"I can't help you there," Raelin said. "I never bet on things. Seems a perfect waste of money to me."

"Not money," Cadfael said. "If I win, Aravel knits me a new lace shawl with the pattern of my choice. If he wins, I embroider him a new petticoat decorated with, ah, well. Let's just say its to be embroidered with Aravel's favorite things."

He flipped his free hand then drank the rest of his punch and set the cup down. Without difficulty because he somehow bent the vast bell of his kilts so that he could step to the buffet and then away without brushing the kilts against anything. Raelin just about swallowed her tongue. For more than one reason.

She turned at stared at Aravel who was still flirting with about twelve different women, only two of which were of a vaguely proper age.

"He wants petticoats decorated by women's vulvas?" Raelin hissed at Cadfael.

"What?" Siobhan gasped.

"...I can see that," Prince Toryn said and then rolled his

eyes when Siobhan glared at him. "For Aravel. Goodness, he's practically a prostitute."

"Oh, no, not at all," Cadfael said while Raelin pondered taking some of Anwyn's habits to heart and punching both Siobhan and every single woman flirting with Aravel. "He's certainly as enthusiastic about sex as I'm not. No one can deny that. But he doesn't bed anyone and he's quite careful about siring children. He said something about preferring to use fingers and his tongue a bit back that I'm steadfastly refusing to understand so don't you explain it, either of you."

He wagged a scolding finger at Siobhan who was turning purple with outrage and Prince Toryn who was snickering at Cadfael. And Raelin, who suspected that her face was nearly as purple as Siobhan's.

"If you don't stop talking about that right now," Raelin said through her clenched teeth, "I'm going to be the one to start the fights."

"Rae," Cadfael said, patting her right arm with fond condescension that she only then realized was completely fake, "you don't start fights. You end them. If you throw the first punch, there won't be a second."

Raelin glared at him, forcing herself to push the idea of her twin wearing petticoats with vulvas away. And the idea of all those women seducing him away from the clan. And everything else, Anwyn, the party, everything.

What was Caddie trying to distract Siobhan from? Or was he communicating with Prince Toryn? They were friends, sort of. More like distant rivals, frankly, though that was far more their twin places as the pinnacles of fashion and society as the two richest and most fashionable men in all of Aingeal.

She rolled her eyes, very deliberately, turned away as if she was about to start yelling and didn't want to. Siobhan was huffing with outrage. Most of the women who had been seducing Dana men looked hesitant as Raelin swept the room with as stern a glare as she could manage at the moment. The women looked... a bit frightened. Worried, even.

And there was the reason why.

Gwen had just swept in with Nolan on her arm. Where Caddie and Prince Toryn were bedecked in lace and ribbon, skirts belled out to frankly ridiculous levels, Nolan's outfit was the definition of discretion. Calm distinction. The sort of class and breeding that neither Dana nor Delbhana men were known for.

He wore Dana blue, of course, shot through with gold and silver threads that Rae knew had to be hand-sewn in. Instead of dozens of petticoats and miles of lace, Nolan had kilts only a yard or so wide at the ankle with one wide band of ribbon along the bottom of his kilt adding a touch of shine. His shirt was plain white with a thin ribbon of the same sapphire blue edging it. The vest, necessary for any man, had a single line of buttons rather than the currently fashionable double-breasted version with huge lapels that both Prince Toryn and Caddie wore.

Even his embroidery was muted, tone-on-tone with sapphire blue instead of gold or silver threads like Cadfael. Prince Toryn's elaborate brightly colored embroidery on his vest looked positively garish compared to the slender line of abstract swirls Noland had on his vest.

"How does he do that?" Cadfael complained to Prince Toryn.

"I know, he walks in and every single eye is on him." Prince Toryn huffed and then laughed quietly. "It's so frustrating. He thinks he's plain and yet the commands the room without even trying. And here he comes, dragging Gwen along with him. No fighting. You promised."

"Still don't think that was a fair promise to force me to make," Siobhan muttered just quietly enough that Raelin heard it but perhaps neither Caddie nor Prince Toryn did.

They ignored it, one way or the other. Raelin stepped back as both Caddie and Prince Toryn stepped towards Nolan, smiling as Nolan held out his hands and smiled at them both with clear joy. Gwen smiled ruefully and joined Rae and Siobhan at the punch bowl.

"Look at you," Nolan said, staring at Cadfael and then Prince Toryn with admiration. "You look wonderful. I love that lace, Caddie. And Prince Toryn, your vest is perfect."

They started talking about where they'd gotten the fabric and lace and who'd done the sewing, both Cadfael and Prince Toryn rightfully admiring Nolan's simple outfit. Raelin shook her head in amazement, then nodded as Gwen silently offered to refill both her and Siobhan's cups.

"Every time," Gwen murmured, stationing herself so that Raelin was between her and Siobhan. "Every single time the three of them get together it's mutual admiration society. I don't know how they do that."

"I wish they wouldn't," Siobhan grumbled.

She looked like she wanted to drag Prince Toryn away but was mildly worried about getting stabbed if she tried. Honestly, Caddie might try to hurt her for it. For that matter, Prince Toryn probably would even though he'd be beaten for it in private.

"It's Nolan," Raelin said, shrugging. "He's oil on the waters, calming everything down. The man works miracles without half trying. Worth every penny you paid for his hand, Gwen."

"Don't I know it," Gwen said with an utterly besotted smile.

Raelin sighed at her. Loudly. Obnoxiously. With

enough force that Siobhan snorted a laugh into her cup of punch. Thankfully, while Father had done a lovely job creating the punch, it wasn't heavy on the alcohol. Siobhan would have to drink a dozen more cups before she got tipsy enough to throw fists in all directions with no provocation.

As long as Anwyn and Gwen stayed away and polite, respectively.

"What?" Gwen demanded with just the right level of annoyance for it to be playing to Siobhan's desire for Dana discord rather than her getting ready to punch Raelin in the face.

"Must you?" Raelin asked. "Some of us don't have any desire to have your lovesick attitude drop its load on our heads."

She made sure that her head was turned so that Siobhan couldn't see the roll of Raelin's eyes. Hopefully it would be enough to prevent an immediate fight. Though with Nolan there, there was less likelihood of a fight. From Gwen at least. Nolan did a lovely job keeping Gwen on an even keel.

"Well, forgive me for being in love," Gwen huffed. She rolled her eyes right back so maybe she got it, maybe not. "He's perfect."

She went red as Raelin's flat stare matched up with Siobhan's glower. Not that she tensed or made a fist but then Nolan did step to her side, hooking his arm through her elbow. Nolan's smile was so rueful that Raelin backed off half a step and Siobhan smiled back just as ruefully.

"I do apologize for interrupting your conversation, Princess Siobhan," Nolan said in the least apologetic tone possible. "We need to go get Gavin and Mari. I'm afraid there's a very minor issue."

"Who broke what during Daire's wedding party?" Gwen immediately asked.

"Don't go there," Cadfael said so snappishly that Raelin stiffened, too. "No, not you, Rae. This is fully a Gwen thing."

"Ah," Raelin said. "Well, that means you don't get to go either Caddie."

He snorted, tossed his head which made the gems nestled into his flaming curls gleam and then smiled so nastily that Prince Toryn willingly stepped to Siobhan's side. She immediately seized his wrist. Not too roughly but with enough force to make it clear he wouldn't be leaving her side for the rest of the night.

Poor man.

"I have more sense than to get mixed up in this one," Cadfael declared. "Come on. I need to go dance with more idiots who think they're charming. The least you can do is drive Anwyn to be a tiny bit sociable. It'll distract everyone from the problem."

Raelin pressed her lips together as she bowed to Prince Toryn, then to Siobhan who nodded grandly like she was the one getting respect. Prince Toryn's eyes wrinkled at the edges but it wasn't a smile. At all.

"I suppose that's my cue to go haul line on the gossip patrol," Raelin said. "Do enjoy the evening, your Highnesses. Someone should. I certainly won't be."

Caddie hooked Raelin's good elbow and hauled her away, barely giving Raelin time to put the cup down on the table where the used ones went. As he pulled her away, she heard Siobhan's snotty laugh. It almost drowned out Prince Toryn's annoyed hiss at her to behave.

Interestingly, the number of women flirting with Dana men was significantly less. There were still looks, significant glances. But no one was ardently pursing a Dana man, now. Or, more accurately, only the normal, expected, women were pursuing Dana men, instead of everyone.

"What did Nolan do?" Raelin murmured to Caddie.

"I have no idea yet," Caddie said. "I'm going after Lady Bethany's idiot daughter. Keep watch on us as we dance. And make sure to tell Anwyn to glare at her extra hard. She always tries to get handsy during slower dances. We're due for one next."

And, because Caddie knew the musician's schedule of dances better than they did, he was quite right. It was a slow dance. Lady Bethany looked cautious about the dance while her daughter leered outright at Caddie. For perhaps two whole seconds before Anwyn growled and Raelin cleared her throat.

"Let's go," Cadfael snapped, seizing her hand and pulling her out onto the dance floor so sharply that she stumbled and nearly stepped on his kilt hem. "Do be careful. That lace is worth more than your entire year's share of Clan-Crannach's profits."

"...I'm almost sorry for her," Raelin murmured to Lady Bethany. "Pity she ended up in a slow dance with Caddie. She's doomed to step on that lace."

"I'm surprised you spoke with Princess Siobhan so... calmly," Lady Bethany replied with a nod and then a wince for the first hem-stomping.

Raelin shrugged. "I've never been the one to battle with Princess Siobhan. That was Sinead. Annie and Gwen are the ones who can't talk to her. Though, stunningly, Gwen managed to be perfectly polite. You could have knocked me over with a hatchling horse's feather."

Both Anwyn and Lady Bethany snickered at that. They looked not at Siobhan and Prince Toryn who had set up court in the spot next to the buffet table that Anwyn had vacated, but at Gwen and Nolan. No one doubted who was truly in command of that marriage. All you had to do was look at them to see how Gwen doted over Nolan.

Raelin wasn't sure that Nolan realized it, though. Poor man. He still hadn't gotten over his mother and sister's abuse. She wondered sometimes if he ever would. Which didn't help her figure out what was going on and why Nolan's arrival, or perhaps Gwen's, had put a stop to the predatory behavior.

4. PLOTTING WIVES

The feel of the ballroom had shivers running up Anwyn's spine. The instant Nolan walked into on Gwen's arm, he'd switched something. She had no idea what the plot really was but it was all about marriages and money. That much Anwyn could tell for sure. The price that Gwen had paid for Nolan had been so damned high. The highest price anyone anywhere had ever paid for a husband before.

Even off in other ports on the far side of the world, Anwyn had heard about that. Lots of people had said that the Dana, Gwen especially, had been idiots to do it. At first. Then as the months had passed and they'd come close to a year of marriage, the rumors and gossip had claimed that the Dana had gotten as steal with Nolan.

It wasn't even a lie. He was brilliant, talented, and better at soothing people than even Raelin. Nolan had to be the best person they'd added to the clan in a generation.

So why were they stopping their ham-handed attempts at seduction when Nolan arrived?

"Your daughter doesn't appear as delighted with the

dance now," Raelin commented with more than a little amusement.

Lady Bethany snorted, her matching amusement mingled with irritation at her daughter. "Benvy isn't the sort to find your Cadfael that interesting. Aravel? Certainly. Cadfael?"

She snorted, prompting Anwyn to grin and Raelin to laugh low and sweet. Like everyone in the city didn't know about Aravel's love of sex. Caddie was just as likely to bite someone's head off as to allow them to touch his fingertips. Not the best match of dance partners there.

Still, Benvy was trying very hard to get Cadfael to smile. Unsuccessfully. Most women would've given up by this point just because of his attitude. And. Huh. All the other women who'd been trying seduction had given up already.

"I'd have Anwyn rescue her if Caddie wouldn't cut my throat," Raelin said, utterly ignoring Anwyn's glare.

Lady Bethany swallowed a startled laugh. "I think you'd be rescuing him, not her."

"Oh no," Raelin said in that warmly encouraging tone of voice that was always so good at getting people to open up when she was working on a trade or dealing with a Delbhana stupidity. "Caddie prefers to have his dance card full. The more he's dancing, the less he has to entertain questions and talk to people. He's terribly shy. Hides it by being ridiculously snappish."

Lady Bethany went alert. Inside. Not physically. It was like she'd been caught on a line, the hook sunk so deep that she didn't realize that she was on a line now. And yeah, Raelin was very aware that she had Lady Bethany, not that Anwyn could tell how Raelin knew it.

"I would have thought it was just temper," Lady Bethany said.

Her voice was even but there was just enough strain there that Anwyn had to shove her fist right against her mouth not to grin. Damn but Raelin was good at this.

"Mmm, it's certainly temper, too," Raelin said. She smiled and canted one hip, looking at Lady Bethany as if she was a friend of the Dana instead of a firm, life-long ally to the Delbhana, especially Siobhan's mother Lady Etain. "But Caddie always hides his emotions under the temper. Finding him a wife is going to be next to impossible. Whoever it is will have to find him not only cute but also be able to deal with the temper. And help him feel safe enough that he doesn't tear them into shreds on a regular basis."

"Rae, you're dreaming if you think we can find someone like that," Anwyn commented because Lady Bethany was so busy running through Clan-Crannach women in her head that Anwyn caught glimpses of their faces before they were rejected. "I still think he's going to end up married to another man. Or single for life. It's not like Caddie's interested in sex."

Wrong thing to say, damn it. Lady Bethany snapped back to the moment, frowning at Raelin and then at Anwyn. She was furious about it, though she managed to show only confusion with the anger wrinkling the corners of her eyes.

"What do you mean?" Lady Bethany asked.

"Caddie's virginal," Anwyn said, shrugging. "Completely and utterly virginal. I mean, he's literally Aravel's opposite. Where Ravi outright rejected any thought that men should hold themselves apart until marriage, Caddie accepted it whole-cloth. I heard Gavin complain, before he and Mari moved into their apartment, that Caddie doesn't even ah, take care of his arousal."

That rocked Lady Bethany right back on her heels and

set her to plotting a whole different set of Clan-Crannach women to set after Caddie. They really wanted one of the men. All of them? No, only some of the men were being targeted.

Anwyn pursed her lips once Lady Bethany turned back to watching Caddie with Benvy. To her relief, Raelin was scanning the crowd, watching patterns of behavior, too. She felt of the need to see who was doing the seducing.

So Anwyn focused on who was being seduced. Caddie, obviously because he was the jewel of the Dana and he'd been a target for seduction and marriage since he left off his boy's short kilts. Aravel, always, because he was out there doing the seducing as well as being seduced. Daire had a lot of women looking at him with annoyance that he had gone and gotten married.

There were women trying to sound out Anwyn's little brother Andros even though he was only eleven. Cousin Grady, twenty-nine and as celibate as a nun, had women trying to flirt with him. Very unsuccessfully because he was so completely clueless about sex and relationships that the whole Clan had given up on him marrying a decade ago. Finn and Rafferty, Aunt Derva's sons, were being flirted with, too, even though Finn was already engaged and Rafferty was completely uninterested in women.

Frankly, Raelin was kind of surprised that Rafferty hadn't come to the party in trousers. He'd threatened to do so since that was what he normally wore. Annie was pretty sure that he'd declare himself a woman if he could get away with it.

Siobhan had made changing your gender nearly impossible legally. At least if you were Dana. And that, actually, had been done within the last month. Part of the plan? Could be. Very well could be.

Benvy escorted Caddie back to their sides, then

breathed a huge sigh of relief as a Clan Ruadh woman, lower rank whose name Anwyn couldn't for the life of her remember, swept him off for a fast-paced reel. Raelin grinned at Benvy, as engaging with her as she'd been with Lady Bethany.

"Well done," Raelin said. "You only stepped on his lace three times that I saw."

"Why?" Benvy immediately groaned. "Why do men wear that many petticoats? It's ridiculous! And so hard to manage. I could barely even look at him. I was too worried about stomping on that damned lace and getting torn to shreds by his tongue."

"Oh, he'd have used knives if you really damaged the lace," Anwyn commented. Then shrugged at both Benvy and Lady Bethany's horror. She ignored Raelin's irritation. "Caddie's dedicated to his lace. Drives me crazy listening to him go on and on about backing this, stitching that, weights and widths and gah! Give me a good argument about Minoo paperwork any day over that. It's less painful."

Benvy snickered and nodded while Lady Bethany rolled her eyes. For the paperwork comment. She was still running through potential women in her head.

"I'm surprised you chose to dance with him," Raelin said. "I'd have thought you'd go after Aravel. Or one of the cousins. They're certainly easier targets for a dance than Caddie."

Both Benvy and Lady Bethany went sour. It was like a sudden burst of lemon in Anwyn's mouth. Her breath caught as the same thought swept through their minds. There weren't many other options if you wanted to get a Dana husband. And they needed one.

Quick.

But all the single Dana men were too old, married, or

too young. Or totally uninterested in women. Caddie was the focus along with Aravel and Andros specifically because whatever Siobhan was plotting needed a Dana man of marriageable age. Right now. And if it was someone closely related to Mother, all the better.

Anwyn shifted to head for the door, where Mother was, only to growl as Raelin blocked. Her.

"Rae."

She ignored Anwyn. Utterly. "Unless you're looking for more than a dance. Though there are still much easier targets than Caddie on that front, too."

How the hell did she do that?

"Rae."

"I would prefer that Benvy settle down sooner rather than later," Lady Bethany said without looking at Anwyn, either. Or Benvy who rolled her eyes and groaned loudly. "A Dana man would at least keep her eyes and hands from wandering."

"She wouldn't have hands," Raelin said with a huge grin for Benvy who glowered at Lady Bethany just like Anwyn glowered at Raelin. "Especially with Caddie. I mean, Aravel might just enthusiastically join in. He's ah, not at all shy about enjoying things though he does prefer women. Entirely."

"Noticed that," Benvy said. She waved at Anwyn and then snickered as Raelin blocked Anwyn from leaving the conversation yet again.

"Rae!" Anwyn shouted and didn't even care who turned and stared at them.

"What?" Raelin looked like she had no idea whatsoever Anwyn was annoyed about but she radiated amusement. And worry.

"Sometimes when you have a lot of punch you need to go use the toilet, Rae," Anwyn said in her very best sickly-sweet tone of voice. "And unless you want me to pee on your damned boots, you're going to let me leave."

Both Lady Bethany and Benvy burst out laughing. Raelin went so blazingly red that her slicked down hair was less red than her cheeks. She took a deep breath, stepped aside and then snorted when Anwyn glared at her.

"I promised not to pick a fight," Anwyn said. "I don't need a baby sitter."

Benvy's choked laugh, hidden behind one raised hand, said otherwise. So did Lady Bethany's snickers. Raelin did it, too, grinning at Anwyn so broadly that the raft of scars on her cheek twisted dramatically. She really didn't smile that broadly anymore. Good to see, even if it made Lady Bethany wince behind Raelin.

"We both know that's not true," Raelin said. "Go on. And keep your promise, Annie."

Anwyn flipped a rude gesture at her, pure dock-side sign that pretty much everyone in Aingeal knew, then stomped off towards the hallway. Along the way she pushed 'toilet' thoughts at Mother in the hopes that she'd feel it, realize what was going on, and join Anwyn in the toilet. At least for long enough that Anwyn could explain what she'd figured out so far.

This whole thing was a trap. Somehow. Anwyn wasn't sure what Siobhan was going to get out of one of their men marrying out of the clan but it couldn't be good if she'd convinced all her allies to push hard to find a Dana man who was willing to leave the Clan. Maybe the whole 'men cannot even speak to non-family women if they're being courted' rule that they passed when Gavin and Mari were courting?

Except no, that wasn't being enforced anymore.

Didn't matter. What mattered was that Mother saw Anwyn heading for the hallway, patted Father on the shoulder and headed out into the hallway just as Anwyn reached the door. Made it look like she'd decided that Anwyn needed a keeper so okay, she needed a keeper or there'd be a brawl. Anwyn could live with that as long as they figured out what Siobhan was up to.

Somehow.

If she was really lucky, Raelin would figure out what this was all about.

Yeah. Anwyn's luck never went that direction, not since her visit to the City of the Ladies. It always went the other direction and she had to spend huge amounts of time and effort foiling Siobhan's stupid plots.

5. EVENING CLEANUP

Raelin collapsed into one of the spindly little chairs in the formal entrance, her good hand over her burning, exhausted eyes. The chair screeched against the wall. Probably put a dent in the expensive blue paint that Mother had just had touched up but Raelin couldn't bring herself to care.

What a mess.

"You figure this out?" Mother asked.

"Only bits and pieces of it." Raelin sighed.

She opened her eyes and sighed again, more loudly, to find Gavin, Mari, Anwyn, Aravel, Father, Mother, most everyone who'd been stuck with 'escort the guests out now that the party was done' duty staring at her. Anwyn had her thinking glower on while Ravi was fidgeting so nervously that Raelin held out an arm.

"That was so scary!" Ravi blurted as he ran over and hugged her tight enough to make Raelin's ribs creak. "They wouldn't leave me alone. All of them kept asking me, over and over, what it would take for me to leave the Dana. I don't want to leave! I like it here. Though I did offer to sire a bunch of babies if they wanted. None of them did, which was really weird. I mean, a Dana blood baby is good enough, right?"

"They want one of our men in marriage right now," Anwyn said, still glowering. "It's a Delbhana plot, no surprise. The whole point is to get one of our men out of the clan. Somehow. It doesn't really matter which one but they'd prefer that it was someone closely related to you, Mother."

Raelin frowned at that. She'd noticed Anwyn flinching, glaring, responding to things that weren't spoken all through the party. Very helpful in the moment to see when someone was hiding something. Though, frankly, most of the Delbhana allies were terrible at hiding their motivations. They didn't have to do it very much with Siobhan. As long as they said the right things to her, Siobhan would believe whatever they said without paying any attention to their body language or behavior.

"Where's Gwen and Nolan?" Raelin asked. "Nolan implied that there was some problem. Was there an actual problem or was that just a way to get Gwen away from Siobhan?"

"Headed back into the offices," Mother said. She frowned. "He didn't say anything to me."

"Gwen commented that they'd found someone roaming the hallways on their way in," Father said. "I didn't ask who but I assumed it was a Delbhana daughter. They do that every time."

Raelin hauled herself upright, barely managing it because Ravi didn't want to let go. He did, finally, standing to follow on her heels as Raelin went hunting for Gwen and Nolan. Wasn't a tough job. If someone had been searching through the warehouses, they would've been stashed in one of the conference rooms and locked in. It happened often enough that there were several designated for that purpose scattered all through the warehouse level.

Gwen's voice raised in anger was the tip-off that they'd stashed whoever it was in the conference room near the crew bunks. There were a few sailors there, two with bruised jaws, one with a huge black eye. Whoever it was hadn't wanted to be locked away, that was for sure.

"You can't just say that there's a plot and not tell us anything," Gwen snapped.

Nolan nodded respectfully to Raelin, stepping aside so that Raelin could see who it was. Beaten, bloody nose, hair a wild mass of blond curls making a halo around her head, Delbhana Danica sat tied to a chair. Her arms were tied behind her back and her feet, shod in battered old boots, were tied to the legs of the chair.

"I thought you were dead," Raelin said.

Danica's head snapped up. She stared at Raelin, then over her shoulder at Gavin and Mari. The instant she saw Gavin, she sagged as if so relieved that she couldn't hold herself up anymore.

"Real relief?" Raelin murmured to Anwyn who pushed past Gavin to stand at Raelin's side.

"Oh, yeah," Anwyn said. She shuddered. "Ah, we're looking at assassination, murder, the complete destruction of the Dana, again, and Siobhan fully intends it to happen as soon as the Queen dies."

"Ah."

Raelin nodded. She waved everyone else to stay outside the conference room. Mother didn't. Anwyn did. Gavin didn't, stomping in to take a seat next to Danica who smiled for a fleeting moment at him, there and gone faster than the flash of green at sunset.

"Shut the door, Mother," Raelin ordered.

"Sometimes I wonder who really leads this clan," Mother said as she did just that.

Raelin snorted. "Gavin and me, who else? We're the only level-headed ones in the whole place. You just have the title. And the only reason you people hooked me into it is because of my stupid scars. If I could still use my arm properly, I'd be out with the Tourmaline Dreams."

Danica stared at first, mouth dropping open to reveal missing teeth on her right side. Then she breathed a little laugh while shaking her head at Raelin. Gavin just rolled his eyes. Both he and Mother had heard that complaint a thousand times before. Pretty much every single time that Raelin was in port, actually.

Wasn't the best thing to have the door closed. Danica had obviously been living on the streets or hiding away somewhere without baths. She stank to high heaven, worse than a horse whose feather shafts had gotten infected during a molt. Raelin breathed through her mouth, studying Danica.

"So, the latest plot we're aware of is getting a Dana man, particularly one close to Mother, in marriage," Raelin said because Danica, here, meant something truly big was going on. "Not sure why. Related to the murder, death and destruction you're telling tales of?"

"I didn't say anything!" Danica yelped. Her eyes were so wide with terror that Raelin leaned forward, elbows on her knees. "You didn't hear that from me."

"True then," Raelin said. She snorted at the way Danica shuddered. "Come on. Give us a hand and I'll smuggle you out of Aingeal. We've got a ship going out tomorrow that you could get on. Not a big one, or fast, but it'd get you away from here and you'd be able to survive."

Danica snorted, glaring at Raelin. "Like you did for Siobhan? Tell me another one."

Raelin shrugged. "Didn't realize the Delbhana knew about that but yeah, just like Siobhan. Though you, thankfully, don't have all her injuries."

All the blood drained out of Danica's face. Well, all the blood other than what was slowly dripping out of her nose. Her mouth opened, incoherent noises coming out instead of words, then snapped shut again. Next to her, Gavin sat with his fingertips pressed against his mouth. He looked like he was about to burst into laughter. Or perhaps hysterical giggles.

"Rae, don't do that to someone who probably has a concussion," Mother drawled. "She'll pass out on us."

"Well, I thought she knew when she said that," Raelin replied. She shook her head and studied Danica whose face was as open a book as any Raelin had ever seen. Even Siobhan usually wasn't quite this obvious about the hope, fear, despair and fury that cycled across her face.

"Siobhan lives?" Danica asked finally.

"Mm-hmm," Raelin agreed. "Barely survived the beating she got. Her leg's hopelessly tricky, barely holds her up. Lost one eye. We ferried her all the way to the other end of the world, set her up there and she's living there now. I can't tell you where. It wouldn't be safe for her or you. But yeah, Doctor Bernice saved her and called in a favor to get her on the Tourmaline Dreams when we shipped out. I really did think you were dead."

"The Delbhana believe I am," Danica said. She sagged against the ropes, sat up straight and then pulled her arms around in front of her, the rope in her hands. Untied. "I've been hiding from them. If Siobhan had her way, I'd be dead and buried in the royal garden, feeding Prince Toryn's roses with my blood. And no, he has no idea that Siobhan does that. He asked for some blood or bone meal for his roses and she murdered one of the cousins who was giving her trouble, then had her body buried under the roses."

Raelin leaned back. A chill ran up her spine. Danica was far too calm and disgusted for that to be a lie. Abruptly, Rae wished that she'd asked Anwyn to stay in the room with them. Having a lie detector right now would be very, very useful.

"I always knew Siobhan would murder someone," Gavin whispered. He looked so queasy that Raelin almost went to comfort him. Mother beat her to it, rubbing Gavin's back.

"Not the first," Danica said, shaking her head. "Won't be the last. The old Queen is on death's doorstep, Rae. It'll be soon. Siobhan has plans when it happens. Wicked plans. She needs to get one of your men so that she can claim the right to unite your clan with the Delbhana. Then everything you have, everyone here, will be hers. She thinks she's found a law in the old books that will let her do it."

"I'll cut her throat before that happens!" Mother snarled.

"Which law?" Gavin asked at the same time, clutching Danica's arm and making her wince.

"That's why she needed a romance to happen right now," Raelin said much more slowly. "Any of her allies could do it, then. She's got all of them under contract so that they're basically just subsets of the Delbhana."

"...How do you know that?" Danica asked, staring at Raelin with horror. "No one is supposed to know that."

Raelin shrugged. "We gave Siobhan the pigments, told her where to look to get the deal set up. Found out that the Delbhana were raiding the royal treasury and that if they went down the whole country would go with them. Caddie found the pigments originally and I snuck the knowledge of them to Siobhan at a party."

Danica stared. And stared. Her face went red. Then white, then back to normal again. At least the bloody nose had slowed to a stop. She didn't have blood dripping down her face anymore.

She turned to Gavin who nodded while shrugging. Then Mother who grinned and wagged her eyebrows at Danica.

"You should have let the Delbhana die," Danica snapped at Raelin.

"No, it would have destroyed all of Aingeal," Raelin said. She waved her weak hand, brushing away Danica's anger. "The borders would have changed. We'd have lost north and west Aingeal. And you know that Tahirih, Kohinoor and Mairsille would have invaded right away. Even Gobnait would have taken a whack at us if given the chance. No, we had to shore the Delbhana up because there was no way it wouldn't have torn the country apart."

Danica frowned, nodding slowly. "I see your point but you still should have allowed it to happen. Aingeal has survived other upheavals. However diminished and changed the country would have been, it would have been better than Siobhan on the throne."

And that was the key, wasn't it? Raelin stared at Danica. It wasn't so much the Delbhana that was the issue. It was Siobhan. There was always something that could be done to stop her mother, Lady Etain. Not that it was usually very hard. Lady Etain's plans were always far too complicated.

Siobhan? Well, all her plans were far too bloody. And complicated, too. Raelin hummed as she cocked her head to the side. Danica eyed her warily, playing with the rope in her hands. She hadn't tried to free her feet yet so that was good. A show of strength, capability, but also trust that they wouldn't kill her out of hand.

"You taking the deal?" Raelin asked. "Tell us what you can, help us figure this out, and we get you out of the country. Because, honestly, we can't just let you go at this point."

"Do you trust the sailors that saw me?" Danica countered. She swallowed and the sound was like a sanding block against a newly hewn beam it was so loud. "Will they talk to anyone else about who I am?"

"They don't know who you are," Raelin said. "Right now, you're a spy and thief with information that the Dana can use against the Delbhana. Happens at least once a week, you know."

Danica choked on a startled laugh. "Ah, so good to know that I managed to be creative in my method of contacting you."

Gavin grinned and patted her arm. "Makes you less noticeable. We usually hire the women who do that. And find good homes for the men. They're usually just fleeing bad marriages."

"Hasn't happened for... oh, months now," Mother said very thoughtfully. She hummed. "Gonna have to check on that. The rumor mills might be spewing chaff again. The Delbhana like to make it seem like we enslave or beat the men like they do."

"So, yes or no?" Raelin asked as Danica flinched away from Mother's thoughtful, completely vicious comment.

She stayed still, calm, as Danica stared at her. Eyes wild with terror again. Terror and hope. What an awful mix to be caught in. It took long enough for Danica to find her answer that Gavin was twitching on his chair and Mother was growling. Raelin just waited. Danica was a good person, one of the few in the Delbhana. She'd pick right.

Hopefully.

"I don't know much," Danica finally said, "but yes. I'll

take your deal. Answers and what help I can give in exchange for an escape from Aingeal. To whatever country you think will not deliver me back to the Delbhana. If they catch me, I'm dead. Siobhan promised to slit my throat herself if she saw me again."

6. FLEETING SHADOWS

Mari hummed tunelessly as she stood next to Anwyn. It was like standing next to a mast as the wind rose for a gale. For more than one reason. Anwyn could feel the worry and anger rising inside of Mari.

Never as much as it did for Gwen as she geared up for a fight but it was there. Honestly, it was like looking in a mirror because Anwyn was humming with the knowledge that a fight was coming, too.

A very big fight.

Even with the door shut, Anwyn could feel Danica's terror. Her determination. She was here for a reason and it wasn't because she thought she'd survive. No, Danica was completely convinced that she was going to die in the next week, no more than two weeks. Her only reason for being here was Gavin.

She wanted to save Gavin. Somehow, someway, she wanted to protect him from whatever Siobhan had planned. And from the emotions roiling off her, this plot was a doozy. Anwyn could see images of dead women, roses, and Siobhan hissing in someone's face. Danica's? No, maybe Prince Toryn. Or the Queen. It was hard to tell when Danica's emotions were all over the place that way.

"Surprised you didn't charge right in there," Mari murmured.

"I'm stunned you didn't," Anwyn said. She tilted her head up until she could meet Mari's eyes. The woman was way too tall.

"Eh, I like Danica an' I trust Gavin," Mari said. "It's fine. Jus' worried what brought her t'that state. Hair is loose, not glued down."

Anwyn burst out laughing despite herself. The sailors who'd been standing guard had moved off to the little common area up the way, playing cards. They craned their necks to see what was going on, then grinned at Anwyn and Mari. None of them felt like they knew Danica. That was good. The fewer people who knew, the more likely it was that Danica would survive.

That they'd all survive.

Because the emotion from the other side of the door was bleak, grim, as angry as anything Anwyn had ever felt outside of Siobhan. She shuddered. The images in Danica's head were damned scary, like out of the Morrigan's Hell but real life.

"You okay?" Mari whispered. "Shakin' pretty hard."

"Just... worried," Anwyn said. She tried not to show her gifts around non-family. The sailors weren't family. Hired staff, yes, but not family. "Siobhan is up to something and I don't know what it... is."

Raelin flared bright, fast and hot, her mind sorting through a thousand different images and emotions. All of them centered on laws, on marriage, on what a new Queen could and couldn't do. Okay, so, it's that sort of thing. Not beating people to death and asking questions later but legal traps and then beating people to death.

"I'm gonna go get our lawyers," Anwyn told Mari. "I think we're going to need them. Stay put."

"Wouldn' leave my Gavin unless he told me to," Mari said with a confident little nod. "Think they're still here, talking to Great-Uncle Jarmon about some treaty work or somethin'."

That gave Anwyn a place to start, at least. Great-Uncle Jarmon had been at the party. For all of about ten minutes. He'd slipped in, then out again, even though officially no one was supposed to enter or leave after 'Princess' Siobhan and Prince Toryn arrived. Not that Great-Uncle Jarmon cared about that. At eighty-three years old, he could get away with it. But having come downstairs for the party, he probably ended up in his office once he'd made his appearance.

Both his and Gavin's offices were just off the warehouse, easily accessible to people with paperwork and officials who came by to discuss business. While Gavin's office was closed, no light under the door, Great-Uncle Jarmon's office door was open a crack and there was light.

"Yes?" Great-Uncle Jarmon called before Anwyn could knock.

"Ah, Mother needs our lawyers," Anwyn said, blinking at him when he grinned at her. It wrinkled his face up like a prune, especially when he chuckled at her. "There's another plot starting up."

"We're discussing it," Curran Dairine said. She leaned back and then hummed to see Anwyn standing there. "I'd expected Raelin, not you."

"Raelin's asking questions," Anwyn replied. "She's better at that than I am."

Dairine was nearly sixty, oldest of six sisters in the

Curran Clan who'd become lawyers. They'd worked with the Dana for decades now, ever since Great-Grandmother Anwyn had chosen them for handling some legal issue that no one would ever explain to Anwyn. Her smooth black hair was going iron-grey at the temples but she looked just as hale and hearty as Mother.

"Do we know what the plot might be?" Dairine asked as she pulled a notebook from her pocket and tapped on it with a fine little pencil.

Anwyn took a deep breath, stepped inside, and shut the door. Then ignored the worry that bloomed on both of their faces. And in their hearts. Not too surprising. Most people did worry when Anwyn got serious.

"Siobhan's put the word out to all her allies that they're to snare a Dana husband somehow," Anwyn explained. She rocked on her heels, hands behind her back and shoulder stiff. "Apparently, Siobhan's found an old law somewhere that'll let her claim our clan and all our belongings if we marry into the Delbhana or any of her allies. Seems like there's an outright goal to take all the men and kill the women, no surprise given that it's Siobhan, but it looks a bit more serious now because it's... tied? Somehow linked to Siobhan becoming queen. She has to do it as soon as she's queen or she can't, I guess. I don't know. That's why I came to find you. This is your route to sail, not mine."

That got both Great-Uncle Jarmon and Dairine up and heading for the door. Anwyn got the door open, got out of their way and then let Great-Uncle Jarmon lean on her as they hurried back to the conference room where Raelin was still questioning Danica.

The hallways were dark now. This late at night, most everyone who wasn't at the party was asleep. All the warehouse workers, the sailors, pretty much all the little kids were asleep. Made the shadows loom and flicker around them as their passage made the oil lamps, turned low, flag and flare.

Mari was still there, leaning against the wall and humming. Door was still shut. Sailors had gone off towards bed. Anwyn could hear them gloating and complaining about the end of their card game.

Everyone in the conference room was coldly furious.

"In there," Anwyn said. "Probably in a fine mood, just to warn you."

Dairine nodded, taking the warning as only logic. Great-Uncle Jarmon squeezed her shoulder with enough strength that Anwyn's bones creaked. Even at his age, he was terrifyingly strong, despite his loss of balance and speed. He shoved the heavy sliding door open as if it weighed nothing, then waved Dairine into the now-silent room.

"Never could figure out how he does that," Mari murmured once the door was shut again. "So fragile an' all."

Anwyn rolled her eyes. "He's old and slowing down but he's not fragile. Strong as an ox, that's Great-Uncle Jarmon. He just looks weak."

They stared at the door together, Mari with nothing but the distant murmur of voices to listen to, Anwyn with the sharp stab and drifting tides of their emotions to batter at her. Didn't take long before Anwyn found herself pacing in the hallway.

"Y'hate waiting even more'n I do," Mari commented.

"Yes, I do," Anwyn agreed. "I wish there was more that I could do. I hate this waiting and not knowing. Something's happening. No one knows what. It's bad. It's terrifying. We're all in danger but no, Annie, no. You can't do anything about it. Just sit there quietly and don't pick a fight. Damn them all to the Morrigan's Hells, I'd pick the mother of all fights if it meant that Siobhan couldn't hurt anyone anymore."

"You pick that fight and the whole clan'll be tipped load over wheels, straight down a cliff," Mari said though she nodded her agreement to Anwyn's complaints. "Leave going head-on at the Delbhana to Gwen and Rae. They handle it better'n you do. Or me. I always end up laughing at 'em."

"Must be nice to be so big that everyone looks cute and harmless," Anwyn grumbled.

Then glared because Mari just grinned at her, wagging her eyebrows. Right. No. She wasn't staying here. No one had told her to. It wasn't going to do anyone any good for her to stay put. Anwyn could feel Danica cooperating, answering all of the questions put to her with painful honesty. There was no point to Anwyn sticking around.

"Going to check on Caddie," Anwyn told Mari.

"Y'do that," Mari said, nodding encouragingly while twin relief and wistful envy bloomed behind her breastbone. "I got this. Don't need two of us t'hold this wall up."

Anwyn snickered as she searched for Cadfael. He wasn't at the ballroom which no long looked like a ballroom. The cousins had already put the moving walls back in. All the spare chairs had been rearranged and the conference tables were back in place. They'd even gotten the leftover food on the buffet table out of the ballroom and off to who knew which kitchens in the clan house.

He also wasn't in their apartment, the library on the third floor, Uncle Athos' rooms which were dark, or the baths downstairs in the warehouse.

Finally, Anwyn closed her eyes, opened her mind and dealt with the surge of nausea as she felt for her twin. He wasn't in the clan house at all. He was out on the dock by the Tourmaline Dreams with Aravel.

Both of them had switched out of their party clothes. They had on regular kilts, Ravi's with one petticoat, Caddie with a dozen. They'd covered up their vests with shawls. Ravi of course had one of his knitted shawls while Caddie's was made of richly embroidered spider silk imported from Chinwendu. Despite the normal clothes, their hair was still up in the fancy loops and curls that fashion required. Gems gleamed from Caddie's hair.

"What are you two doing?" Anwyn asked as she marched over to their sides. Only the night watch was on the Tourmaline, eyeing both Ravi and Caddie with worry on her face. "You're frightening Bahb. And me."

"I had hoped that Captain Vevina would be available," Cadfael said, softly enough that Anwyn moved right to his side so he'd feel safer. He never talked that gently unless he was afraid someone was going to hurt him. "Ravi and I had a question for her."

"It's not too important," Aravel said even though his fingers shook as he tugged and fussed with his shawl. "We just hoped..."

That she could get them out of Aingeal.

That she could smuggle all the Dana men, all the younger boys especially, out of the city. Out of the country. Anwyn rubbed Ravi's back. Tugged Caddie into her arms. He bit back a whine as he shook in her arms. Both of them felt of fear, stank of worry and desperation and the complete inability to protect themselves.

"It can wait until morning, you two," Anwyn said in her best approximation of Gwen's superior older sister knows best voice. "Come on. No humoring Ravi's tipsy ideas, Caddie. You know you always end up furious and embarrassed when you do that."

"I am not tipsy," Aravel declared with such offense that

Bahb had to turn away up on the deck of the Tourmaline Dreams, snickering into her hand.

"You try talking him out of one of his wild ideas," Cadfael replied, words muffled against Anwyn's shoulder but hopefully clear enough for anyone listening in from the other ships on the dock.

"Nothing doing," Anwyn declared. "I still remember that ball of scrap yarn you bought in Nasrin, Ravi. I know better than that. I just go get Mother. Or Father. That works."

Ravi played his role perfectly, tucking one hand into Anwyn's elbow as she steered them both back to the Clanhouse. They went in through the people door next to the two-story high warehouse doors. No one looked to be around to see them but Anwyn could feel people watching the three of them. At least a couple of those watchers felt of avarice and fear.

Siobhan had spread her plot far and wide. Damn her.

"Do not go outside without escorts, you two," Anwyn said once they were inside and presumably safe. "I mean it. There's a plot to marry the two of you off against your will and it wouldn't take all that much to do it if you got yourselves kidnapped. Stay inside where it's safe."

Caddie nodded, the fear instantly transmuting to sheer delight. He'd always loved being a stay at home. If he had his way, Anwyn knew that Caddie would never go outside at all, even to get more silk for his embroidery.

"That's not fair!" Aravel cried. He flapped his hands at Anwyn, so dismayed that he looked on the verge of tears. "I don't want to be stuck inside all the time."

"No going out without an escort, Ravi," Anwyn repeated. She wagged a finger at him. "And no, you can't play the 'too innocent and sweet' card with me. You're as smart as any of us. I know you like your lady friends but any one of them could turn you over to the Delbhana and then..."

Ravi paled. She felt the moment that he realized that she was serious. That the threat was a real one instead of the standard warning that all boys got about strange women and rape. He caught Anwyn's hand, squeezing hard. She squeezed back.

"It's friends, too," Aravel whispered. "Not just Delbhana women. Their allies. Our allies, too."

Anwyn nodded. "It is. I don't know the whole story. Rae's figuring that out right now. All I know is that all the boys, all the men, need to know to stay safe. If Siobhan can get any of you, just one of you, she can destroy us all. You have to stay inside and only go out with an escort, Ravi. Once the old Queen is dead and Siobhan is the new Queen, I think it'll change. There's some plot for the transition. It's not forever. Maybe."

Ravi nodded slowly, biting his lip. "All right, Annie. I'll be good. Caddie, we should go tell everyone. If they're that desperate, even the little kids are in danger."

Caddie straightened up and took a deep breath. It felt like he pulled on armor inside of his heart. One minute he was full of fear and rage. The next he was coldly determined and completely controlled.

"Thanks, Annie," Caddie said. "We've got this."

He and Aravel marched off, leaving Anwyn standing by the warehouse doors. Yeah, they had it. The question was what they could all do when Siobhan was heading for ultimate power in Aingeal with nothing at all to stop or block her plans.

7. PRIVATE DISCUSSION

Dairine's suite in the Curran house was... small. Raelin stood and waited for her to return from the Curran library, doing her best not to stare at everything. A small couch fit for no more than two small women sitting side by side. A small area table that would hold one small pot of tea with less than four cups. One small arm chair that was too narrow for Raelin's hips. Caddie could sit on it. Not many other people could.

And bookshelves.

Every single wall was covered in bookshelves filled and piled and stacked with books. Law books in thick leather covers embossed with gold. History books wrapped in Dana cloth. Popular novels with tattered paper covers. Folios filled with mystery papers jostled with scrolls from Chinwendu. Raelin had thought that Darine's office held a lot of books.

Her suite made that office look like a show piece in a play, made for looks, not for reading. There were books under the sofa, under the chair, stacked on the table. Propping open the door to Dairine's bedroom which held a single-width bed and more bookshelves almost hidden by the piles of books.

"Be helpful and clear the table off, Raelin," Dairine said as she pushed the door to her suite open with her shoulder, one elbow working the door handle.

She had a stack of books topped by a tea tray with a large pot of tea and two mugs. Raelin snorted and set to work leveling the books on the table rather than getting them off. No point to struggling to get rid of them all. There was nowhere for them to go anyway. They'd just have to be careful not to spill their tea.

"I assume that your rooms always look like this," Raelin said as she took the tea tray from Dairine. "This isn't research from last night's discovery?"

"Oh, no," Dairine said. She laughed, as rueful as Aravel realizing that the scarf he'd intended to make had turned into an epic blanket instead. "No, my reading habit is the joke of the clan. Makes me a good lawyer but it does make my suite a bit crowded."

She set her stack of books on the sofa, then retrieved the tea tray from Raelin. Two cups of tea, served black, with a scone each, Dairine shook her head and stared into the distance. No scowl. Also no smile.

"You've no idea which law she's planning on using, do you?" Raelin asked.

Dairine grimaced. "I do know which law. I simply can't see how she can use it to any positive effect. For her or for the Delbhana. There's a very old law, three dynasties ago, that was never overturned. In times of turmoil, and yes, a new Queen and new dynasty counts, the Queen can rearrange the clans as she wishes. But only if there's cause. She couldn't take, say the Griogal and tie them to the Crannach. Too different, no real connection between them. And no marriages between them."

"All right." Raelin sipped her tea, raising an eyebrow at the sweetness of it. Far more fruity than she expected. "I want to know what tea this is, just so you know. It's lovely and we can sell it."

"My youngest sister's husband makes it," Dairine said with a huge grin. "And no, you can't. It's literally peasant tea, just dried fruit mixed with the leftover dust from the tea bags."

"No, seriously, I can sell this," Raelin insisted. She shrugged away Dairine's disbelief. "I can. It's delicious and all we have to do is find the right line of patter to convince people to buy it. Which doesn't really matter right now. The plot is to get a Dana man into the Delbhana or one of their allies."

Dairine nodded. "Which won't happen. Laoise has already said so."

"But I think that more than just the Delbhana and their allies are angling for it," Raelin said. "Anwyn saw that there were... far more than just Delbhana fishing for one of our men. Danica had a worry, too. She's afraid that her being in the Dana warehouse would be... leverage. That Siobhan could claim that she had joined the Dana and thus there was a tie."

"Both ways..." Dairine breathed.

She stared at Raelin, then stared into space with her eyes both distant and darting side to side. At any other time, Raelin would have thought that Dairine was reading a book. Incredibly quickly, perhaps, but reading. Perhaps she was like cousin Daire, able to see anything he'd ever read and recall it perfectly in his mind's eye.

Would explain why she was such a vicious, effective lawyer.

"That... could work," Dairine said. "If, of course, Danica was still alive. Which we know that she is not."

Raelin raised one eyebrow and then nodded. "As you say. Either way, Mother was worried that every single marriage we've had, every alliance and contract, could be used against us."

"No, that wouldn't work," Dairine said. She set her tea down, half drunk, and picked up the stack of books. As she flipped through them, searching for something, she kept talking. "According to the law it would have to be recent, during the times of unrest. The language is rather archaic but it's quite clear about alliances made during the unrest take priority over those made previously."

Raelin stiffened. She set her tea down, carefully, and then reached over to put one hand on Dairine's arm. The little touch made Dairine start, then stare at Raelin with wide eyes. The stare turned into a frown as Raelin's heart pounded hard enough to make it hard to form the words.

"Alliances made during the unrest take priority over those made previously," Raelin repeated. "Could a new, or a forced, alliance be ruled to overturn an old contract? An old alliance? Could Siobhan say, oh, let's see. You've allied with Lady Bethany from Clan-Crannach because her daughter Benvy is engaged to Caddie, so your alliance with the Affrica is null and void. Could she say, Mari and Gavin are no longer married because the alliance they were married for is cancelled?"

All the blood drained out of Dairine's face. She bolted to her feet, nearly knocking over the tea tray. Raelin caught it, lifted it up and then carried it outside Dairine's suite. Clearly, Dairine wasn't going to finish her tea and scone. Neither was Raelin.

There was a little table obviously intended for holding Dairine's tea trays sitting by the door. So, Raelin used it and then headed back inside, carefully shutting the door and then locking it because no. No one else needed to hear this. No, Raelin flatly didn't want anyone else to hear it, either from the Curran or the Dana.

Not with Dairine cursing like a dock worker while hauling book after book from the shelves. She cursed as she skipped through the books, as she grabbed folios and tore them open, scattering pages that drifted like horse feathers to the floor. Dairine cursed and read and cursed some more, calling Siobhan every name imaginable.

Raelin sat down and waited for Dairine to reach an end to either her cursing or her research. It took half an hour, but eventually Dairine stopped cursing. She opened one thick book, leather bound, so old that the lettering on the spine had worn off. Flipped through it to a page about three quarters the way through the book and then stood reading the page.

Fast, eyes flicking over the writing. Then slower. Then staring at one point while her lip curled up in a snarl that would do any cat from the warehouse proud. Dairine snapped the book shut before stomping over to fling herself onto the couch with a growl that would have done Anwyn proud.

"I was right," Raelin observed.

"Yes," Dairine agreed. The words barely made it through her clenched teeth. "You were."

"Lovely," Raelin said and then sighed deeply. "Next question."

"That wasn't enough?" Dairine asked with enough rage that Raelin rocked back a little bit. "That...! She's going to tear apart the fabric of Aingealese society and you're just calmly asking questions as though it's nothing. This law could destroy our family. Yours! Every alliance and marriage in Aingeal is on the lines, Dana!"

Raelin nodded slowly, not rising to the anger because that only ever made it worse. Really, Dairine had spent far too much time around the Dana if this was her response to Delbhana stupid plots. She smiled as Dairine glared at her, teeth still gritted, eyes narrowing to slits.

"That's happened so many times before that I can hardly count this as serious," Raelin said. "The one thing the Delbhana, especially Lady Etain and Siobhan, do is overcomplicate their plots. That's why they fail. And our simple, blunt plots are the ones that succeed. You know that."

Dairine huffed, waving one hand for Raelin to get on with it.

Still gritting her teeth but that was all right. Raelin chuckled. So much work that had to be done and no time left for it. All Raelin could do was ask her questions, duck as Dairine got to work finding the answers, and then pray that the old Queen didn't die for long enough that they could come up with a counter. Or at least a plan to mitigate the effects.

"First," Raelin asked, leaning forward with elbows on her knees, "what laws have been put in place since then on this issue? As old as that book is, there have to be subsequent modifications to the law. I believe the Queen gets to roll back three rounds of revisions at most. So. Have there been three modifications? If so, we're safe. If not, we have a problem."

"That's... very important, yes," Dairine said, blinking and relaxing as her eyes started darting as if she was reading again.

"Second, does this law apply to marriage alliances or other forms of alliances?" Raelin asked. "Both? Neither? If there's one thing I know about Siobhan, it's that she's impatient. She doesn't verify or check deeply when something catches her attention. What are the full details of the law? The implications and applications of it. What it says in it's bald, unadorned state may not be at all what it says with however many decades of judicial rulings."

Dairine stared long and hard at Raelin, mouth opening and closing in the slow, lazy motion of a fish in an eddy.

"...You should be a daughter of my house," Dairine said finally.

"No, thank you." Raelin laughed and leaned back in her too-narrow armchair. Then forward again because truly the thing was just too slender for Raelin's shoulders. "I'd much rather be on the sea, even if I can't actually captain the Tourmaline Dreams."

"You and that ship," Dairine said. She shook her head and then stood, the law book in her hand still. "I'll research it. You'll have an answer by morning."

"Good," Raelin replied. "I'll be waiting for your reply. No matter what time it's done. Send whatever you have by dawn. And any updates after that every two hours. We've another wedding event tomorrow afternoon, a charity event that the men have to attend. I need to know what to watch for before that happens."

The grim nod Dairine gave her promised information well before that. Raelin left to the sound of Dairine bellowing her sisters and nieces out of their beds. If she mobilized her entire family, then yes, Raelin might have the answers she needed before the charity ball.

Right now, Raelin would have preferred to cancel the damned thing. But she, out of everyone, couldn't do that. Raelin was the one who'd insisted last year that the Dana would be doing charity again. She was the one who'd suggested that they have a ball where people could come and make a donation to talk or dance with one of the Dana men.

It had seemed like a good idea at the time but now Raelin's skin crawled at the thought of it. All the men, married or not, were going to be there. Old, young, even the children were supposed to attend. There was no way to keep anyone away because it would be noticed and commented on.

So they'd have to be extra careful about security and make sure that all the men understood to go nowhere alone, accept no offers of anything, and definitely not drink or eat anything that wasn't provided by the Dana. She didn't know if that would be enough but it was the best she could figure out right now. Hopefully, Gwen and Anwyn and the others would have some ideas of how to keep the men safer during the charity ball.

8. CHARITY BALL

The Grand Market ballroom was packed. Anwyn shuddered and backed away from the door as the wash of too many tense people and far too many voices raised in excitement pounded at her. She'd felt it from a block and a half away but she hadn't wanted to believe it would really be this bad.

So much fear. Excitement. Lust. Anger. Sorrow. Every emotion in the human heart and all of them stabbing into Anwyn's head in ways that she'd yet figured out how to convey to other people. The older she got, the worse her control was over this stupid gift.

No wonder Great-Grandmother Anwyn was such a brawler. And a pirate. She'd been able to see what was in everybody's heart and mind, knew what they wanted before they said it, and she'd been at the mercy of their rampaging emotions all the damned time. Normally people's emotions were the tide coming and going, the waves washing over Anwyn relatively painlessly. Only a few big waves that swamped her now and then.

This was a hurricane. A gale so strong that it battered

the shutters open and shattered windows. One that ripped the sails right off the mast and snapped the keel of the ship before sending the ship and all her crew to the Ladies.

Right now, Anwyn would gladly take the Ladies talking in her head, making her so sick that she couldn't breath for throwing up so hard. It'd be better. A lot better.

"You all right?"

Anwyn opened her eyes, starting when she realized that there were three Delbhana men staring at her with worry and fear. Worry for her. Fear for themselves. Oh, damn Siobhan to the Morrigan's claws, she was using the Delbhana men as lures.

"Yeah, just not fond of crowds like this," Anwyn said. "I'd rather be up in the crow's nest on a ship in a storm than deal with that."

She hooked her thumb at the crowd and got three shy, frightened smiles out of them. Plus a whole bunch of determination to seduce her. Goddesses, Siobhan would laugh her tits off if any of them succeeded.

"My best friend Iola would laugh so hard at me," Anwyn continued as if she hadn't seen their shift of expression. "She's not Dana so she didn't get to come. Pity. I'd spend the whole afternoon glued to her side. At least then we could make snide comments to each other. No one I'd rather be with than Iola, especially at something like this."

And there, that worked. All three of them got the 'suggestion' that Anwyn was more than friends with Iola. The oldest of the three, maybe nineteen with fine blond hair that he'd put up into a complicated knot on the back of his head flinched. The youngest, maybe fourteen and still wearing his braid straight down his back, felt relieved. The middle one just blinked at Anwyn, confused.

"Well, I better go find my sister Gwen," Anwyn said. "She's the next best for snarky comments. Enjoy the party.

I'm sure Princess Siobhan will be delighted to have you guys eat your weight in our food and wear us all out entertaining you."

She strode off before they could do more than open their mouths. None of them felt as though they had the slightest idea how to stop her. They'd been given a script, that was it. Anwyn had thrown them off the script and once out of familiar waters, they'd been sunk.

Poor things.

They'd been so stifled by the Delbhana women, so beaten down, that they couldn't cope with anything new or unexpected. Opposite of the Dana men who were working the crowd with practiced ease. Ravi was in his element, right in the middle of the room flirting with twenty women at once. Gavin was standing next to Mari, answering questions about Minoo paperwork that actually had the women taking notes. Nolan was sitting in the back of the room with several women who were also taking notes while nodding thoughtfully. They all had the look of bookkeepers, dowdy clothes, ink-stained fingers, hunched shoulders.

And there was Gwen, flirting with four different men at once under Mother's watchful eye. And Raelin. Who looked like she was about to leap right out of her skin for how ferociously she watched everyone in the ballroom. The level of fear in her was a big part of what had battered Anwyn when she first tried to come in here.

Odd. Usually Raelin was the calm one. Anwyn scanned the room, both with her eyes and her gift. Nothing too urgent. No men doing stupid things like going off alone. No Dana women but Gwen thinking about going off by herself with one of the flirting men. So. Time to rescue Raelin for a bit.

"You look like you've got the worst headache," Anwyn

said to Raelin. Then snorted when Raelin whirled and nearly popped her one in the face with her left arm. "Yeah, come on. You need a break, Rae. Normally it's me on edge at these things."

"We shouldn't go off alone," Raelin snapped at Anwyn. With wild eyes and a lump in her chest that Anwyn could feel like a hot coal of pure fear.

"...What part of I'm going to be with you is alone?"

Mother started snickering. Which attracted Gwen's attention. She grinned and came over to drape an arm over Anwyn's shoulder.

"Finally made it, Annie?" Gwen asked.

"Yep," Anwyn said, popping the 'p' so obnoxiously that the men Gwen had been flirting with edged away. "You are not seducing them."

"Oh, come on, it's not that big a deal," Gwen complained. She glowered as the men scurried away, reporting back to their mothers who were all clustered across the far wall.

"We're all targets, Gwen," Anwyn murmured to her. To her surprise, Raelin was the one who started at that. "You go anywhere with anyone who's not a relative, you're a target and Nolan pays the price. Besides, how do you think that flirting is making Nolan feel? You may think he hasn't noticed but it's Nolan. He saw it."

Gwen went so white that every single freckle on her face went bright as blood. She strode right off, dodging and tacking through the crowd on a path that led straight to Nolan's side. Raelin grinned as Nolan blushed and then all but melted at having Gwen sit by his side, just barely touching their knees together.

"You cheat," Raelin said. Admiration flooded in, then washed out and left nothing but that heart-clutching anxiety.

"Seriously, Mother, I'm taking Rae outside for a bit," Anwyn said. "She's as nervous as a new cabin girl on her first climb up the rigging in a storm."

"Go," Mother said. She flipped her fingers at Raelin. "We're not fools, Rae. They're pretty damned obvious and yeah, you can tell us after this what you've found out."

As Raelin nodded, reluctantly, Anwyn grabbed her elbow, the bad one, and hauled her straight for the door to the ballroom. Given how little strength Raelin had in her right arm, she got dragged along spluttering. And, given Anwyn's reputation, no one got in their way.

A lovely path cleared for them, right to the door and then outside, too. The Market building was huge enough that the fifth floor held not just the ballroom, six times the size of the ballroom back home, but also hallways wide enough for Mari and all three of her sisters to walk shoulder to shoulder and still have room. Meeting rooms, council chambers and the archive room where all the old files went when they were too old to be used every day were on this level.

Plus there was a beautiful balcony that overlooked the market below. Anwyn dragged Raelin over to the balcony, glowering the Delbhana women murmuring to each other away. They scattered, hurrying back to the party. Felt like complaints about their favorite boys potentially going away. Not anything Anwyn was going to worry about right now.

"Spill," Anwyn demanded. The single word was barely audible over the chatter of bargaining people, carriages and horses screaming at each other five stories below.

"This is very public," Raelin hissed at her.

"Rae," Anwyn said. Flatly while gesturing towards the market below.

It took a second or two before Raelin's cheeks went red.

She sighed, leaned against the railing and scrubbed her hands over her face. Whatever had her upset was a big deal. Her hair was more of a poof of tiny coils as fine as Aravel's smallest lace knitting needles than normal. That only ever happened when Raelin was too sick or too upset to spend the time taming her curls.

"Fine," Raelin said. She glared towards the ballroom. "Siobhan can, if she can get an marriage or engagement or even one of the Delbhana working for us, cancel marriages. Break old alliances. Claim that we've cast off all our old partners for this new thing she's trying to set up with the Delbhana. And then she can claim everything and everyone as Delbhana."

"Huh," Anwyn said, nodding slowly. "Explains the three Delbhana boys trying to seduce me."

"You don't even like men that way!" Raelin spluttered. "That's like trying to seduce me at all."

"Stupid and pointless, just wastes everyone's time," Anwyn agreed. "I think that's why no one bothered to follow us out here to flirt. The whole family feels it, Rae. They all see it. They may not know the details you've figured out but no one's stupid. They're being careful and not... taking any risks."

Lady Etain appeared at the doorway to the ballroom. She glowered at both Raelin and Anwyn as if it was a personal insult that they'd retreated for a while. To Raelin's horror and Anwyn's amusement, Lady Etain gestured and then stomped over with six young Delbhana. Three women who warily eyed Anwyn and three young men who tried to smile at Raelin.

Anwyn started snickering before Lady Etain even got there. "Oh, Rae. Your face is a study!"

"What is so funny?" Lady Etain demanded.

"Her!" Anwyn said.

Her voice went squeaky because Raelin was all but climbing over the railing despite the five-story drop, eyes wide and bottom lip quivering as if she was about to run screaming from the Market Building. The Delbhana men peered at Raelin, and yeah, it was the same three as before, then looked at her sympathetically.

"What... is wrong with you?" Lady Etain asked, frowning at Raelin.

"Romance," Anwyn said and then started cackling as Raelin blanched. "Oh, may the Goddesses bless you, Rae! You're so hopeless! I mean, I'm bad enough stuck on someone who's not interested in women. Or sex. But you!"

"Annie, shut up," Raelin groaned. "You're not helping."

Except that, yeah, she was. Not with Lady Etain. Nothing was going to help her. She was getting madder by the year. Granted, she'd never be as bad as Siobhan but Lady Etain's crazy went right down to the bone.

The Delbhana with her, though, they got it. The women relaxed, smirking at Rae. The men had nothing but sympathy for Raelin's hatred for romance and a good bit of charity for Anwyn being in love with someone she couldn't have. It was good enough. Especially as more guest for the party came up the stairs and spotted them all together. Witnesses, perfect.

"You... you don't want to get married?" Lady Etain spluttered.

"She'd marry the Tourmaline Dreams if she could," Anwyn said. Then ducked because Raelin tried to punch her in the face with her good left arm. "You would! Rae, the entire world knows how much you love that ship. You'd never set foot off her if you could."

Raelin snarled at Anwyn just as ferociously as Siobhan ever had but the fury wasn't there. Fear, sure, lots of that.

And an awareness of everyone watching the confrontation that went right down to the soles of Raelin's shoes.

"I'm going to beat your head through a wall if you don't shut up, Annie."

Lady Etain snorted, amusement mixing in with her irritation at them both. "And you?"

"Eh, I've got my eye on someone but she's not interested in marriage," Anwyn explained. "Iola's from Archaelaos. Marriage is ah, not exactly the sort of thing she's got a good opinion of, if you understand my meaning."

All the women, Rae and Lady Etain and the Delbhana women flinched. The men frowned. Not a clue, any of them. They clearly hadn't ever heard of Archaelaos. No surprise there. Anwyn couldn't imagine that Lady Etain would want them to know that there was a country where men ruled and women stayed home to cook, clean and take care of the kids.

"Still," Lady Etain started to say only to stop when Anwyn shook her head.

"Sorry, but no way. I'm not allowed to even talk to you. No. Seriously. For real. Mother made me sign an actual contract that I wouldn't talk to you or Princess Siobhan at any of these parties all week. This is too much already. I'll have to pay her a fee for this."

"Week's wages for every instance," Raelin said, smug now though she was edging her way behind Anwyn in an effort to get as far away from the men and Lady Etain as possible. Just slowly so that it would be painfully and ridiculously obvious that she was trying to be casual about it.

Lady Etain opened her mouth, left it open and then snapped it shut. She held up one hand while rubbing her forehead.

"You signed a... no. No, I don't care," Lady Etain said. "I

honestly don't care. The both of you are impossible anyway. Come on."

She strode off, gesturing for the others to follow her. They did, the women without a second look. Only the youngest of the men looked back. He waved to Anwyn so she threw a little wave, just a couple of fingers flipped up, at him. It made him grin and walk a good bit more bouncily.

"I can't believe she walked away," Raelin said. She sagged against the railing, watching the new guests as they warily edged to the door and then darted away from the balcony where Rae and Anwyn stood.

"You shouldn't doubt my ability to be effective, Rae," Anwyn said. "And again, everyone knows something big is going on. No one is doing anything alone. No one is accepting anything. Gwen was the only one being stupid and it was just her normal flirting. One mention of Nolan and poof, even that was gone."

"We've still got a huge problem, Annie," Raelin replied. "A huge one. We have to get a handle on it before the Queen dies."

"Mmm," Anwyn hummed. "We'll hold the line, Rae. We're all good at that."

It didn't reassure Raelin at all. Nothing did. Made Anwyn really curious what, exactly, Siobhan could be up to. And how much of a threat it would be once she was finally Queen Siobhan, ruler of Aingeal.

9. FAMILY MEETING

Thank Chin, Tahira and Ragna that there weren't any wedding celebrations tonight. Mother had deemed the charity ball sufficient to show of the Dana's power so they all were free tonight. Raelin sat at the head table next to Dairine as her entire family filtered into the warehouse. They couldn't fit everyone into the conference rooms. None of the rooms in the Clan house were big enough other than the warehouse staging area.

So Great-Uncle Jarmon and Mother had given all the staff and crew the night off. They'd closed the doors, moved all the staged bales and barrels and boxes. Then the kids had set up chairs between the shelves and the great double doors as Mother called an all-hands family meeting.

Raelin couldn't remember the last one. She'd been less than a year old when it happened. According to Mother, she'd been on Father's hip the whole time while Mother carried Ravi around with her during the meeting. Great-Grandfather Tau had still been alive then. He'd called the meeting and ruled it with an iron fist. And his whip when some of Raelin's aunts had gotten disruptive.

It'd been the meeting where Great-Grandmother Anwyn was finally declared dead after disappearing years earlier.

"Your mother's... quite tense," Dairine commented to Raelin as she carefully straightened the paperwork she'd brought to support their arguments.

"The last all-hands meeting was when Great-Grandmother Anwyn was declared dead," Raelin said. She smiled, heart hurting, at the surprised comprehension in Dairine's eyes. "It'll be all right. If I have to punch anyone, though, I'm using my left arm. This is too important for anyone giving us lip."

Dairine nodded, her lips going thin. "I may join in if people do start questioning us. I've spent far too much time figuring this out and not enough time sleeping or eating. It's too important to make any mistakes."

"Just make sure you sleep after this," Raelin said. She wagged a finger when Dairine shook her head no. "You'll make more mistakes if you're not rested. Even in a gale you need to rest, Dairine. Don't let the threat of a wave wash you overboard before the deck is even wet. We need you alert when it happens, not falling asleep in your ink pot."

"Always so colorful, Dana language," Dairine murmured as Mother shouted for Gwen and Nolan to hurry up and get to their seats.

Once they sat, up front and center next to Gavin and Mari, Raelin stood on her chair so that everyone could see her. Got all their attention. Must've expected Mother to open the meeting. A sea of red hair, blue clothes and concern sent straight at Raelin. Good. Everyone knew how significant this was because there wasn't one person smiling, whispering or looking like they'd fall asleep on her.

"I hate to intrude on your wedding week, Daire, but we've got a major crisis," Raelin said. She projected her voice so that everyone in the back could hear her too. "The old Queen is dying and Princess Siobhan has found an old law, several dynasties back, that'll let her dissolve old marriages and alliances, even ones that've lasted for decades in favor of ones that she likes better. Once she has that, she can start tearing apart the clans, all of them, and putting them together how she likes. And you know how she'd like us to be."

That got voices going. Murmurs, whispers, a few quiet profanities about Siobhan and what she should do with her old laws. Anwyn, sitting on the side of the crowd towards the back, nodded slowly as if she'd just heard good news.

"I got news of the threat last night," Raelin said. "Dairine of the Curran spent the last... what is it?"

"Close to a full day," Dairine said. "Nonstop."

"Day," Raelin continued, "researching the law and what Siobhan could do to us with it. But it's not just a threat to us. Yeah, everyone knows that the Delbhana hate us. Thing is, the Delbhana have used their contracts with their allies to take money from them. Sons. Daughters. Whole businesses. That's history. We've got proof of it."

The uncles were the first to still like a baby seal, down feathers not yet dropped and swim feathers not yet grown in, with a wild horse on the prowl for flesh. Then the kids, all of them. Finally the women, old and young, started shifting like they wanted to start brawling.

Didn't say anything, though, so that was good. Raelin nodded, ran her hands down her thighs and wished that this was the Tourmaline's bridge. That she was at sea, safe from all these stupid plots and ridiculous threats. Not that the sea was safe, anymore. Her scars more than proved that.

"Dairine's research shows that this law'll be used against every single clan in Aingeal," Raelin said. She nodded at Anwyn's shocked look, Ravi's bitten lip. Even Caddie's anger had gone to fear as he clutched Andros in his arms. "We're the wedge. We're the start. If she can get us, she'll be able to go after everyone else. It's perfectly legal for her to do whatever she wants to her own allies. That's normal, expected. You get that whenever a new dynasty comes in and everyone expects that the Delbhana allies'll shift around."

"If she manages to get something that says there's an alliance with the Dana," Dairine interrupted, "anything at all, then she can do it to you. And given all the alliances, contracts and deals you've got with everyone across the planet, it would give Princess Siobhan the leverage she needs to grab everything."

Raelin nodded as her stomach churned. "She could claim sovereignty over Chinwendu because of our ties there. Not effectively but she'd could try. Ntombi? She'll claim our work there as her own. Minoo, don't know that she'd go after Minoo but you never know. Every single clan, most every country we do business with, they'll all be in danger."

"She's crazy enough to try," Gavin said.

He probably intended it to be a quiet murmur but the warehouse was so silent that everyone winced. Because he was right. Very right. Anwyn shuddered in the back, scrubbing her hands over her thighs in that about to crawl her way out of her skin way she had when the Ladies' gifts got to be too much for her.

"Is there anything we can do to stop it?" Caddie asked. He raised his chin when Dairine frowned at him. "She needs something to tie us together. Well, let's assume she's already got it. What can we do to block her? How do we say that her claim is invalid and we refuse to accept her power on that? Because I will stab her in the gut myself before I let her have any power over me."

All the men, even little Andros, nodded at that one. Great-Uncle Jarmon huffed and slapped his palm against his thigh, hard enough that Raelin started from the crack of sound. Dairine pursed her lips and then slumped in her chair.

"We haven't found anything," Dairine said. "The law has never been overturned. It hasn't been used in hundreds of years but it was never legislated, never amended, never overturned. There is nothing in the legal code that will stop her."

"I could care less about the legal code," Caddie snapped at her. "I want to know what contracts I can use. I want to know what customs she's breaking. I want to know what the last response was to someone trying to use that stupid law against a clan she didn't like! Who was it and how did they die because if Princess Siobhan tries to do this it's going to end in her death."

"Very messy death," Gavin agreed.

He and Caddie exchanged angry, fierce looks and then nodded at Dairine who'd gone pale at Caddie's ferocity. Normal response there. Most people were unprepared for Caddie's steel wrapped in lace and ribbon froth. Just like most people were unprepared for Gavin to be as steel-spined as he was.

"That... wasn't something that we researched," Dairine admitted. She pressed her fingers against her forehead for a long moment.

"Well, then," Caddie said with the little lift of his chin that promised a screaming match complete with knives flung at people's heads, "we'll just have to make sure that absolutely everyone in Aingeal understands what she's up to."

Raelin almost fell of the chair. Her jaw dropped. Her stomach dropped. Her knees nearly dropped her right down to the floor, too.

"No, Caddie," Raelin said.

"I agree with him," Gavin said. He glowered at Raelin.

"As do I," Great-Uncle Jarmon said and there went any chance of Raelin keeping control over this. "The risks of this extend far beyond our family. While I'm... somewhat worried about how to phrase it when telling everyone--"

"Siobhan's gone insane at last and she's trying to take over the world!" Caddie snapped.

"--We definitely do need to inform our allies," Great-Uncle Jarmon continued as if Caddie hadn't interrupted him.

"And everyone else!" Caddie insisted even as Raelin waved her hands to try to stop the rising tide of angry chatter. "We need to make sure that the entire country knows what she's going to try to do them. All of them. It's not just us. It's everyone and they deserve--"

"Enough!" Raelin bellowed.

Her shout echoed throughout the warehouse, 'nuff' coming back half a dozen times from the warehouse shelves. Dust filtered down onto the suddenly silent relatives that stared at Raelin. None of them said a word. They all stared at Raelin with wide, blinking eyes. Even Caddie sat there with his mouth open.

All of them except Anwyn.

"Rae, they're right," Anwyn said into the fragile silence.

She was far too calm. A bit pale, a bit twitchy. Anwyn looked over her shoulder at the great double doors that led out to the port and sighed as she shook her head.

Damn it all. Someone had listened in. They'd heard this.

"We can't keep something like this silent," Anwyn continued in as grim a tone as Raelin had ever heard from her. "It's not right and its not fair to do so. I'm not saying that Caddie should write a thousand stern letters and post them to all his friends but we need to get the news out. There's so little time. We can't hold back."

"And when the riots start," Raelin replied, setting her hands on her hips and glaring at Anwyn, "we'll be the ones blamed for it all. Not Princess Siobhan. Not the Delbhana. Us."

"...Tomorrow's our day of donations," Daire said into the silence that followed. He winced as everyone turned to him. "I know we planned on giving away goods to everyone but why don't we just... tell people as we do that? It's not graceful. It's not tricky or smart or anything that we'd normally try for when fighting a Delbhana plot. But the news will fly if we just... tell people about it. The old law. Our worries about Princess Siobhan breaking up our clan with that law. And definitely our fears of having marriages broken up."

He clutched Caitlin's hand, shaking in his seat. She pulled Daire right into her lap, murmuring something into his ear that made him nod and hug her right back. Grandma Treva rubbed Daire's back while scowling.

Daire was a surprise baby, born long after Grandma Treva thought that she'd never have another. Three miscarriages previous to him had made it unlikely. Getting pregnant with him and then having him survive all the way to birth had made him precious in the family. Sort of like little Erlina in Raelin's family. After how hard the birth had been for Mother, they all knew that there'd not be another baby coming. Father had said that outright, publicly.

Raelin turned to Dairine who grimaced while checking with her notes. They'd discussed a dozen different ways of getting the word out, of dealing with the threat of Siobhan's plan, but none of them had been anything like Daire's suggestion.

Tell everyone. Rich, poor, related to the Dana or not. Just tell them what the law was and what it meant and how they feared it would be used. Be open and blunt and...

"Right," Raelin said. She threw up her hands. "Annie, what's your feeling on the luck of that one? Gwen? What do you think? You two are the best other than Caddie for riding the luck this way. Think it'll work? Can we ride that wave long enough to protect the Clan?"

Because that was one idea that depended entirely on riding the storm surge of fortune until it ran out. All of Raelin's plans had been focused on their circumstances and how to manage events, people and politics until they got what they wanted.

Luck might work better.

Maybe.

Gwen winced as eyes turned to her. She wrapped an arm around Nolan's shoulders. The other hand was clutched around Nolan's fingers. No surprise. If anyone was going to get un-married by Siobhan, it'd be Gwen and Nolan. Siobhan favored Nolan's abusive mother, not Gwen. She'd shove Nolan right back into his mother's clutches despite the epic bride price Gwen had paid.

"I think it's our only chance," Anwyn said. She stared up at Raelin with enough confidence that Raelin knew she wasn't going to win. "I know you, Rae. You're trying to logic this out. You can't. We're dealing with a madwoman and logic won't work."

"Yeah, I agree," Gwen said. "The only thing that's ever slowed Siobhan, excuse me, Princess Siobhan, is too many people going up against her for her to beat them all up. We get enough people up in arms about the law and she won't be able to use it."

"Sadly, I think that will be the only effective tool we have," Nolan said into the rising murmurs full of worry, fear and the faintest hints of excitement. "I... won't be taken from Gwen. Or the Dana. Not now. Not ever."

All the men, and all the women, who'd married into the Dana nodded. Grim and determined, most of them, which made a stark contrast to the nervous excitement rising in the Dana faces that turned to Raelin.

"Well, that's our plan, then," Raelin said. She rubbed her hand over the scars covering her cheek. "Just be careful, everyone. We don't know how the Delbhana will react. You can't say, ever, that it's something Princess Siobhan will do. Or that the Delbhana have plans. It's 'we fear'. It's 'this could be used to'. Say 'I'm terrified that'. Make it all about our fears and worries for our families, our friends, our allies and businesses. Don't make it about Princess Siobhan."

"Everyone else will do that," Caddie said with a little snort that echoed in the rafters overhead.

10. RISING WAVES

Anwyn stood at the window over the formal entrance to the Clanhouse, letting the Dana-blue curtains hide her from the people below. Mother had gotten permits to close Dana Lane off entirely from the port right out to two blocks past the Clanhouse. It was the best way that they'd been able to find to do the donations that Daire and Caitlin had decided on.

Several booths gave away food for those who wanted it, staples like flour and sugar as well as dried fruit and meat that the poor could hoard and use during the middle of winter when there was nothing fresh. Clothing that Caddie had gathered from every single second-hand store in the city, all repaired and washed and pressed. There were three tents giving away shoes, one for women, one for men and a third, much bigger, one for kids.

Plus books and lessons and gear for a thousand different jobs in the city. Toys for children and pens for scribes, ink and paper for students in need. Daire and Caitlin had wanted to do something wonderful for the whole city with their wedding.

Pity the gossip about the old law was turning the whole thing sour.

Daire and Caitlin, in their wedding finery, were right below Anwyn serving soup and bread to anyone who came up, even if they'd already had two or three bowls. Good hearty soup with plenty of tubers and meat. Anwyn could smell it. Frankly, she was halfway tempted to go get a bowl herself so her stomach would stop rumbling.

Even though she knew already that she didn't dare set foot outside, not with all these rumors going. Wouldn't take much for the rumors to turn against them. People were already thinking about how Siobhan and Anwyn fought. There was a couple of poor people in tattered clothes right below her who radiated their worry about getting between Anwyn and Siobhan when it all came to a head.

Didn't stop them from taking the soup and drinking it down. Or from going to get new clothes, new shoes, and because Caddie was the one passing out coats, sturdy new coats that would keep them warm all winter long that somehow still managed to make them look much better off than they were.

Anwyn's head throbbed as she focused just on those two people. Two women, both so far down on their luck that bad luck would count as good. The fear and suspicion slowly transmuted as they were given more and more stuff into anger. Outright fury that the donations that were keeping them alive might go away.

"You staying up here all day?" Mother asked from the doorway.

"I'm no help down there," Anwyn said as she turned, then made grabby hands at the bowl of soup Mother had for her. "I'll just push people's minds to the feud instead of to the potential problems from the law."

Mother snorted, waiting as Anwyn drank the broth and then shoveled the meat and tubers into her mouth. "I'll grant you that but we need to know how people are reacting."

"Mmm, not too bad," Anwyn said. Her fingers tapped against the side of the bowl as she let herself reach out and feel everyone in the street below instead of just those two. "Overall, people are delighted by the gifts. No one thinks of it as charity, more like Dana showing off how rich we are by giving gifts for the wedding instead of getting them."

"Accurate enough," Mother said, amusement in her voice. "Daire did want to give instead of getting."

"Under that, though," Anwyn continued while watching people walking by, "there's a lot of anger. A lot. The richer people are irritated that we're not following Siobhan's plans. The less wealthy are angry that they haven't been able to do more, to raise their clans up instead of down. They blame the Delbhana for that but we're very visible right now so there's a lot of resentment. I'd send more people to the teaching tents, make sure there are more instructors and that people know they can keep coming back for lessons if they need it."

"We can do that," Mother said. Her voice sounded farther away now even though her hand cupped Anwyn's elbow as she took the empty bowl away. "That's enough, Annie. You can stop."

"No, I can't," Anwyn said because no. She really couldn't stop. She was never able to stop and the older she got the stronger her gifts got. If she survived to twenty-five it'd be a miracle. "The poor, though. That's where the real anger is. They know the Delbhana are behind it. Especially Lady Etain and Siobhan. It's outright fact to the poor. There's so much resentment, Mother. So much anger bubbling under the surface. Riots are one bad word, one mistake away. The

Ladies know it's happening but they don't understand why. There's a lot of them in the port right now, watching and listening."

"Annie, stop!"

Mother shook Anwyn sharply enough to snap her out of the street and back into her head. For a second, Anwyn was alone in her head, stunningly clear-minded and only a little startled that Mother was staring at her with desperate worry in her eyes.

Then the pain hit so hard and fast that Anwyn's legs gave way. She nearly threw up the soup she'd just eaten, barely keeping from it by swallowing hard and clenching her teeth. Mother caught her, eased her to the floor and then knelt next to Anwyn as she panted against the pain.

"Went too far, didn't you, Annie?" Mother asked in her softest, most soothing voice.

"You think?" Anwyn replied and then clamped her mouth shut again.

The pain was bad. Really bad. Not the true nausea she usually got from talking to the Ladies. This was as if she had people hammering iron spikes through her skull from the inside out. There was a red-hot iron band tightening around her forehead and every couple of seconds someone with a sledgehammer smacked it down on the top of her skull as if she was trying to pound Anwyn's spine through the floor.

Not good. Very not good. And there really wasn't anything to do about it but suffer through the pain.

"Mom!" Andros shouted as he ran into the room, skidding to a stop in front of them. "Oh, sorry, Annie. But um, Princess Siobhan is on her way in. She wanted to drive her carriage in but Gavin and Great-Uncle Jarmon told her that she couldn't because the queen had already signed off on no carriages on Dana street until the fair is over. She'll be here any second."

"When it rains, it pours," Mother said. "Andros, help Annie upstairs. She's got another of her headaches. I'll go deal with Princess Siobhan."

"Won't work," Anwyn said because she could feel Siobhan coming and her rage was all for Anwyn. "She's looking for me. Help me downstairs quick so it seems like the headache hit down there. Better than letting her upstairs and see that I was spying."

Mother wanted to protest. That was obvious on her face, much less in her emotions. Andros wanted to, as well. He pouted but helped Anwyn up, steading her for the three steps she managed to take on her own. Then Anwyn's legs went out, Mother cursed, and Anwyn got swept up in her arms like she was two years old again.

"Mother," Anwyn complained despite knowing it would do her no good at all.

"We don't have time for your pride, Annie," Mother said.

She strode out of the room, down the stairs and to the spindly little formal chairs that lined the formal entrance room. Anwyn's butt was barely perched on one of the wobbly little things when Siobhan slammed the door open and strode in ready to yell.

"Ow," Anwyn squeaked.

She hated it when she squeaked like that but the door slamming against the wall and rebounding was horribly loud. Mother patted Anwyn's shoulder at the same time that Andros cuddled up next to Anwyn, keeping her from falling over.

"Princess," Mother said. "Is there something we can do for you?"

"...What is wrong with her?" Siobhan asked.

There was so much in that question, so much more than just asking why Anwyn was too pale, shaking and sweating from the pain in her head. Siobhan radiated rage that could never be satisfied. The world was against her, every single person and animal. They were... not quite real in Siobhan's eyes. Yes, they, Anwyn, experienced pain but it wasn't real pain like what Siobhan experienced.

Animals didn't experience pain.

Men, in her eyes, were less than animals and they enjoyed pain.

It was like slipping into a bath of sewage, dipping into Siobhan's mind. Blood and pain and death, all wrapped in vengeful, paranoid rage. The plot wasn't as clear as Anwyn had expected. Siobhan thought she could use the law, certainly, but her plans for using it were vague and distant things.

She was making it all up as she went. There was no grand plot, no carefully arranged scheme. Someone else had the plot and the details. Siobhan was just using those around her.

Anwyn shuddered.

"Could you possibly be a bit quieter?" Anwyn said. Her voice shook horribly.

"What...?" Siobhan said, not one bit quieter but a good bit more hesitantly. It kind of looked like worry for her but Anwyn could feel that it was worry of being infected with whatever Anwyn had.

"It's another of her headaches," Mother said. "Annie gets them pretty regularly, especially when she's in port. Something about the air, I think. Gets a lot less of them at sea."

"Winter's the worst," Andros agreed and he wasn't even lying. He really believed it.

Their faces were all blurry, coming into focus and going out of focus as Anwyn's head throbbed, her stomach churned and her cheeks went wet. She tried breathing but Siobhan's disgust turned to triumphant superiority that she, Anwyn, was so weak as to be laid low by a fireplace.

"Andros, go get Doctor Bernice," Mother ordered. "Annie needs her."

"I'll be fine," Anwyn protested even though she really wasn't fine. She wasn't going to be all right until she could go up to her bunk, close the curtain and hide her head under her pillow. "I don't need poppy milk."

"Annie, you're shaking so hard I'm afraid you're going to go into convulsions," Mother said. She came and sat next to Anwyn, holding Anwyn's shoulders that yes, were shaking violently. "Really, what did you need, Princess Siobhan? I'd like to get Annie up to bed as soon as Doctor Bernice gets here. Poppy milk at Annie's doses is pretty powerful stuff."

"I can wait," Princess Siobhan said. "My issue was with the slander your daughter is spewing against me and my Clan."

"I haven't even been outside the door," Anwyn protested in what felt like the right direction. She couldn't be sure that the reddish shape near the door was Siobhan but it should be. Or maybe it was one of her guards. Hard to tell. "Been inside the whole day because of this stupid headache."

"She's here!" Andros yelled only to flinch and whisper 'sorry, Annie' when she whined at him.

Doctor Bernice was a pillar of cool control compared to Siobhan's raging fire. Andros was quicksilver, every emotion at once flitting through his eleven-year-old mind. Mother, wary, watchful, strong and determined to keep everyone safe. And yes, there were guards, all of them terrified of Siobhan. Most of them were so scared of Siobhan that they couldn't even spare a thought for

Anwyn who found herself on the floor shaking uncontrollably.

"Seizure," Doctor Bernice said, still cool and blue and steady. "Give me that cushion, Andros, there, under her head. I'll need you to hold her shoulder for me so I can inject the poppy milk, Laoise. Should take the edge off enough that we can get her upstairs. I've told her to be more careful with these headaches. She's going to end up with a bleeding artery in the brain if she doesn't watch out."

The poppy milk washed away everyone's emotions other than the Ladies whose singing came through much more clearly now. They were worried about events on the land, but in that distant way that said they were studying things of only mild importance rather than the sort of worry that Anwyn felt.

"I've got her," Mother said. "Thanks, Bernice. Andros, get the doors for me. Let me get Annie settled and I'll be back down, Princess Siobhan."

The world shifted around Anwyn and suddenly she was flying the same way the Ladies flew through the water. Anwyn's body went one direction, carried off by Mother with Andros and Doctor Bernice in tow, while her mind stayed right there in the lobby. Siobhan's rage was still there, banked now instead of flaming up into the sky like a bonfire.

"Ah, Princess Siobhan?" one of the guards said. She swallowed when Siobhan whirled to glare at her. "Um, Lady Etain did ask that you not interfere with the donation fair. We should--"

"Are you the princess or am I?" Siobhan snarled at the guard who paled and backed off several paces. "I thought not. They're slandering me and I know it. That little monster is plotting against me. I won't have it. They'll all pay for it when I'm Queen. If you don't want their fate then you should think carefully about what you say and do."

She strode out of the Clanhouse. Her guards hesitated for a long moment before following, all of them afraid and praying that the Queen lived a long, long time.

Without hope.

Because they, just like Anwyn, knew that the Queen was hours from death.

11. MIDNIGHT BELLS

Bells echoed in the night.

Raelin jerked awake. That was the grand temple bell, the big one that was too wide for her to stand inside and touch either side. A moment later the smaller bells in the market began to ring. Then bells at the smaller temples. More bells near and far rang out until the entire city was filled with the sound of bells chiming over and over and over.

"Damn it," Raelin whispered as she threw her blankets off and shoved back the curtain on her bunk.

Anwyn was rolling out of her bunk, slow and clumsy from the poppy milk she'd been dosed with. Treva poked her head out of her bunk over Gwen, eyes wide. Little Erlina started crying on the bunk underneath Raelin. As Raelin swung down, Erlina crawled out of her bunk and ran to Anwyn who scooped her up and patted her back.

They both ended up on their asses, sitting in the middle of the girls' bunk room.

"The Queen?" Treva asked in a voice so soft that it was barely audible over the clamor of the bells.

"Yeah," Anwyn said.

She shut her eyes and leaned back against her bunk, nearly boneless in her exhaustion.

"Get back in bed, Annie," Raelin ordered. "Come on. You're in no shape for getting up. Help us get her in bed, Erlina. I think you're going to need to cuddle with her to keep Annie from doing something silly."

Erlina's bottom lip pouted out but she shoved at Anwyn as Treva and Raelin manhandled Anwyn right back into her bunk. Then, thankfully, Erlina curled up next to Annie, snuffling against her confused tears. Took only a few moments before Anwyn dropped back to sleep. Before Raelin could shut Anwyn's curtain, Erlina was sleeping, too.

"They'll be okay?" Treva asked with her hands clenched in the hem of her night shirt and bottom lip gnawed between her teeth until she saw Raelin looking.

"Lina's too bitty to know what's going on," Raelin said. She ruffled Treva's soft crown of curls, chuckling at the way she growled. "And Annie's too drugged up to do anything but sleep. She needs it. You know she's been… thinking too hard."

Even here, in their bedroom at the heart of the Dana Clanhouse, Raelin didn't want to say openly that Anwyn had been using the gifts the Ladies gave her too much. It wasn't safe. Frankly, Anwyn was going to be lucky if Siobhan, Queen Siobhan and wasn't that a horrifying thought, didn't have her executed.

Treva nodded. When Raelin held out one arm, Treva gratefully leaned into Raelin's side. At eight, Treva really should go back to bed too but she was too old for that and too young for any of the discussions that were sure to begin soon. Andros would be fussing, though, so perhaps she could get together with him.

"How about you and Andros work on making us a midnight snack?" Raelin suggested. "I'm betting that no one's going back to sleep anytime soon. Well, no one but Annie and Lina."

Treva nodded, squaring her shoulders like she was a good decade older than she was. Raelin chuckled, nodding approval.

"I was only a year older than you when I helped rebuild the Tourmaline Dreams, Treva," Raelin said. Softly because she could hear Mother and Father in the other room. Plus Gwen and Mari and Nolan and Gavin, come down from their apartments one floor up.

"I can't... do that," Treva murmured. "I'm not like you."

"Hey, you're just like me," Raelin said, kneeling down so that she could meet Treva's eyes even with Treva staring at the floor. "You're Dana. Not one of the fiery tempered ones, one of the steadier ones. I mean, nobody's quite as even tempered as me but still. You're not Gwen or Annie."

Treva grinned at that, like a flash of lightning before her face darkened with doubt again.

"I didn't do it all at once, you know," Raelin said. She ignored the bells to focus on Treva. "I did it one day at a time. One lesson at a time. That's all anyone ever does. Even the Goddesses saved our ancestors one soul at a time, you know. So you do one thing. Look around. Find another thing. Do that, and then another and another and another until somehow you look back and you've done... so much. That's all it is. One foot in front of another. One haul of the line at a time. That's what we Dana do. It's what we'll keep on doing."

Treva's eyes went wide as Raelin explained. By the end, she was standing tall, smiling and those little hands that seemed far too small for any sort of work were calm and loose and ready. Just a year younger than Raelin had been.

Time had passed so quickly and Raelin wasn't sure when, how.

"I can do that," Treva said.

"Good," Raelin said. "So, you go corral Andros and make snacks. Something easy like toast and preserves. Make cold cuts of meat and cheese. I'll go corral the rest of the family and get them to not run off and cause trouble."

Treva snorted and then laughed, nose wrinkled as she grinned at Raelin. "Might as well tell the tide not to come in, Rae."

"I know," Raelin groaned. "Go on. Get us all fed."

She stood and watched as Treva ran off to the boy's room for Andros who appeared with Caddie and Aravel a moment later. Raelin headed into their common room with Aravel who caught her good hand and clung desperately.

"Annie?" Mother asked so grimly that Raelin rolled her eyes.

"Asleep with Erlina," Raelin said. "She's dosed too much for anything but sleeping. Probably best thing for her. Erlina was frightened by the bells but she fell back asleep right away. We hear any announcements?"

"Only the bells," Mother said.

Father leaned onto her, pale-faced and shaking, so Mother wrapped her arms around him and hugged him close. As always, he was thin and delicate compared to her muscle-heavy arms and shoulders even though he was stronger than most any other man around. Raelin looked at Gwen, holding Nolan close, and Mari who was like a tree trunk that Gavin had wrapped himself around.

"I'll go," Raelin offered. "Someone needs to see what's happening on the ground. I'll grab Bridget and Nuala, bring them as backup. We'll head into the Market, see if anyone's posted notices. If not, we'll head for the Delbhana Clanhouse, then up to the Palace. The streets are sure to be chaos but the three of us should be able to make it."

"You should take Eoghania," Gwen said.

"I don't think you could get her away from Sean," Raelin said.

Mother chuckled at that, as did Mari. As much as Gwen adored Nolan and Mari loved Gavin, Eoghania doted on Sean and his baby daughters. She'd never leave them alone when there was a chance of trouble.

Raelin was single and likely to stay that way all her life. Nuala was a brawler but one of the slower to anger ones. And Bridget was whip-fast and scarily smart. Between the three of them, they should be able to find out what was happening without setting off a riot.

"Go," Mother said. She rubbed Father's back. "Be careful, Rae. We can't afford to lose any of you."

Raelin nodded, hugged Aravel who whined before letting her go, then changed clothes. By the time she was dressed in her oldest, most worn clothes with a cap over her hair so the red wouldn't give her away instantly, Nuala and Bridget where there, both in worn dark Dana blues that wouldn't stick out on the streets. The three of them left the Clanhouse by the little side door along Port Street that was lined with tiny restaurants.

None of them were open, even the ones that served sailors and dock workers on night shifts. The cooks were out on the street, watching people, talking, worrying. The streets were full of people, all women, gossiping in whispers. The whispers died as Raelin emerged with Nuala and Bridget at her back. Then sprang back up again, louder, once they'd passed.

That held true as they made their way though the still-calm streets towards the Great Market. None of the stores were open there, not even the Delbhana store with all the dyed goods that Siobhan had sacrificed herself for a year ago. The people there barely noticed Raelin, Nuala and Bridget at all. Better than back home but worrisome, still. Everyone was far too wary, watching the red brick walls of the Market as if they expected attack at any second. Even Raelin felt too nervous to meet other women's eyes as the three of them moved through the market, checking all the message boards.

"No notice," Nuala said.

"No one knows anything," Bridget agreed, eyes darting as she watched the people around them.

Raelin nodded. "It's too soon for a formal notice. That'll come tomorrow, maybe in the afternoon."

Neither Nuala nor Bridget said anything about the potential for riots delaying that notice. They didn't have to. The electric tension in the air, like lightning about to strike, wasn't quite there. Raelin had been through riots before, both in Aingeal and elsewhere. It was possible, yes, but not likely right this second.

That could change at any moment.

People were moving through the market, not staying, not even lingering in hopes of an announcement. They weren't heading up Admiralty Lane towards the Delbhana Clan-house. They were all heading straight up the Royal Road.

"Let's go," Raelin ordered.

"Lead on," Bridget replied.

They stayed behind Raelin, one on either side, as Raelin followed the crowds building in the streets. By the time they arrived at the Royal Palace, there were rich and poor mingling together in the streets. A few men, mostly the severely poor men who had no clan to support them, slipped between the masses of women. But only a few. It looked as though every single man who could afford to had stayed home behind closed doors.

What had Raelin's skin crawling was the silence of the crowd. The closer they got to the Royal Gates, which stood open as they never, ever were, the quieter people got. No whispers. No murmurs. Just the sound of breathing, boots against the cobblestones. The occasional quiet apology for jostling someone but nothing else.

She found herself panting just from the stress of it all.

Annie wouldn't have been able to handle this. At all. She would have started screaming and swinging wildly long before they passed through the gates and onto the broad lawns that surrounded the Palace.

Which was quiet, windows closed but lamps obviously lit. Every single room had lights in it. Raelin bit her lip, glanced at Bridget and then nodded towards the great balcony that the Queen sometimes used to use to make addresses. Bridget bit her lip and then shook her head no. When Bridget headed towards one of the trees, carefully pruned and shaped by the royal gardeners, Raelin followed. Nuala hesitated and then stuck to Raelin's right side.

Guarding her. Making sure that Raelin wouldn't be attacked on her weak side. Nice, if somewhat embarrassing. Needed, if this did go as badly as Raelin feared it would.

When the bells suddenly stopped, people screamed. Raelin shouted and then clamped a hand over her mouth. It couldn't have been an hour already. Could it? But no, it had to have been. They'd walked all this way so yes, it was an hour.

Bells tolled the hour of the old Queen's death. Silence

marked the new Queen's assumption of power. A new dynasty?

Well. That hadn't happen in long enough that Raelin wasn't certain what should happen. The Vanora dynasty had taken over Aingeal one hundred forty-seven years ago but it had been an easy transition from one cousin in the Saraid to another cousin in the Vanora. The Saraid dynasty had ruled Aingeal for two hundred eighty-nine years, growing it from a tiny little country into a powerhouse of commerce and manufacturing.

Raelin had to wonder whether the Delbhana dynasty would see the fall of Aingeal after thirteen dynasties had watched it grow and prosper. Watched them, the people of Aingeal. Seriously, thinking of Aingeal as though it had any reality outside of the people was stupid.

It was the people that counted, not the maps or the laws or anything else. As people appeared on the Queen's Balcony, Raelin stared up at Prince Toryn and Princess Siobhan. Did they know that? Prince Toryn, no, King Toryn. He was King Toryn now for all that he looked like he wanted to cry his eyes out.

King Toryn seemed to understand what mattered. He stared down at the gathered crowds with sorrow and pride. Sorrow for the loss of his mother, pride in the people so silently waiting.

Siobhan.

Huh. She looked down at the crowds with a smile that was, even at this distance, cruel. Greedy. More than a little mad.

Queen Siobhan, first of the Delbhana Dynasty, leaned her hands on the railing of the balcony and smiled down at the crowds as if their presence was her due rather than a warning. Raelin hissed and backed up as the crowd began to murmur, to talk, to call to one another with anger in their voices, their faces, their clenching fists.

"We can't leave," Bridget hissed at Raelin.

"I know," Raelin said. "I know! Damn her, doesn't she understand what's happening here?"

12. DYNASTY CHANGE

Raelin's heart pounded in her ears. The rising voices of the crowds around her grew until it was enough to drown out her heartbeat. It drowned out Siobhan, too, as she first raised a hand while smiling smugly then frowned, then waved a fist and finally shouted.

Unheard.

Her words were less than a whisper in a hurricane against the growing roar of the crowd. It was uncoordinated, the shouting, the screams, the bellows. Too many people saying too many things for any sense but as King Toryn caught Siobhan's arm, stopping her from summoning the Royal Guard, women lifted their arms to pump a fist into the sky.

The shouts changed it a chant. One that swept across the crowd, unifying the voices into one.

"Va-No-Ra!"

A chill ran down Raelin's spine. Vanora. The old Queen, the old Dynasty. The rule they'd all been born and lived under. That had shaped Aingeal to what it was.

"Vanora! Vanora! Vanora!"

Nuala started chanting with the crowd. Then Bridget. Both of them with the burning ferocity of a Dana ready to beat someone through the floor. It would have worried Raelin but the women around them were just as fierce, just as loud, just as defiant as they shouted and thrust their fists up to the Goddesses.

As Raelin watched, lifting good left arm to the sky with her cousins, Siobhan's face went the sort of red that was nearly black with rage. When she whirled at King Toryn, the crowd roared at her for daring to touch their king.

He was their King. Raelin's king. All of theirs. Siobhan had married him, yes, but everyone in the world knew that she treated him poorly. Toryn stepped backwards, fear on his face that shifted to shock at the booming majesty of the crowd's fury. It rocked Siobhan, too, draining the red from her cheeks and making her back away from Toryn.

She stood, silent and still, as Toryn took four slow, hesitant steps to the railing. As he raised one hand.

The crowd, Raelin included, went silent.

She heard his sob. Watched him dash away tears with a trembling hand. Then nodded slowly as Siobhan looked away, hands clenched in fists.

"Thank you," King Toryn said.

He projected well. His voice carried over the crowd perfectly or maybe it was that they were all still and silent, holding their breath to hear what he said. Raelin would have sworn she heard the sound of teeth grinding from Siobhan but that was certainly her imagination. That was too small a sound for her to hear it this far away, no matter how angry, how frustrated Siobhan was.

"Thank you for coming," King Toryn said. His smile was weak. "My mother... she never spent much time focused on you. On Aingeal's people. She wanted to. There were always meetings and work that had to be done. But she tried to think of you. To do what was right for everyone. She struggled to live as long as possible. For you. All of you."

He shut his eyes for a long moment. Raelin could see the wetness of tears on his cheeks even though she was too far away to see the individual tears falling. Siobhan, still standing well away from King Toryn, turned back to him. Her frown was puzzled, frustrated. When King Toryn shook his head and pulled out a handkerchief to wipe his eyes, her hands relaxed.

Did she not understand grief? The love a child felt for their parent?

Maybe she didn't. Annie had said that Siobhan was mad. Perhaps she truly didn't understand love at all. It was sad. And horrifying. What would she do if she couldn't understand the most basic things about being human?

"The Vanora dynasty, my mother's line, is done," King Toryn announced so sadly that even Siobhan rocked back a bit. "I was her only surviving child. Her only son. I will carry her blood into the new dynasty. My wife will be the Queen. I do not know what will come but I thank you, oh, I thank all of you for coming here tonight. You don't know what it means to see you all here to mourn for my mother with me."

Shouts of sympathy, of grief, of support echoed across the crowd. Raelin swayed a step forward with the crowd when King Toryn turned to face Siobhan.

Siobhan curled a lip and took a step towards King Toryn, one hand curling into a fist.

The roar of fury knocked her back several steps. She looked so shocked, so stunned that anyone would object to her treating King Toryn as she wished. Not so surprising, really. No one had objected all this time when King Toryn had bruises, when he flinched away from Siobhan. No one had dared.

But it was different now. Thousands upon thousands of women, hundreds of men, too, stood watching. All of them reading and willing to storm the doors, to climb the walls, if that was what it took to keep their King Toryn safe.

Raelin would join them. Damn her to the Morrigan's hands, she'd lead them. That was a horrifying thought that made Raelin gulp. She would, right this very instant, storm into the palace and kill anyone in her way if it meant keeping King Toryn safe.

By her side, Nuala looked ready to charge. Bridget was panting with the sort of fury that led to blackout rages. They both started when Raelin grabbed their wrists. The pull of the mob, that's what it was. It had to be. They couldn't let it pull them under because a mob led by Dana was a hundred, a thousand times more dangerous.

"She hurts him and I'm killing her," Nuala said through gritted teeth.

Several women near them nodded their agreement.

"I know," Raelin said. "But I can't fight, Nuala. Not with my arm."

Again, women around them responded just as much as Nuala and Bridget did. Several looked Raelin's way, taking in her scars and old clothes, making assumptions that probably, hopefully, kept them from seeing that the three of them were Dana. Or maybe seeing that they were and accepting that yes, the Dana had a right to be here, too.

Hard to tell.

"Then stay with us," Bridget said. "We'll keep you safe as we kill her."

Raelin snorted, shook her head and focused on King Toryn and Siobhan again.

"Mother always said," King Toryn said in that perfectly

projected voice that sounded conversational while still carrying so that everyone could hear him, "that the rulers of Aingeal are not like any others in the world. Other Queens have the favor of the Goddesses. They claim a divine right to rule. Not here. We do not give the Goddesses the right to choose our rulers. The Vanora ruled because the people of Aingeal willed it so. They accepted the Vanora and the Vanora took care of them."

He raised his chin as Siobhan opened her mouth to object. The crowd growled and Siobhan snapped it shut again.

"Now the Vanora are dead," King Toryn said. His voice broke on the last word. "You are my wife, Delbhana Siobhan. Through me you have a chance to start a new dynasty. Only through me. Without me, the last of the Vanora blood, you are only Delbhana, only a daughter of a rich clan. And not one that the people love."

Raelin nearly began laughing. She clapped a hand over her mouth that King Toryn would be this bold. That he would dare to set the boundaries of his marriage in public where everyone could hear and see and know if Siobhan violated them. She'd had no idea his spine was that strong. It was something that Caddie would have done, that Gavin had done. It was almost Dana and Raelin could almost love him for it.

The crowd erupted, shouted accusations flying at Siobhan and bellowed support winging to King Toryn. Everyone, even Nuala, went silent when King Toryn held up one languid hand.

This time Raelin was sure that she actually could hear Siobhan gritting her teeth.

"The Queens of Aingeal serve at the people's will," King Toryn said. "They serve the people. I've told you this before. I told your mother, Lady Etain, and yes, I see you there by the door."

Lady Etain came out, jaw jumping and face red as she stared at King Toryn. Siobhan didn't turn to look at her. She stared at King Toryn who nodded slowly.

"The old dynasty is dead," King Toryn said. "Siobhan, daughter of the Delbhana, I call on you to swear oaths of service and protection to these, the people of Aingeal. Will you swear to listen to their voices? Will you swear to put their needs above the needs of the Delbhana, above your needs, above even my needs? Will you do everything that is necessary to help the people of Aingeal grow, prosper and succeed? Will you protect the clans that these people belong to? Or will the Delbhana dynasty die before it even begins?"

"Oh, you brilliant, wicked, perfect man!" Raelin whispered.

She'd clapped her hand over her mouth. She couldn't remember when. Maybe when Toryn called Lady Etain out? Or when he started listing what Siobhan had to agree to.

It didn't matter. Nuala clutched at Raelin's good shoulder while Bridget whispered prayers that alternated between begging Siobhan to say yes and begging her to say no so that they could kill her now.

"I'm your wife," Siobhan said. Her voice was too thin to carry all the way but the words were so clear that Raelin saw them.

"Wife or not, that doesn't matter," King Toryn said. He shrugged. "I'm a man. I can marry again. And if I die, well, the civil war will be horrible but a new dynasty, a new Aingeal, will rise from the ashes. I'm but the tool of the succession. They are the ones who choose. Not me. Not you. Swear. Or do not. But know that there is no second chance. You swear now or you will never be the Queen."

Siobhan made a choked noise that carried perfectly across the now dead-silent crowd. Lady Etain was whispering curses. They had to be curses given how furious her face was. She didn't take a single step closer to King Toryn but her hands were in fists that shook by her sides.

As Siobhan shut her eyes, Raelin sucked in a breath because she'd been holding her breath, staying as still as she could so that she wouldn't miss anything. She couldn't miss this. It was too important. Raelin didn't even know what she wanted Siobhan to say.

"I swear," Siobhan said and this time her voice did carry properly, dead calm and serious though her eyes bored holes into King Toryn's head. "I swear that I will uphold the clans and the listen to the voices of the people of Aingeal. I will work to help everyone in Aingeal grow, prosper and succeed, even the idiot Dana and I still think that's asking too much of me. I will... I will protect you, as well."

Prince Toryn shook his head. "I don't need your protection, Siobhan, daughter of the Delbhana. I belong to the people of Aingeal. They will protect me."

The roar that tore itself from Raelin's throat was a surprise but everyone else was roaring, too. She would. Whenever she was in Aingeal, Raelin would be watching out for King Toryn. And as a Dana and one of Mother's older daughters, she had the chance to actually see how he was doing.

King Toryn let them roar for long enough that both Siobhan and Lady Etain went still and quiet. Fearful. They were afraid. Good! They should be afraid. The Delbhana always thought that they could steal power, take what they wanted and destroy those who opposed them. Maybe now they'd learn that no, they couldn't.

Huh, and maybe the Ladies would swim right up on the land to put the crown on Siobhan's head.

Raelin went quiet as King Toryn held up a hand again. So did the crowd though Bridget whined next to Raelin. At least she'd chosen to grab one of the neighboring women rather than grab Raelin's bad arm.

"Then in the morning," King Toryn said in a sad, distant voice, "as all the Clan leaders watch, you will be crowned Queen of Aingeal. And may the Goddesses have mercy on your soul if you fail to remember this night, wife. For the Morrigan herself will walk among Aingeal's people, raising them to war if you forget. I would not wish that on anyone."

Not even you.

The words hung in the air, unspoken, but Raelin heard them. She could see the women around them nodding their agreement with those unheard words. Siobhan lifted her chin despite the way her hands shook.

"So be it," Queen Siobhan said.

13. CORONATION DAY

The silence woke Anwyn. She blinked up at the ceiling, not sure at first what it was. Then she realized that it truly was quiet. Dead still. Her fingers felt like they were somewhere off by the door, completely disconnected from her body, while her mouth was full of cotton. But her ears still worked despite the poppy milk.

No giggles from Erlina. No snappish comments in the kitchen as Cadfael argued with Father and Andros about what to make. Raelin wasn't stomping around. Nothing, not a single person in the apartment.

Her mind slipped away from her body and oh, good, her fingers were still where they belong. It was her mind that'd been touching things it shouldn't. Stupid poppy milk always made things go weird. Weirder? Definitely weirder than normal for Anwyn what with her body and mind being disconnected, extra senses zooming in and out of focus without her having the slightest control over them.

Ladies sang quietly under the bay. There were a pair of them under the dock, right beneath the Tourmaline Dreams. Strange part was that there was only one person on the Tourmaline. And just two in the whole Clanhouse other than Anwyn, one guarding the warehouse door and another at the formal entrance biting her nails.

Where was everyone? It was midmorning. They should be working.

The whole city was still and silent. Well, almost. There were Royal Guards escorting Mother back to the Clanhouse, all of them scowling as Mother cursed under her breath. At least she had the good carriage, the little one that you only needed one horse to run with.

Anwyn looked around again, trying to focus. It wasn't easy but she managed to drag her attention, her mind, gifts?

She dragged herself back to the Clanhouse, back to their suite, to the kitchen table where a note sat. Waiting for Anwyn.

"Annie," it said in Mother's firm script, "the Queen died so we're all off to attend Princess Siobhan and Prince Toryn's coronation. If you get up, go back to bed. Don't be stupid, girl. You had convulsions from that headache of yours and I'll not have you risk yourself by moving. Sleep. Rest. We'll tell you how it went. Rae's pretty sure it'll go all right."

It was signed "Laoise" rather than "Mother" which said a good bit about how nervous Mother actually was about the coronation. Anwyn hummed thoughtfully, the sound coming out of her physical mouth and apparently from her floating mind because all the Ladies in the bay brightened.

"Chaos-Daughter Anwyn free-swimming," one of the Ladies said, slipping free from her body to come up and swim around Anwyn.

Free of her body she was far more a mass of light and color than the blobby head, many tentacles and needle-pointed teeth that Anwyn was used to.

"Eh, had a really bad headache," Anwyn said. "Gave me convulsions so they medicated me. Poppy milk. It always makes my mind slip free of my body though this is worse than normal."

She glanced at her body, glad to see that it wasn't convulsing. Didn't seem like she was in any more pain than she'd been before. That was good. Normally, talking to the Ladies made her so damned sick.

"Problem that is," the Lady said as she wrapped glowing not-tentacles around Anwyn's left wrist. "See us. Measure to take there can be."

The actual words were completely disassociated from the images that the Lady gave to Anwyn. Something about alterations and controls that really made little sense to her, especially with the poppy milk making her mind move both too fast and like molasses at the new year. The Lady laughed as several of her sisters swam free of their bodies to cluster around Anwyn. They ran glowing tentacles over Anwyn's mind-body, too, singing things that she couldn't follow about changes, testing, advances.

They all froze as Mother strode into the suite with the Royal Guard at her heels.

"Shoot, I better get back in my body," Anwyn said. "Sorry, Ladies. Gotta go. I'll do my best to get somewhere that I can talk to you without it being noticed. Might take a couple of years, though. I'm... watched."

She shrugged, surprised that the Ladies all glowed that they knew and understood that Anwyn wasn't free. Huh. Well, as long as they knew that she'd have come back to sing with them if she could. Pity that they couldn't fix whatever it was right now but if they couldn't, they couldn't.

"Annie!" Mother snapped, shaking Anwyn's shoulder.

"Mngh," Anwyn grumbled, trying to swat at her hands

and failing because her arms were like lead. So were her eyelids.

"What's wrong with her?" one of the Royal Guard asked.

"Migraines," Mother replied as she levered Anwyn up and patted her cheek until Anwyn managed to open her eyes. "Come on, Annie. Need you up and dressed. We're all required at the coronation. They're all waiting on you."

"Not fair," Anwyn complained. She peered at the Royal Guard, pouted and then shuddered because sitting up made the pain come right back. "Ah, damn her to the Morrigan's very bosom. Stupid headache's a cluster, Mother, not a migraine."

"Shit."

Mother sighed but she still made Anwyn struggle into pants and a shirt, then wrestled a proper vest and jacket onto Anwyn. By the time they managed that, the Royal Guard who'd spoken had Anwyn's shoes. She even helped Anwyn get them on her feet which was good because there was no way that Anwyn could bend down to tie them up without passing out or throwing up.

"What's a cluster?" the Guard asked. Her eyes were as green as Caddie's but her hair was black and her skin a dusky rose like she'd come from Western Aingeal. No accent. Maybe her parents had moved here?

"Migraines leave in a day or so," Anwyn explained as she carefully, with both Mother and the Guard's help, got to her feet. "My headaches cluster. I'll get one, then another, then another, days and days of them. Sometimes five and six days in a row of migraines bad enough that I can't... think, eat, move. Nausea, light hurts, convulsions when the pain gets bad enough. This? Is a cluster. It's going to be a bad one. I really have to go?"

"Sorry, Annie," Mother said.

The poppy milk had been keeping everyone's emotions far away, up in the clouds. It cut suddenly and Anwyn was chin-deep into all their emotions. Mother was riddled with fear, rage and guilt so strong that it nearly knocked Anwyn to her knees. The guard was worried, stunningly about Anwyn, and not just because Siobhan was being made queen. Other four guards were watchful, wary, concerned. One, way in the very back, suddenly had a new way to describe the headaches her husband got.

At least that was a good thing out of this mess. She'd be able to go to a doctor and get proper help for him.

"I think I'll just pass out. Sorry," Anwyn said to Mother who started, cursed and caught Anwyn as she did just that.

Her mind didn't go all the way away. Not with poppy milk in her system. No, Anwyn hovered over her body as Mother scooped her up and carried her down to the carriage to tuck her in. The guards whispered between themselves, feeling bad now about forcing Anwyn from her bed when she was so obviously sick.

At least outside of her body she didn't have to feel all the jostling in the carriage, didn't have to see the light that would stab through her brain if her eyes were open. The streets were empty until they got close to the Royal Palace. Then they were lined with people. Anwyn almost jolted back into her body as she realized that most of the people in the city were there, standing, sitting, waiting outside the Palace.

Those that weren't outside were inside, waiting as tense as Caddie when he was in a room with a bunch of strange women. Mother carried Anwyn in, the guards surrounding her like an honor guard instead of the near-jailing that it was probably meant to be.

Anwyn kind of wondered whether Siobhan realized that by dragging Anwyn here she was giving Anwyn a sort of importance that everyone in both the Dana and the Delbhana had been trying to avoid. Like making Anwyn into the most important part of the coronation.

Then they arrived in the grand hall where the coronation was to be held and Anwyn realized that yes, that was exactly what Siobhan wanted. Neither she nor Prince, no, King, Toryn were there. But all the Delbhana were. And so were all the Dana, standing across the aisle from each other while glaring. There was a spot for Anwyn and Mother, right up front where they'd be forced to watch every single second of Siobhan being crowned.

"She's still out?" Raelin asked once Mother took her spot with Anwyn still in her arms like a little boy getting cuddled.

"Woke up for a minute or so and then passed out again as we got her dressed and standing," Mother replied. She glared at Lady Etain who sighed, pursed her lips and then nodded a faint-hearted apology.

The coronation wasn't a fancy thing. Anwyn slowly edged her way back into her body, taking it by bits and pieces because she really wasn't looking forward to trying to stand up while her head hurt that bad and she was filled to the eyeballs with poppy milk. She managed to get her feet under her as King Toryn came up the aisle in a beautiful gold kilt that rustled like it might just be made of actual cloth of gold. His vest was silk, obviously, heavily embroidered with roses in gold thread but the base fabric was just silk. White and gold, with angry dark eyes and pursed lips and every square inch of his body covered other than his fingertips and face.

Even the back of his neck was covered because he'd put a sort of lace veil on that hung down his back. A slender gold crown with moonstones held it in place. Once he was in place at the throne, a Delbhana boy who couldn't be more than five next to him with the Queen's Crown on a pillow next to him, Siobhan emerged from the back of the room.

Mother turned so of course Anwyn turned with her. She wasn't quite steady on her own feet yet. It was Mother's grip around her waist that kept her from falling to the floor in a whimpering heap.

Siobhan smirked at seeing Anwyn not-quite standing there. Yeah, she definitely wanted to have Anwyn watch her take the throne. And to have everyone else watch Anwyn watching. Probably made her even happier that Anwyn was sick while it all happened.

Stupid poppy milk making her gifts worthless.

Unlike King Toryn's slow, stately progression up the aisle, Siobhan strode up it. She looked like she was in a hurry, like she expected someone to object. Anwyn didn't roll her eyes, much as she wanted to. No point to it. It'd only make her headache worse.

"Siobhan of the Delbhana," King Toryn said in one of those wonderfully theatrical tones that carried for miles, "I call on you to swear oaths of service and protection to these, the people of Aingeal. Will you swear to listen to their voices? Will you swear to put their needs above the needs of the Delbhana, above your needs, above even my needs? Will you do everything that is necessary to help the people of Aingeal grow, prosper and succeed? Will you protect the clans that these people belong to?"

The whole room went as electric as the rigging during a thunderstorm at sea. Anwyn stared at King Toryn, shocked that he'd try and impose that sort of thing on Siobhan of all people. He had to be covered in bruises and yet he was demanding that? In public?

"As her oaths," Raelin whispered while grinning like a mad woman. "Formally!"

She flinched away from Mother's glare so there was more that Anwyn had missed while unconscious. Probably a lot more because Siobhan didn't protest, didn't even glower at King Toryn.

Siobhan knelt in front of him, bowed her head as if she was completely and totally willing to be a selfless queen who never did anything for her own sake.

"I so swear," Siobhan said in nearly as good of a theatrical voice. "I will listen to, protect and serve the people of Aingeal. I will put their needs above the Delbhana, my or even your needs. I will do all that is necessary to help the people of Aingeal grow, prosper and succeed. And I will protect the Clans of Aingeal to which the people belong."

King Toryn nodded once. He turned to the boy, picked up the Queen's crown and slowly lowered it onto Siobhan's head with a grim sort of finality.

"I declare you Queen Siobhan, First of the Delbhana dynasty," King Toryn said. He shut his eyes, stood silently for a long moment that had Anwyn's heart pounded despite everything.

"Long may you reign."

14. FIRST MEASURES

The Royal Council room was as hot as the inside of an oven. There were so many women packed into it, standing in front of the Council on their walled-off dais that Raelin could've lifted her feet and not fallen to the floor. She'd packed crates of trade goods less tightly than this. Every single Clan Head, all their heirs and a good number of women like Raelin who were called on as seconds or occasional replacements were there.

All of them silent as Siobhan took her place, smirking, in the middle of the Council dais.

Lady Etain was on the floor, not on the dais. That was a surprise. Raelin had expected Siobhan to put her mother at her left hand, in a place of honor, but no. She'd very firmly sent her mother to the floor with everyone else. Right then, there was no one on the dais with Siobhan.

Queen Siobhan.

Damn but it was going to take a long time to get used to that. Raelin wasn't sure she'd ever manage it. From Mother's scowl, she didn't think she'd manage it, either. She had her arms crossed on her chest, her chin tucked like she was ready for a battle and a snarl already forming on her face.

"Breathe," Gwen murmured to Mother.

"Please," Raelin agreed, nudging Mother. "This is not the time for your temper, either of you."

"Oh, do share," Siobhan said, raising her chin and smirking at Raelin. "What's so fascinating that you'd interrupt before I can begin to make assignments?"

Raelin snorted, clapped her bad hand over Mother's mouth and kicked Gwen in the shin, making her jump and glare.

"Not interesting, just Dana tempers being as bad as it's possible for a temper to be, Queen Siobhan," Raelin drawled. She got a lot of snickers, a few people edging away and a raised eyebrow from Siobhan.

"I've not said one word," Siobhan said so innocently, complete with batting eyes, that Raelin raised an eyebrow.

"You don't have say anything, your Majesty," Raelin said. She glared at Mother when she tried to tug Raelin's hand away from her mouth. "Dana pick fights in our own heads and then expect everyone else to know what we're angry about. And you, both of you, need to breathe and calm down. Goodness, you're as bad as Erlina when she doesn't get a treat."

Both Mother and Gwen made hurt noises at Raelin. Justified hurt noises because Erlina's tantrums at four were little better than they'd been at two. Just louder and more studied than the epic screaming and tear-fests Erlina had thrown a couple of years ago.

"What?" Siobhan asked. She, thankfully, dropped the innocent act to scowl at Raelin.

"Erlina's my littlest sister," Raelin explained. "She's just four and has figured out that tantrums will get her things sometimes if she does it just right."

Siobhan choked on a laugh and then threw her head back to laugh good and long. There was an edge to that laugh that made Raelin nervous. Vicious, too pleased in having Mother and Gwen humiliated in public, but at least she was amused instead of faking being suddenly good, kind and wise.

When she finally, after laughing an uncomfortably long time, stopped, Siobhan's eyes glittered with amused malice. "Far be it for me to keep you from tending to your family's tempers. I would have thought it an impossible task."

Raelin nodded grimly. "Mostly, it is, your Majesty."

The titles, however wrong they felt, did soothe Siobhan's malice a touch. Just enough that she smiled and hummed as she studied all the women looking up at her. Siobhan, ever the sadist, let the silence stretch until pretty much everyone including Lady Etain was fidgeting nervously. Only once Raelin allowed herself to huff and shift her feet in a display of nervousness that she didn't actually feel did Siobhan open a folio and pull out some paperwork.

"As the Queen," Siobhan said, "it is my duty to form a Royal Council. Tradition says that I should retain the same council that my predecessor had however we have long agreed that it was not working well."

Truth delivered in a sly, fake-innocent tone of voice that made Lady Etain hissing something at her daughter that Siobhan completely ignored.

"Given that this is the start of a new dynasty as well as a new reign," Siobhan continued, looking at her paperwork instead of the women in front of her, "I will be seating an... altered council. Some will remain. Others will be new. And perhaps shocking."

She looked straight at Mother who went so still that

Raelin peered at her in worry before turning back to Siobhan who nodding to the right side of the room.

"Lady Mab of Clan Griogal, I would have you retain your place," Siobhan said. "We can discuss your replacement when you choose to retire as I know you are considering it. During this transition, though, the military needs your firm hand."

"Thank you, your Majesty," Lady Mab said.

She hobbled up the stairs to take the seat directly to Siobhan's right. Her scowl said that no matter what Siobhan claimed, this wasn't what she'd wanted. As old as Lady Mab was, Raelin was sure that she'd been actively working towards retiring and had expected the transition to happen right now, not at some point in the future after 'discussion' of her replacement.

"Lady Fiora," Siobhan said, smiling viciously as Lady Fiora started cursing, "you are released form your duties in the Royal Archives."

That one was purely punishment. Raelin could see it. So could Mother who was cursing under her breath and Gwen who grumbled. Lady Fiora had taken the position only three months ago and set out on a huge project to get the Royal Archives up to date on... pretty much everything. Trade, finance, inventions created inside Aingeal and outside of it. Books, history, music, she'd created teams to work on every single thing that anyone could think of.

And now that was gone.

Raelin watched Lady Fiora as Siobhan let two more recently appointed councilors go. All three of them had been put in at Lady Etain's suggestion. All three of them had done pretty good work. Focused more on making Aingeal and the Delbhana look good but still, good work. The ones Siobhan retained were older councilors, the ones who were tired and ready to retire. Just like Lady Mab, they glowered as they took their spots on the bench.

"Lady Bethany," Siobhan said with a smirk for her start and blush, "I appoint you to take over the Royal Archives. I expect that you will work closely with Lady Fiora to continue her good work."

"Thank you, your Majesty," Lady Bethany said. Sweat dripped down her temple as she took her spot on the bench. Not too surprising when she was well known to not like anything at all to do with records, archives and reading.

Siobhan lifted her head and stared right at Mother who stiffened. "Our country has long relied solely on nobles for the Royal Council. My husband brought up a very good point that this is foolish and does not serve our country. Thus, I appoint Dana Laoise to the Council in the position of Councilor of Commerce. Also, Tierney Yvon, you will take the position of Councilor of the Treasury. Your skills are well suited to those tasks, both of you."

Mother sighed, scrubbed her hands over her face and then strode up to the bench to take her spot. Gwen switched from clutching at Mother to clutching at Raelin, not that Raelin was much better. How the hell was Mother going to have time to run the Clan when she had to do all of this, too?

"Your Majesty," Tierney Yvon said in such an angry, brittle tone that people edged away from her, "while I am honored by your request, I do not feel that it is a good choice."

Siobhan leaned on the bench, malice glittering in her eyes as she smiled at Yvon. "My husband, personally, selected you. He is the one who felt you were the correct choice. He is the one who feels that you, above everyone else in Aingeal, is the correct person to lead the Treasury. I, personally, would not have chosen you. Nor would I have chosen Dana Laoise. My personal feelings in this matter do not matter. I swore a vow when I took the crown to serve this country and that is what I am doing. If you cannot do the same, perhaps another country would be better suited to you."

Shit.

Raelin stared at Mother who was seated two chairs away from Siobhan's left hand. She had on the sternest, stone-face that Raelin had ever seen from her. It didn't look like she was happy but King Toryn was right.

Of all the clans in Aigneal, the Dana were the best at commerce. And Mother was their leader. Officially. In reality, it was Great-Uncle Jarmon and Gavin who led them while Mother was the front who said the right things and signed official papers.

So no, this wouldn't actually be that big of a hit for the Dana. Mother could spend time and go battle against the stupidity that was sure to come down from Siobhan and the Royal Council. She could fight for what was right.

Not much likelihood that it would work out because Siobhan's vicious smile as Yvon bowed, mouth pursed over her fake teeth, promised that no matter what either of them wanted, it wasn't going to happen.

And that was likely the point for Siobhan.

She'd put in the people that King Toryn recommended, let them try while undercutting them in every single way possible, and then declare that it wasn't working so obviously changes must be made.

When Yvon took her seat at Siobhan's left hand, the Council was filled. Not one Delbhana other than Siobhan was on the bench. Lady Etain growled so loudly that Siobhan raised an eyebrow at her.

"Mother, I must be seen not to give special treatment to my family," Siobhan said. "That is the world we live in."

"...Of course," Lady Etain said. She ground the words between her teeth, hands in fists. Raelin was pretty sure that Lady Etain's glare could strip the tar off a ship's hull. Might take a few inches of wood along with the tar.

The rest of the meeting was short, just an announcement that the policies that had existed before Siobhan's rule were going to be reviewed and revised as necessary. The secretary for the Royal Court, a mousy little man with tear-reddened eyes and a trembling bottom lip, gave each of the Councilors a stack of folios a full two feet high.

"These are to be reviewed for our next meeting," Siobhan announced. She nodded to the crowd still watching. "They are available for you all to review as well. As is tradition, anyone will be able to comment and request revisions for a period of one month. Our next meeting will be held in one month's time. Use your forty days wisely."

She closed the meeting with a solid thump of her fist on the bench, then stood and left the room by the side door the little clerk had come through.

Lady Etain started cursing immediately, calling Siobhan everything from the Morrigan's hand upon the world to a stupid, cock-blinded bitch. A good number of the other people listening in nodding their agreement though most of them kept their cursing well under their breath.

None of which mattered that much to Raelin. Mother and Yvon came down from the bench and headed straight for the door, their stacks of folios piled high in their arms. Yvon was cursing, too, more at the sheer amount of work she had to do than anything else. Mother was dead silent though her jaw jumped in her anger.

"Come to the Dana Clanhouse," Raelin suggested to

Yvon who stared at Raelin like she'd sprouted a second head. "We've the best records on the Treasury outside of the Royal Archives and we're better organized. Besides, you use the Curran as your lawyers, too. Dairine is there waiting to see what news we bring back."

"This is a trap," Yvon hissed. "How can you be so complacent about it?"

"Of course, it's a trap," Raelin said. She snorted and rolled her eyes as everyone around them stared, not just Mother, Yvon and Gwen. "But you were placed on the board by King Toryn. Personally. As such, it's not the same sort of trap as the rest of that nonsense. I'd think you'd want to give it a good try just for his sake."

Mother sighed before shoved the stack of folios into Gwen's arms. "Rae, sometimes you're the worst person in the world."

"You mean that I'm the most practical person in the Dana family and thus you don't like it when I make you be level-headed and reasonable instead of punching everyone in the face," Raelin replied.

She went with sarcastic and loud enough that even Lady Etain heard it over the rumble of her continued cursing. Not surprising that everyone laughed. Even Mother laughed, ruefully, rubbing the back of her neck. Yvon barked a single laugh, looked down at her stack of folios and then nodded sharply.

"I'll take you up on that offer, Dana Raelin," Yvon said. "Though I suspect that my idiot son won't be pleased about it."

"Oh, he won't be," Gwen said. Her glance at Raelin was so disapproving that Raelin's cheeks went red for a second. "But I won't let you talk to him, anyway, so it hardly matters. He's busy with our records anyway. Quarterly audit, you know."

"Quarterly?" Yvon asked, striding towards the front door where everyone's carriages waited. "That frequently?"

To Raelin's surprise, Gwen nodded and calmly, patiently, explained that yes, the Dana audited their books every quarter, rotating through businesses and concerns to ensure that everything was examined at least once a year.

Not what she'd expected out of either of them, especially after Gwen knocking all of Yvon's teeth out after she married Yvon's son Nolan. And, more importantly at the moment, the entire meeting was not what she'd expected of Siobhan. Raelin followed Yvon and Gwen, trying to decide whether it was good or bad that Siobhan was making an effort to be a good queen.

She hadn't decided by the time they reached the carriages. Raelin suspected that she might never figure that one out. At least, not for as long as Siobhan's 'good' behavior lasted.

15. CITY PULSE

Anwyn held back both grumbles and the sort of sighs that got her smacks upside the head as she followed Caitlin and Daire out to their next wedding engagement. Just one more. They'd skipped the ones yesterday and the day before out of respect for the old queen dying. No one would've thought it was appropriate to celebrate a wedding then.

But now there was a new queen and a new dynasty, horrifying as that was, so Daire had declared that they were going to the Temple of the Goddesses and praying. Publicly. Together. Both of them. No matter what the Delbhana regulations said about it.

"Still not sure about this," Mari murmured next to Anwyn. She was tall enough that she towered over Anwyn, half again as tall as Anwyn was and at least twice as wide in both shoulders and hips.

"You and me both," Anwyn agreed. She held up her hands when Caitlin glowered over her shoulder at the two of them. "We're coming. We're entitled to worry. We are playing bodyguard, you know."

"I know," Caitlin said with a tiny wince because it was probably completely necessary to have bodyguards. "It's important, though."

"You wanna pray for a baby right away, go right ahead," Anwyn said just loud enough that a few women walking by smirked at Caitlin and Daire. "That's your choice. Not what I'd do, of course, but hey, your marriage, your body, you get to choose."

That got her highly amused grins from the passing women and twin glares from both Caitlin and Daire. As long as they'd been courting, going for babies right out of the dock made sense. Caitlin was twenty-nine. Having babies soon was logical.

Even if that wasn't at all why they wanted to go to the Temple.

Daire had, always, been close to Mother. He was her baby brother, youngest sibling in Mother's family, so she'd always doted on him the same way everyone in Anwyn's family doted on Erlina. And, because of how close it had been when he was born, he'd been prayed over, blessed and taken to the Temple a million times as a child.

At least until the Delbhana began blatantly outlawing the old religions. First the smaller ones, the ones that immigrants followed. Then rules against who could worship when at the Temple. What displays they could have. How often there could be festivals and prayer nights.

Any mention of the Ladies as objects of veneration was outright forbidden.

Anwyn couldn't really disagree with that one. The Ladies were people, powerful, alien, but people. Worshiping them was outright odd. No one agreed with her on that but then no one else in the city had ever actually gone and talked to the Ladies.

Sad part was, no one in the world seemed to agree with

Anwyn. Everywhere else, people openly venerated the Ladies. They made offerings, prayed, went on actual pilgrimages to where they could see the Cities of the Ladies. Every time Anwyn had sailed to Atalya, the other country with a City, they'd had a handful of people who took passage with them just so that they could go and see the City there.

"You're such a pest," Daire grumbled to Anwyn as they turned the corner to Temple Road and headed up it. "Must you say things like that?"

"I'm your niece," Anwyn replied with a grin that had Mari start hooting with laughter. "I mean, you're only ten years older than me but still. I think it's required to tease you."

Daire huffed, stomping hard enough that the rather restrained lace on his kilt bobbed as he walked. The heels of his boots hit the cobbles like hammers, echoing up Temple Road.

Which was empty.

Worryingly empty. The shops that usually stood open on either side to offer candles, prayer boards and ribbons for blessings were shut. Boarded up. The bits of paper and burnt ribbon that always drifted away from the great urns with their always-burning fires hadn't been swept up even though it was mid-morning.

Anwyn dared to open her mind up a little, rising a return of the stupid headaches that'd haunted her the last few days, but there was nothing to fear. The only people there were for the four of them.

Temple Road, all the way to the Great Temple of Aingeal, was empty.

"Wait," Anwyn said as her heart started to pound. She pulled her mind back in again, or tried to, but fear had her reaching out for people and threats that weren't there.

"Yeah, this isn' ri'," Mari agreed.

Daire kept going for two steps before Caitlin caught his shoulders and made him stop. Apparently, he'd actually been angry because only once he'd stopped did he seem to notice how quiet Temple Road was.

"What happened?" Daire whispered. He clung to Caitlin's hands, face going pale. "I've never seen it closed down this way."

"We should go home," Caitlin decided.

She shook her head no when Daire looked up at her, betrayed and pouting. At first, Anwyn thought his hands were the ones shaking but no, when Daire pulled one hand free to gesture up the street, his free hand was completely steady. Their clasped hands shook. Hard.

"Mari, take them home," Anwyn said.

"Nothin' doing," Mari said. "They can take themselves home. Or all four o' us go home together. I'm nae about ta let ya wander abou' by yerself, Annie. They gotta be targets because of the wedding. Yer always a target."

Anwyn glared up at her even though Daire and Caitlin both nodded their agreement. "That's not fair! Don't say it!"

"Life's not fair," Mari, Caitlin and Daire all said with huge grins.

"Damn you all to the Morrigan's hands," Anwyn groaned. "Fine. Life's not fair, but you should be because that's what makes life better for everyone. There. Are we done quoting Great-Uncle Jarmon?"

"Nope," Mari said with an even bigger grin. "Got one more for ya."

Anwyn just stared up at her through narrowed eyes. This was not going to be good. She could tell without her gifts. There was too much laughter in Mari's eyes.

"He told me before we set out," Mari said and yes, she was definitely a half-second away from belly laughter.

"'Don't you let that girl wander off on her own or there'll be riots in the street, Mari. You known Annie. She's a trouble magnet. Escort our wedding seals and then come straight home.'"

"I hate you all so much," Anwyn declared.

Then rolled her eyes because Mari's laughter won. It set Caitlin off, then Daire, too. Daire's laughter was quieter, more nervous, which was understandable given the situation. All of them stilled when Anwyn held up a hand. She didn't hear the horses coming. Her gifts told her they were coming.

"Out of Temple Road," Anwyn ordered as she grabbed Daire's wrist. "Move!"

They ran, Anwyn pulling Daire and Caitlin holding his other hand. Neither of them protested. Not that it would've done any good with Mari striding along behind them. Her long legs made their run into a fast walk, damn her for being so tall.

They'd made it out of Temple Road and up the street nearly a full block when the Royal Guard appeared. Turning the corner from Royal Road, no less. A company of women, all in the Royal black uniforms with all the gold braid and trim of a formal unit that saw no combat.

Except that their horses wore combat saddles and had gleaming, sharpened claws. The halters they wore left their wicked beaks free to slash and cut and bite anyone in their way. And every single one of the Royal Guard had swords that were well used, leather worn and comfortable on the hilts.

Anwyn pressed Daire back towards the building while Caitlin took one side and Mari the other. When Anwyn bowed her head, the Royal Guard ignored them though she could feel the women's responses. The captain felt it was appropriate, that Dana should be bowing to them now. Her followers, every single one of them, was a nauseating mix of fury and despair. None of them wanted Anwyn to bow. None of them wanted to be there at all.

They rode on past, turned up Temple Road, and disappeared.

Something like a keen of despair that only Anwyn, or maybe the Ladies, could hear echoed inside Anwyn's mind.

"Home," Anwyn said grimly enough that Daire hiked up his kilts without protest and ran along with them.

Half an hour later, Anwyn was back on the streets, this time with Eoghania by her side and Mari on her heels. The two biggest women on the clan with the smallest. But between them, Mari and Eoghania could take down anyone coming at Anwyn. For her part, Anwyn could feel, see, taste, exactly what people actually thought.

Five minutes after they'd left to go to the temple, Siobhan's first royal decree had come out.

The Temples to the Goddess were 'outdated' and 'contrary to progress'. They were to be closed, the priestesses to resign and their buildings converted to other uses. People were, of course, free to continue to worship the Goddesses but it was to be done at home, in private. Siobhan had decided that organized religion was no longer needed in Aingeal.

Anwyn could've told everyone what the response was to that before she set foot outside the Clan house. Anger. Disbelief. A little relief but only among the rich and powerful who found getting scolded by the priestesses to be annoying. Terror from the poor who had one less place to go to get food, clothes, education, support.

"Why?" Mari asked in a soft, frightened voice as they made their way past the Market which was also strangely quiet. "Doesn' make sense."

"Of course, it does," Eoghania disagreed in much the

same tone. "Fewer people to scold her. To tell her what to do."

Anwyn ignored them. She paused in front of the Delbhana shop, open but empty. The Delbhana women working it looked out at Anwyn, Mari and Eoghania, worry echoing in their minds.

"Come on," Anwyn said as she headed straight back towards the port.

This is only the start. That was what she heard in the shop keeper's minds. It was only the first step towards creating the country that Siobhan wanted. She had sworn oaths but that wasn't going to stop her. All she had to do, and Siobhan was truly gifted at it, was find a convincing enough excuse, a papered-over lie that would be just plausible.

Then she could do whatever she wanted.

And the one thing that the Delbhana had hated for as long as Anwyn could remember was that the Dana ships were better than the Delbhana.

"Where're we goin'?" Mari asked.

"Sunrise Shipyards," Anwyn replied. "We'll stop and get Rae before we head over there. We'll need her. No one in the family understands as much about building ships as Rae does, both on the construction side and on the regulation side. Rae's our expert. We need her before we see if there are… new regulations coming down on how ships can be built. And for who."

She nodded at the startled stares and then furious cursing that both Mari and Eoghania gave her. How many times had the Delbhana tried to keep the Dana from building their ships the way they wanted? How many times had they tried to outright steal the Dana ships, Dana cargo?

Too many to count.

It was just the beginning.

That's what the shop keepers knew. Anwyn knew it, too. Siobhan's luck was strong right now. She had a lot of power, the entire weight of the Aingealese government behind her. There was no doubt that she'd use every bit of it to destroy them all once she figured out how to make it look good enough.

Looked bad. Very bad. But if they could figure out where Siobhan would strike next, perhaps, given Mother's position on the Royal Council, they could stop her from doing too much damage.

Maybe.

If they were very, very lucky.

Anwyn would just have to hope that she could ride the luck well enough to find a way to save her family, her clan, and Aingeal itself from Siobhan.

16. SUNRISE SHIPYARDS

The big double doors leading into Sunrise Shipyards were closed. Raelin hesitated by the smaller people door with its plain blond wood scarred by the passage of decades of women carrying thousands of tools. She could trace which tool caused which scar. That one was an adz used for smoothing the beams and shaping them to fit into their slots along the keel. This long one was a shovel where someone had banged the door open after shoveling snow during a mid-winter storm.

That one might have been Raelin, actually. Her winter spent working on repairing the Tourmaline Seas had included one of the worst snow storms in generations. She smiled and pushed the door open, Anwyn a vibrating presence at her back. Mari and Eoghania loomed behind Anwyn. They fretted, each in their own ways. For Mari it was bitten lips and fidgeting. Eoghania was all stiff shoulders, clenched fists and worried frowns.

Befind stood, arms crossed over her chest, watching as Ornice bellowed at the crews hauling a beam up into place worked the lines. There was grey in Befind's dark hair. She was still tall and strong and had a faintly mischievous air, but she was getting old.

"Hey, Rae," Befind said. She took in Raelin, Anwyn, Mari and Eoghania looming behind them. "Trouble?"

"Maybe," Raelin replied. "Beefy beams. Big keel. Not one of ours though."

"Hmm, no." Befind hummed, mischief definitely there in her eyes now. Her lips quirked. "What else you see?"

There was no sign of Mistress Chie, owner and driving force of Sunrise Shipyards, so Raelin huffed before turning back to the ship. It was broad, flat bottomed from the shape of the beams. The keel was nearly as thick as the ones the Dana used in their ships which faced the worst seas and the longest voyages across the world. But the beams going in were also short, so it wasn't going long distance. It didn't have the breadth and beam for that.

"Cargo hauler to Tahirih," Raelin guessed. "The Boid finally paid for another ship?"

Befind grumbled without answering which mean that Raelin was right and Befind didn't want to admit it so Raelin punched her in the shoulder with a laugh. Behind her, Anwyn shifted in that 'something's wrong' way. Raelin waved one hand at her. She already knew. Something had to be wrong for Mistress Chie to be away during beams being set.

"Mistress Chie?" Raelin asked.

Befind shut her eyes, opened them and put on a blank-mask expression that did nothing to hide how upset she was. "She's off on the side, watching. She's retired."

Raelin stared at her. All Befind did was shrug and jerk her chin in Mistress Chie's direction. When Raelin waved for the others to stay in place, Anwyn was the only one who protested. Just a little noise and a frown that went away when Raelin shook her head. Still a protest. That she would protest, here, at the one place that could possibly have tempted Raelin away from her beloved Tourmaline Dreams, said a lot about how much had to be wrong.

Mistress Chie.

Retired.

The words did not belong in the same sentence. Raelin had been convinced that Mistress Chie would die on the job. Half the city was convinced of that. Curious that she had finally taken that step. And potentially very revealing if she retired within days of the old queen dying.

Raelin found Mistress Chie sitting by the wall, watching Ornice and Befind working the teams with a blank expression. The last time Raelin visited, she'd noticed that Mistress Chie had gotten older. Fragile. As delicate as antique bone china shipped all the way around the world from Chinwendu.

Now she looked broken. Her golden skin had gone yellowish, dark eyes sunken. The spot that she had always kept shaved where she had twin dragons tattooed, one red, one black, was filling in with bristly hair.

"You dying or is it just killing you to sit here and watch them work without you?" Raelin asked as bluntly as Mother would. Or Great-Grandmother Anwyn.

Or maybe as bluntly as Great-Grandfather Tau would have because everyone, Mistress Chie included, said that Raelin was very much like him. Mistress Chie snorted and shook her head, patting the rough bench she sat on. Raelin sat, watched and waited.

"I've outlived everyone," Mistress Chie said.

"You did that a generation ago," Raelin replied. "Serious now. Are you dying?"

"Mmm, perhaps," Mistress Chie said.

She sighed and shook her head. When she spoke, her words were in Aingealese-accented Chinwenduese with all the wrong grammar and no proper respect markers. It was the weirdest thing Raelin had ever heard and virtually incomprehensible. Which could, possibly, be the point.

"I'm almost a hundred years old, Rae," Mistress Chie said so sadly that Raelin turned to stare at her. "I've lived in Aingeal for eighty-one years. Watched your family grow and prosper. Made ships the likes of which I only dreamed of when I was a girl. I left Chinwendu without any regret. No hesitation. Until a few days ago, I had no wish to ever go home."

"What did Siobhan do?" Raelin asked in her own weird mix of rolling Chinwenduese and the clipped tones of Atalya.

It took a second for Mistress Chie, blinking and frowning, to figure out what she'd said. Then she cackled and smacked a still-strong hand against Raelin's thigh.

"That's what I've always liked about you, Rae," Mistress Chie said. "You catch on so quickly. I almost wish you would have chosen to be my heir."

"Mother would have beaten us both," Raelin countered, rubbing her thigh. Going to have a bruise there. It was worth it to see Mistress Chie smile instead of being so blank. "So?"

"It wasn't her," Mistress Chie said. "Well, it was but it wasn't. I'm old, Rae. So old. I'm forgetting things. Befind's been covering for me, trying to make sure I don't notice it, but I do. Little things. Big things. Which ship we're on and what to do next. Who's working what position. What modifications we should use for this specific ship. I can't keep working when my mind's going that way. Even with notes it's not going to work. I won't let a ship leave here with mistakes like that. So I'm retired, Befind bought the shipyards, yesterday, and I'm pondering asking you or your sister there to help me go back to Chinwendu. I haven't been home in, oh, more than fifty years."

"Would they even know you?" Raelin asked, stunned at the sheer thought of Mistress Chie not being here at the shipyards.

Mistress Chie snorted and glared at Raelin like her old self. If it weren't for the wrinkles. The sad downturn to her mouth. The way her wrists and hands had gone skeletal instead of just thin.

"I may not have visited but I did send letters," Mistress Chie snapped. "Besides, family is as powerful a concept in Chinwendu as it is here."

Raelin nodded. "Yeah, I know. Aravel found that out on his last trip there. You should go see the silk offering he made at the temple when you get back."

"He didn't," Mistress Chie breathed, eyes brightening again. "That boy. He knitted something, didn't he?"

"Knitted them an altar cloth and foiled a Delbhana plot at the same time," Raelin said, grinning even though her heart hurt. "When'd the sale go through?"

"The day before the old queen died," Mistress Chie said and there was the sharp mind, the vicious heart that Raelin was used to. Her smirk was one that sent a shiver up Raelin's spine. "Good thing, too. The Records Office, that boy who works there."

"Sean?"

"That's the one," Mistress Chie agreed. "He said that they'd just gotten orders not to accept any sales of businesses or major property after the old queen died. Something about new rules, taxes and procedures."

"That bloody bitch," Raelin hissed.

Mistress Chie nodded and patted Raelin's thigh a great deal more gently. Appreciated given the bruise Raelin knew she had growing there. She started as Mistress Chie stood, waved for Raelin to follow and then strode, slowly, far too slowly, over to Befind.

"Going over to the Dana Clanhouse," Mistress Chie said, glowering when every single worker in the area turned to stare at her. "Don't you be paying attention to me! I'm not your employer anymore. This fool is."

"And thank you so much for giving me crews that have to double-check every single order," Befind said. She rolled her eyes and then strode off to yell at Team Two who weren't keeping pressure on their line as Team One hammered the beam into place.

The walk back to the Clanhouse was slower than Raelin expected but then Mistress Chie was retired. And old. She could be excused for dawdling. It took Anwyn making a little noise of fury for Raelin to realize that no, it wasn't that.

They were being followed.

She'd been completely certain that no one followed them to the shipyards. To have someone follow them back meant that yes, this was another of Siobhan's plots. Raelin waited until they were inside, the door shut behind them, before turning to Anwyn, Mari and Eoghania.

"Were we followed on the way there?" Raelin asked.

"No," Eoghania said with complete certainty.

"Didn't see anyone," Mari agreed.

"No one was following us because the shop keepers were paid to keep an eye for us coming," Anwyn said. Her tone could have scorched paint right down to the base wood. "We definitely were followed back but it was for Mistress Chie, not us."

Mistress Chie nodded. "Been like that for a good three, four months now. Everywhere I go, I'm followed. You know you got spies in here, right?"

"We always have spies," Raelin said. Both Eoghania and

Mistress Chie rolled their eyes. "Annie, go tell Mother about the spies. Mari, Eoghania, let Gavin and Gwen know. We're headed to Great-Uncle Jarmon."

That got surprised looks from all of them but really, there were different tasks to be accomplished all at once so splitting up made sense. Even if there were spies in the Clanhouse, those spies were known.

Besides, booking passage for honored allies and suppliers was something that Great-Uncle Jarmon always handled.

They found Great-Uncle Jarmon in his office, sipping Jasmine tea. He looked up, beamed and waved Mistress Chie right in. She laughed, bowed quite properly and then sat smiling with a sort of delight that warmed Raelin's worried heart as he poured her tea. Well, first tea for Mistress Chie, then tea for Raelin even though she'd never been very fond of Jasmine tea. Give her a nice hearty cinnamon tea or a thick black tea with stewed fruit any day.

None of them said a thing until the first cup had been drunk and the second poured. Then Great-Uncle Jarmon beamed at Mistress Chie who snorted and wagged a skeletal finger at him.

"None of that flirting now, boy," Mistress Chie said. "I helped change your diapers."

"Why, I have no idea what you're talking about," Great-Uncle Jarmon said with every bit of the flirtiness that Aravel was so well-known for. "Though I am quite glad to see, you, Chie. It's been far too long since you've come to visit."

"Tell him," Mistress Chie said, waving to Raelin to do the honors as she settled into sip her second cup of tea.

So, Raelin did. By the time Raelin was done telling the whole thing, in order of what she'd seen because Great-

Uncle Jarmon always preferred things in sequential order, Great-Uncle Jarmon had been surprised, horrified, saddened, and then furious. He huffed, drained his cup of tea in three great gulps, and then scowled at Mistress Chie.

"I've taken care of my business," Mistress Chie said. She shrugged. "And I think I'm ready to go home. Might not survive the trip across the world but I'd like to make the attempt." She glanced at Raelin and then grinned so wickedly that Raelin snickered. "After all, I should at least make an attempt to see the new altar cloth that Ravi knit, now shouldn't I?"

Great-Uncle Jarmon choked. "That boy. He finds more trouble than anyone other than Gwen and Annie. Ah, well, if you want to go home, I can certainly arrange your travel, old friend. We'll miss you. Rae, do go get Gavin for me. I want his input on which ship would be best."

"Of course," Raelin said. She swallowed down the last of her tea and then stood. "Let me know if you need anything else, Mistress Chie. Other than kicking the teams into action back at the shipyard. That's Befind's job."

Mistress Chie shouted a laugh at that, wagging her eyebrows before flipping her fingers to send Raelin away. They started gossiping about Great-Grandmother Anwyn and Great-Grandfather Tau's early days together, when the Dana clan was new and young so Raelin shut the door.

Whatever it was they wanted to talk about, Raelin could let them have the time. Especially since what she really wanted was to go find a quiet closet to curl up in and scream. Aingeal without Mistress Chie. It didn't bear thinking about. Except that she had to.

How many other immigrants were thinking of going home? How many had discovered that their work, their businesses were at a disadvantage? Raelin had seen it growing over the last few years. Since Siobhan got engaged to Prince Tory, honestly; that was when it started.

Aingeal was closing itself off to everything and everyone that was different.

How long did they have before the Dana themselves were too foreign, to strange, to survive?

And what in the name of the Goddesses and the Ladies was Raelin going to do about it?

17. TEMPLE ROAD

"Still don' think we should be out here," Mari said as Anwyn stood at the end of Temple Road. "No' a good idea, Annie."

"I know that," Anwyn said without look at her. "Heck, I knew that before we left yesterday with Daire and Caitlin. But I'm curious so I'm going snooping. You coming?"

Mari groaned loudly enough that the spies hiding half a block away behind a shop-keeper's door grinned. So did the one merchant still in her shop up Temple Road. Anwyn started walking, poking her head into every doorway and looking down the tiny alleyways that led to the shops' back doors.

Completely empty. Well, other than that one shop which only had the one woman in it. She felt like she was packing things up to sell them elsewhere. Made sense. Her shop sold wool scarves, cheap ones, ribbons that could be used for anything really, and pretty bits of paper for writing prayers to the Goddesses. All of that could be sold in other shops that weren't focused on the temple.

"You are not going down there," Mari huffed as Anwyn

started up one alley that was barely wide enough Anwyn's shoulders, much less Mari's.

"Oh, come on, I'm just curious," Anwyn complained. "I've never seen what's back here."

"An' yer nae gonna this time either," Mari snapped. She grabbed the back of Anwyn's shirt, hauling her up off her feet before Anwyn could dart down the alley. "Tha's tres-passin' an' yer nae doin' it."

"Ugh, fine," Anwyn grumbled. "Put me down."

Mari lifted her up instead, glowering right back at Anwyn until Anwyn gave in and nodded that she wouldn't run down the alley the instant that Mari let her go. All of which was amusing the hell out of the spies watching them.

Good.

Half the point of this little expedition was to feel out just how many spies there were and what they felt about Anwyn, Mari, Raelin, the Dana as a whole. While Raelin was doing real work, sorting out the laws and new regulations that Siobhan was issuing at a near-hourly basis, Anwyn was stuck with little to do.

Figuring out just how solidly the spies were behind Siobhan, what they actually thought of the Dana, that was something that only Anwyn could do. If she got out of the Clanhouse and poked around.

It was interesting, anyway. Temple Road was usually so packed with people, mostly men, that you could only walk at a shuffle while carefully watching your feet lest you step on someone's kilt. Straight up the road, turn right to the Temple and then shuffle back the way you came. Darting into a shop for a trinket, a scarf, a breather, that was the only variation.

Now, though, Anwyn got to see the carefully carved paving stones. Someone, ages ago, had carved the symbols of the Goddesses on the cobbles. The book, sword and healer's cup were all worn down in the center of the street but there were places near the walls of the buildings where you could see the original carvings.

"Huh, had no idea those were there," Mari said when Anwyn knelt down to run her fingers over some really clear ones that were next to a closed incense shop.

"Me either," Anwyn said. "Super old work. Must've cost an arm and a tit to get all these done."

"Eh, probably something they did with donations," Mari said. "Temple back home does something similar 'cept that it's a wall around the temple grounds. Pay for a brick an' they have it carved in yer honor."

"Huh, nice," Anwyn said, nodding as she stood. "Good idea."

The fire urns were completely dead.

That was the first thing that Anwyn noticed when they turned the corner to the Temple itself. She'd never, ever, seen the Grand Temple of Aingeal City without pillars of smoke coming up from the three fire urns in front of the stairs. For a second, her eyes didn't track what she was looking at. It was so strange to be able to see the smoke-darkened marble façade.

Two stories high which was short compared to the four-story Clan buildings butting up to it, the Grand Temple was long and narrow. Anwyn had been inside exactly three times that she could remember, all three of them for recent weddings. Gavin and Mari had come to offer prayers for the success of their marriage and the alliance of the Dana and Affrica. Gwen and Nolan had come twice, dragging Anwyn along both times.

It'd been twice because the first time Gwen had convinced Nolan to just make offerings at the fire urns. She'd regretted that after Gavin told Nolan all about the special ceremony you could pay for where the priestesses would bless you and your marriage while asking the Goddesses to give you wealth and lots of healthy babies.

That had been a very long ceremony. Anwyn had spent most of it grinning because Gwen was so uncomfortable as Nolan prayed, so very seriously, while occasionally giving Gwen stern little looks for slouching or fidgeting or yawning. Even if Gwen yawned with her mouth shut.

"What?" Mari asked so warily that Anwyn snickered out loud.

"Just Gwen and Nolan's ceremony," Anwyn explained.

Mari guffawed and nodded. She'd been along for that, though she and Gavin had shown up a little late due to a ship going out. Behind them, one of the spies had climbed up onto the nearest building so that she could watch whatever they did.

"Strange not to see the smoke," Anwyn commented. "I had no idea they'd carved the façade with images of the Ladies."

"Mm, it's nice, I guess," Mari said, cocking her head to the side as she frowned at the façade. "Can' say it's very traditional."

Except that it was. Anwyn knew that. She'd asked Great-Uncle Jarmon about the association of the Ladies with the Goddesses ages and ages ago, back when her ankle was broken when she was little. Facades like that where the Ladies lifted up and supported the Goddesses were very traditional, from a time when Aingeal had worshiped the Ladies above the Goddesses.

The idea of it felt very strange to Anwyn. Mostly because she knew that the Ladies were people, not all-powerful beings. She'd talked to them, made them laugh, asked questions and gotten answers while answering their questions. That was where her gift came from.

Admittedly, the Ladies were tremendously powerful, but they weren't like the Goddesses. Anwyn sighed.

"Done?" Mari asked.

"Yeah, I guess so," Anwyn said. "Still very odd to see this like... this. Empty. Abandoned. I couldn't have imagined it."

Mari rolled her eyes. "Let's go, Annie. We don' hurry we won' be back in time for the final dinner for Caitlin and Daire."

"Oh, please," Anwyn groaned. She rolled her eyes as she turned and got a lovely quick glimpse of the spy ducking down up on the rooftop. "That's hours off yet."

"Nae really," Mari said. She pulled out her pocket watch and showed Anwyn. "Temple bells aren' ringing anymore. It's only half an hour t'time to get dressed. I promised Gavin I wouldn' be late."

Anwyn froze, turning to stare at the temple. No bells. Siobhan had shut down the bells that everyone in the city, at least the poor people, used to tell time. She hadn't even realized it until Mari said something. How many women across the city had suddenly lost their sole way to tell time?

More importantly, who sold most of the pocket watches and clocks in the city? And had Siobhan issued a new regulation requiring employers to track their employees' start and stop times to, oh, verify that they were actually getting the work they paid wages for?

Anwyn would bet a year's wages that she already knew the answer to that. She strode back up the street, setting Mari to scrambling to follow her. Also made the spies, all eight of them, scramble, too.

"We don' gotta hurry quite tha' fast, Annie," Mari said.

"Says you," Anwyn retorted. "You only have to deal with Gavin. I have to deal with Dad, Davin, Aravel and Caddie."

"Point made," Mari said. She laughed and let Anwyn set the pace after that.

She kept on rushing mostly because she knew Caddie was going to tear her apart if she was late to the wedding but also because she could feel the spies signaling to each other as they passed.

Organization amongst them. That was... worrying. Anwyn hadn't expected that they'd be able to communicate between themselves, or that they'd know how to handle things when something unexpected happened. It implied that there was a much bigger structure to all these spies than just Siobhan and Lady Etain offering a bounty for information about the Dana. Specifically about Anwyn, of course.

So, if they had an organization, and they clearly did, that meant that they had lines of command. People in charge who had to keep records. Her question now was who was in charge, where they kept their records and whether or not Anwyn could get a look at them somehow. There might be a lot to learn if she could find those records and spend some time poring over them.

There'd be even more to learn if Anwyn could get copies of those records back to Nolan, Great-Uncle Jarmon, Gavin and Aunt Keelin. Between the four of them, they could probably figure out everything that Siobhan was up to.

Of course, given enough unrestricted time around Siobhan while she lost her temper, Anwyn could figure out what Siobhan was up to, too. It wouldn't be admissible to any courts but she'd still know. The gifts of the Ladies made reading Siobhan's mind pretty easy, if ridiculously unpleasant. The older Anwyn got, the stronger her gifts got, and the more she could see.

Also, the less she wanted to see but that was apparently part of growing up.

They made it back to the Dana Clanhouse in record

time. Anwyn was jogging by the time they got there despite Mari's mutters and grumbles and outright questions of why Anwyn was suddenly in a huge hurry. When Anwyn turned away from the door instead of heading into it, Mari snatched her right up off her feet.

"Where you think you're goin'?" Mari demanded.

"Up the block to get a watch," Anwyn exclaimed. "Seriously, I've barely enough time to get one before I have to get ready. If the bells aren't ringing anymore, I'm going to need one, Mari. Come on, it'll only take a minute or two."

Mari glowered at her but set Anwyn back on her feet. They hustled up to the little watch, clock and knife shop that one of the distant uncles ran. The current shop owner had inherited it from his mother who'd been married to one of Great-Uncle Jarmon's sisters' son's brothers or something like that. Either way, Uncle Michael had wonderful pocket watches that should do well for Anwyn whether she was on land or at sea.

Better still, she could ask and see if people had realized that the bells weren't going to ring anymore.

At least she'd thought that she could get a watch.

When they arrived at the door, the closed sign was out. Anwyn frowned, peered in the window and hummed. Mari looked too, frowning at Anwyn because she could see the same counters and shelves full of knives, watches and clocks that Anwyn saw.

"Why's he not here?" Mari asked. "Didn' think anyone aroun' here took a day off."

"He doesn't," Anwyn said. "I've never known the shop to be closed except on a holiday."

She went next door to the sweet shop, waving to old grannie Seannan. "Seannan, why's Uncle Michael not open?"

Seannan scowled and pursed her lips like she wanted to

spit. "You've not heard the new rule, then. Our wonderful new Queen's decided that men need to have a woman in the shop to keep them safe. You know he runs that shop on his own. The Royal Guard came round and told him he had to shut the doors until he got a wife or a daughter, sister or something, to work with him."

"What?" Mari bellowed.

"Oh, wow," Anwyn said, shaking her head. "Right. Okay, thank you for telling us, Seannan. We're off to home to listen to Gavin, Great-Uncle Jarmon, Father and every single Dana man go up in flames."

Seannan grinned at that, nodding and then tossing them both a bit of hard candy. Mari shoved hers into her pocket while Anwyn stuck hers in her mouth to suck on as they walked, no, jogged, back home. This was not good. This was very, very not good in the Mother was going to have to go to court and fight against every single noble not good.

Come to that, Raelin might have to go to court, too. She was doing a good job dealing with all the legal regulations alongside their lawyers. Anwyn nodded slowly, making sure that she caught the door and didn't let it smash into the wall when Mari shoved it open with her full strength.

Report on this latest problem. Get cleaned up for the wedding dinner. Celebrate for Caitlin and Daire.

Then go out again and see what else Anwyn could find out. She still wanted to know how organized the spies were and who was in charge of them. If she could find that, maybe by talking to Danica wherever she'd gone to hide out until her ship left, then she could get fuel to start a fire under Siobhan's ass. Hopefully, it would be a big enough fire to make her stop whatever nonsense she was pulling.

18. SECRET MEETING

Danica stared at Anwyn, brows furrowed. To Anwyn's surprise, she'd not gone all that far away from the Clanhouse. It'd taken almost a full day to wear Mother down, but Anwyn had finally wormed Danica's location out of her by promising not to pick a fight and not to reveal where Danica was.

That had been harder than anything else. Getting out of the Clanhouse without being seen was not an easy thing with so many spies watching them all. Anwyn had switched out her clothes with a boy's vest and kilt, one of Caddie's old ones from back before he went lace and ribbon crazy. Her bust was so small that the vest fit just about perfectly.

Then she'd found an old wig that someone, probably Aravel, had gotten for a masquerade. It was black as night, put up in a bun on the back of her head, and ridiculously itchy. But between that, the bits of makeup and the clothes, Anwyn looked nothing at all like herself. Frankly, she thought she looked like some of her cousins from uncles who'd married outside the clan.

Caddie had given her stuff to carry to have an excuse for being out and miraculously, none of the spies had paid the least bit of attention to Anwyn when she left the Clan-house. Walking in kilts was the weirdest thing she'd ever done but Anwyn was dressed like she was ten or twelve while carrying an obvious Dana donation basket so people had smiled and nodded approvingly at her.

Even as she moved away from the warehouses and into the tenements that Danica had chosen to hide in, people were sweet, kind, welcoming to Anwyn. So very odd. Maybe that was why Aravel always acted like the whole world was his friend? People just treated him well? Or maybe it was because Anwyn looked like a young boy being responsible and helpful. Hard to tell and frankly, it didn't matter once Anwyn found Danica's room tucked way in the back of a tenement with piss-stained floors, crumbling plaster walls and doors that looked like they'd been built to withstand a war.

"Can I… help you?" Danica asked so warily that Anwyn grinned. "Do I know you?"

"I have food donations for you," Anwyn declared. "Plus a new jacket, some small clothes, sixteen pairs of new socks that might fit. The ones that don't fit can always be sold to someone else, you know. Oh, and pastries. With hot-pepper jam."

Danica's eyebrows went up for the pastries. She opened the door all the way for the hot-pepper jam, gesturing for Anwyn to pass the basket over. When Anwyn did so, she made a point of touching Danica's hands. Most of Danica's mind was consumed with worry as far as Anwyn could tell. But sometimes, when her gifts cooperated, Anwyn could see deeper. If she touched.

It worked this time.

Deep inside, Danica was hopelessly convinced that she

was doomed to die. She outright did not believe that she could escape the spies. No matter what Mother, Raelin or Anwyn did, Danica was certain that she would be discovered and killed, more than likely within a few days at the outside.

Anwyn let Danica take the basket, took a deep breath, and then pushed right into Danica's tiny apartment even though Danica made a strangled noise of horror when Anwyn did it. What with the basket, Danica couldn't stop her. As soon as Anwyn was inside, she kicked the door shut.

"Which Dana are you?" Danica snarled.

"...What gave me away?" Anwyn asked, instantly curious about where she'd made a mistake.

"Men, boys, don't kick doors that way," Danica replied. She peered at Anwyn and then went white as bone. "Anwyn?"

"Yep," Anwyn said.

She grinned at Danica's cursing. There was one tiny table for Danica to eat at with one wobbly stool that had legs of different lengths. The bed was a narrow, cramped little thing about the size of a crib with only two very thin blankets. Danica had no dresser, no closet, no place to store food. Nothing of comfort and certainly nothing on the walls.

But the walls were surprisingly sturdy, crumbling plaster over old-fashioned red-mud bricks that had to be a good foot thick. The room was quiet, windowless and as secure as you could ask for.

With just one way in and out.

"Right," Anwyn said. "You really do have hot-pepper jam in there. And socks that you could sell for spare cash. But I'm here because I need to ask you a very serious question that I have to get an answer to. Tonight. If I have to, I will use the gifts that no one talks about, Danica. This is way more important than probably anyone but you realizes."

"I don't know what Queen Siobhan is up to," Danica said as she carelessly set her basket on the table and then very carefully sat on her stool.

"Not what I want to know," Anwyn said. She waved off Danica's frown. "She's insane. I know that better than most anyone. Her mind is like a sewer of violence and paranoia. If I knew how, I'd go in and break her mind fully so that she couldn't hurt anyone else but I haven't figured out how to do that. If it's even possible."

Danica stared at Anwyn. Her cheeks couldn't get any paler but her eyes went so wide that she looked like a dead fish. When she opened her mouth to ask just what Anwyn needed to know because Danica had been out of the Delbhana for quite some time, nothing came out.

"I know you've been hiding out," Anwyn said, answering her unspoken question. "That's fine. That's not an issue. I don't need current news. I need to know who the Delbhana spy mistress is. Where she is would be lovely but a name is the most important thing. I can track everything else down from that but I need that name."

Anwyn could almost hear Danica's heart hammering. It throbbed at her temple, so fast and furious that you'd think that she'd been hauling line in a storm. Or that she was having a panic attack. Didn't feel like panic. Fear, yes, but not panic.

"I'm dead if I tell anyone that," Danica whispered.

"Danica, you're dead anyway," Anwyn said. "If the Delbhana catch you, if they have any clue that you're still alive, they absolutely will come after you. They'll track you to the other side of the world. Great-Uncle Jarmon is working on a trip for Mistress Chie. She wants to go back to Chinwendu before she dies. She's... nearly a hundred.

We don't expect her to make it. But she'll need an attendant. I can say that you've been hired as her attendant for the trip, bring you back with me. The basket of goodies is your hire-on benefit. People will wonder but not that much."

Danica shook her head. She stood and started pacing across the end of her room closest to the door. Her hands shook as she gestured as if to push Anwyn's offer away. No, to push Anwyn's question away. Just thinking about answering had her legs shaking, her stomach queasy and sweat beading up on her forehead. Her shirt was already going wet under her breasts and armpits.

All through it, a face was in her mind. Stern, blond and blue-eyed like all Delbhana. Older, maybe in her mid to late fifties. She didn't wear embroidery on her jacket. The vest she wore in Danica's head was nearly plain as well, which was highly unusual. Embroidered vests and jackets were standard, had been standard since before Anwyn was born. Since before Danica was born.

Interestingly, that image in Danica's mind moved and breathed and lived. This was someone that she'd interacted with many, many times. Someone she knew very well.

"Your grandmother?" Anwyn asked. "Is that who it is?"

"...How in the name of the Goddesses did you do that?" Danica hissed. She caught herself against the door, legs going weak from fear.

"Eh, told you, gift of the Ladies," Anwyn said. "Interesting. You're truly terrified of your own grandmother. Odd."

"Not odd at all," Danica said. She staggered over and sat on her stool, nearly toppling over until she leaned against the grey, crumbling plaster. "Mother... got me with a Dana man. That's why Grandmother insisted I have this name, so that no one would ever forget what I am."

Anwyn blinked, frowned and then deliberately reached

out to touch Danica's forehead with one finger. She'd noticed, occasionally, when her gifts were working best, that there was an echo of sort with Dana family members. Like they were slightly different from everyone else.

Not all of them. Raelin didn't feel that way. Gavin, Aravel, Caddie, Mother, all her relatives who had the best luck and the worst tempers felt of that echo.

"You don't have the blood," Anwyn said after a second. She snorted at the way Danica's jaw dropped. "Seriously, Dana women who have the blood have our tempers and our luck. It's not just… rumor, Danica. Our luck is a real thing. It's what Great-Grandmother Anwyn got from the Ladies in her visit. I guess that's what she asked for. I just tried to talk to them, to understand them, so I sort of… hear things? Know things sometimes. It's unreliable but its there. You don't have the blood because you don't have the luck. I can tell."

"I would almost wish to have you tell my family that except that I most earnestly do not want to go back to them," Danica said. She pressed her lips together and then rubbed her hands over her face, up through her Dana-wild curls, and sighed. "Grandmother is the spy mistress. Mother works with her. She plans on taking over after Grandmother retires. Both of them are quite convinced that I'm dead. It's the only thing keeping me alive."

Anwyn nodded. "All right then. Tomorrow, early in the morning, really early, show up at the warehouse door. Any of them will do but the one on the docks is best. Say that you're reporting for escort duty. I'll let everyone know that you're to be allowed in."

"It's not safe," Danica said even though hope quivered deep inside of her. "They have spies in your warehouse, Anwyn."

"I know," Anwyn said with a snort of amusement. "Danica, seriously, of all of us, I know best who the spies are and what they're looking for. Just show up. Make it as close to dawn or just before dawn if you can. That time of the morning the spies will be groggy and the ones in the clan will still be sleeping."

She didn't want to do it. Anwyn could feel it. In her bones, in her teeth that ached with sympathetic pain as Danica clenched her jaw, Anwyn could feel it. But she also knew that Danica would be there. Terrified out of her mind, disguised as best she could, Danica would show up.

It was the best that Anwyn could hope for so Anwyn smiled, gestured towards the basket, and shrugged.

"Might as well eat a bit," Anwyn said. "I'll see you tomorrow, Danica. Be careful but be there."

Anwyn left the way she'd come, kilts swinging around her ankles and people smiling at her as she went. She got a lot more worried frowns this time because full night had fallen and this part of town had few lights in the streets but no one stopped her. Amusingly, when Anwyn smiled the way Aravel always did, people stopped worrying about her. They smiled and just assumed that she knew where she was and what she was doing. That she was safe and belonged here.

There were a few women, in bars that Anwyn passed, who had lascivious thoughts but it was all for the man they assumed she grow up to be, not for the little boy they thought she was now. How odd. Women really did view men differently. She'd have to tell Caddie about it and apologize for not believing him when he complained about it.

After she told Raelin, Mother and Great-Uncle Jarmon about what she'd found out today. That came first. And hopefully, once Raelin knew, Raelin would find a way to use that against Siobhan and her stupid plots.

19. HIDDEN POWERS

Raelin leaned against the wall by Great-Uncle Jarmon's office door. The only thing keeping her from punching Anwyn in the nose was locking her hands around her biceps. Of all the damned, foolish stunts, Anwyn had to go out at night, dressed as a boy. Not just any boy but one dramatically underage. And then she compounded the stupidity by going into the worst neighborhood of Aingeal City. Alone.

"Quit fussing," Anwyn said entirely too casually as she tilted the chair she sat in backwards so that she could balance on two legs. "I was fine. It was the only way to get past the spies."

"You don't know for sure that there were spies watching," Raelin grumbled. "You could be getting overly paranoid, Annie."

Anwyn snorted and glared. "Rae, I know. We're going to have this whole discussion in a minute or so because Danica has arrived. Mari and Mother are escorting her. Oh, and Great-Uncle Jarmon just joined them with tea.

Good. We'll want to move to the conference room across the hall."

The casual way she said it, as if she was watching things happen, made the hair on Raelin's arms stand up. Anwyn dropped the chair back to the ground and stood, heading for the door as calmly as if the entire fancy of hers was true.

"It's not fancy," Anwyn told Raelin in that same too-calm, too unfocused sort of tone of voice. "You keep pretending that I don't have gifts but that doesn't make the gifts go away. Come on."

Raelin followed. Reluctantly and with her stomach churning, but she followed. Great-Uncle Jarmon did have a tea tray with the biggest teapot and a dozen cups. Mother and Mari did have Danica walking between them. And Danica did look absolutely terrified out of her mind.

Until she saw Anwyn.

Then she blew out a breath and nodded to Anwyn who grinned and waved everyone to follow her into the middle-sized conference room with its extra-heavy door and soundproofed walls. Just how much had Annie's gifts grown?

"A lot," Anwyn said, shrugging when Raelin gaped at her. "Seriously, they've grown a lot lately. The last few years have been... unpleasant. It's where the headaches are coming from. The Ladies strongly suggested that I take some time, find a way, to go and talk to them. They said that there's something they can do to give me a bit more control but I don't have the slightest idea how I'm going to do that."

"Please stop talking like the Ladies are right outside," Danica said, shuddering.

"Of course, they are," Anwyn said with a frown. She rolled her eyes when everyone, Raelin included, stared at her. "They live in the water. Under the surface. They can go anywhere there's water, not just in the river with their City. Don't be stupid. They're right out in the bay and across the planet. The city's a city. As far as I can tell, they've got trade channels and small towns and everything we do."

"Underwater," Raelin whispered. She collapsed into a chair, desperately glad that she'd turned down the offer of the Ladies gift in Atalya.

"You did?" Anwyn asked, staring at Raelin. "Huh. Hadn't caught that from your diaries."

"I didn't write that in my diaries and you're picking things out of my head, Annie," Raelin snapped at her. "That's hardly what we need to focus on."

"No, no, you're right," Anwyn said. "All right. So, it wasn't exactly a distraction because now you all can see that I'm getting stronger. Yes, Mother, that does mean I can see what Siobhan wants. Sadly, she's crazier than a rainbow shark with a parasite during the spring seal hatching. I can't really tell what she's up to without touching and there's no way Siobhan will let me touch."

"Queen Siobhan," Danica interrupted. Then blushed when Anwyn stared at her. "You should say the title."

"Eh, I should," Anwyn said as she flipped her fingers to brush that away as unimportant, "but right now we have very little time for this discussion. Great-Uncle Jarmon has agreed that you'll escort Mistress Chie, Danica. But we need to dye your hair, probably brown, and you need to get punched in the face."

Raelin opened her mouth to object and then nodded slowly. "It does do a lovely job of disguising facial features. Worked very well for Sinead. A broken nose, black eyes, split lip, you'll be virtually unidentifiable."

"And it gives us a reason to be shipping you off to the

other side of the world," Anwyn said, wagging a finger at Danica as she groaned. "We do that all the time. Honestly, I'm away from home more than I'm here specifically because everyone agrees its better to keep me away from Siobhan and Aingeal."

Danica nodded, holding up a hand that stunningly stemmed the flood of words from Anwyn's mouth. "I understand. That's fine. Though I'd prefer that Mari do it. Not either of you, or Laoise. All three of you are too… powerful when you punch."

Raelin grinned at that while Anwyn hooted a laugh and Mother wagged her eyebrows. Great-Uncle Jarmon shook his head as he poured the tea for all of them. Anwyn looked like she wanted to keep talking but one stern look from Great-Uncle Jarmon had her snapping her mouth shut.

Only once the tea had been poured, appropriately doctored to their individual tastes, did Anwyn continue. And only after Great-Uncle Jarmon nodded that she could.

"Right, so," Anwyn said after just one sip of her tea, "I've noticed spies for quite some time. Years, really. We know about the ones in the Clan but there are more spies that watch us when we're outside the Clanhouse and those people are growing in number. This time in port, there's a dozen or more that watch me every time I set foot outside. And yes, Mother, I can actually tell when someone's watching me. Even if they're not visible, I know. It's like shouting without words."

"Grandmother would kill people to be able to do that," Danica murmured. She winced as Great-Uncle Jarmon turned to stare at her.

"That's why I wanted to have this meeting," Anwyn said. She waved one hand vaguely in Danica's direction, so casually that Raelin wanted to reach out and catch her wrist.

"The spies are organized. They're not just people angling for a bounty for information on us. They're organized, able to signal to each other and have a specific hierarchy. I figured that out yesterday. And I realized that if there's a hierarchy, there has to be a spy mistress. Find the spy mistress, look at her files, and there we go, a clearer idea of what Siobhan is up to."

Raelin stared at Anwyn whose eyes were even more unfocused than before. This time, Raelin did get up. She grabbed Anwyn's wrist, checking her pulse. It was way too fast. When Raelin touched Anwyn's neck, verifying, Anwyn didn't even flinch. If it weren't Anwyn, Raelin would've thought that she was drugged out of her mind on poppy milk. Well, if Anwyn weren't so coherent, that is.

"Now, I know everyone likes to pretend that it never happened," Anwyn said, turning to Mother and Great-Uncle Jarmon who were both standing up, too, "but I did go talk to the Ladies. They did give me gifts. Yes, yes, I know, Mother. I'm not supposed to say that out loud. But you need to understand this. I have gifts. Actually, I have Gifts."

The second time she said it, Raelin could hear the special emphasis as though Annie was writing the word down in her scrolliest font, in Aravel's brightest turquoise ink, on special parchment embossed with gold Dana symbols.

"Exactly," Anwyn said, smiling vacantly at Raelin. Her pupils were huge. "That's exactly what I mean, Rae. Thank you. Now, these Gifts are getting stronger. That's why I've been getting more and worse headaches. But, at the same time, they're getting stronger. I see more. Hear more. Feel more. And now, because I know Danica will tell you all about it after I pass out, I'm going to go check on Danica's grandmother. Because she is the Delbhana spy mistress and I know you'll find something useful to do with that."

"Annie, what the hell?" Raelin demanded.

"Oh, didn't I say," Anwyn said as she slowly went limp in her chair, slumping towards Raelin while talking perfectly calmly and coherently. "I'm not exactly tied to my body. This is going to hurt, of course, but I can get you a location. Once you have an address, I'm sure you use it against Siobhan. And Danica can explain things. And then you can smuggle her out of Aingeal. Just punch her in the face really well. Should work."

She stopped talking as Mother started cursing and Danica began whispering prayers to the Goddesses and the Ladies. Great-Uncle Jarmon sighed, stood, and went to the door. He far too calmly told one of the passing warehouse workers to summon Doctor Bernice because Anwyn was having another of her cluster headaches.

"Mother used to do something similar," Great-Uncle Jarmon commented as he closed the door, came over and helped Raelin move Anwyn to the floor. "Hopefully there won't be convulsions. Annie's had far too many of them lately. It's very damaging for the brain, apparently."

"Why?" Danica whispered. "I would have told you anything I knew. It's my only chance of escaping. I would have said, done, whatever I had to."

Anwyn jerked before Raelin could do more than open her mouth. This time when Anwyn opened her eyes, she was all there. Green and sweating, swallowing against vomit, but she was fully focused.

"She works out of a converted tenement," Anwyn said between gritted teeth. "It's all of three blocks from where Danica was hiding out. The big one that has the white brick façade and the functioning toilet."

"I know that one," Mari said.

"As do I," Danica said, shuddering. "I thought I was safe."

"She thinks you're dead," Anwyn said as she pressed her hands over her eyes far too hard. "Both your grandmother and your mother think you're dead. Truly. All we have to do is dye your hair, punch you in the face until you're all swollen up and then get you on a ship. Soon as possible. Mistress Chie's preferably."

Raelin put one hand, her weak one, on Anwyn's shoulder, squeezing firmly enough that Anwyn stilled. She kept her hands pressed against her eyes but she seemed to be waiting. Listening? Something like that.

"Why do you keep insisting on punching Danica?" Raelin asked.

"Lady Etain is on her way here," Anwyn explained. Still through gritted teeth but with that same watchfulness. "At the front door now. With Doctor Bernice so yeah, punching."

"Hurry up and hit me!" Danica exclaimed in a high-pitched voice. "I can play the offended women about to be hired by insane Dana well enough but Aunt Etain cannot see me!"

"Hol' still," Mari said.

Raelin didn't watch. Three meaty thuds were enough for her to know that no one was going to recognize Danica anymore. She focused on Anwyn, instead, checking Anwyn's pulse, the grey-green color of her skin and the way she panted through clenched teeth.

This hurt. It hurt her far worse than was reasonable. Raelin wanted to yell at Anwyn for taking stupid risks but she wasn't wrong.

In fact, Anwyn was dead right. Knowing that the Delbhana employed spies, had created an actual spy ring with a mistress and hierarchy that might rival the Minoo spy network spread across the world, was a horrifying thought.

Useful, but horrifying.

"Gonna try and touch Lady Etain," Anwyn whispered just before the door opened. "Might see more."

"Don't you dare, Annie," Raelin scolded her and absolutely meant it. "You'll do no such thing. You're going to take your medicine and go straight to bed if I have to drag you buy your hair."

"Agreed," Great-Uncle Jarmon said. Raelin wasn't sure that he'd heard Anwyn's whisper but she'd bet that he had.

"What happened here?" Lady Etain asked.

"Nae your business," Mari said. She grabbed Danica by the back of her coat and dragged her straight out of the conference room. "Back in a sec for Annie. I'll tuck her in after I ge' this dealt wi'."

While Lady Etain frowned, Doctor Bernice shook her head and came over to kneel by Anwyn's side. She pulled out the little bottle of poppy milk, shaking it slightly before getting her needle out.

"I hate poppy milk," Anwyn said with forced clearness.

"It's the strongest pain medication I have," Doctor Bernice replied. Raelin frowned because Anwyn's scowl might be half hidden by her hands but it was still quite clear. And Doctor Bernice wasn't paying attention to it.

"Wait," Raelin ordered, much to Mother, Doctor Bernice, Great-Uncle Jarmon and Lady Etain's surprise. "Annie, why do you hate it? It makes the pain stop, doesn't it?"

"No," Anwyn said. She shuddered and whined, shifting her shoulders as if she was trying to edge away from Doctor Bernice. "Still hurts, it's just distant. And it makes me sick, can't think, can't move, but my mind is still awake. Weird, horrible dreams. Hate that stuff."

Doctor Bernice went so pale that Raelin caught her shoulder to keep her from collapsing to the floor, too. "It's not supposed to work like that, Annie. You should have told me!"

Anwyn shrugged one shoulder. "Thought that was just what it did."

"Right," Raelin said and sighed. "Doctor Bernice, if you would be so kind as to follow Anwyn and Mari up to the apartment. You and Annie can talk about a better choice once she's in bed."

Doctor Bernice nodded, hands shaking as she put the poppy milk and needle away. She didn't say anything else. Not when Mari came back, not when Anwyn choked and almost threw up after being picked up, not the entire time until the door shut, leaving Raelin staring at Lady Etain who still had a puzzled frown on her face.

"What can we do for you?" Raelin asked Lady Etain.

Lady Etain straightened her shoulders, firmed her lips to the point that they disappeared into a slash across her face, and met Raelin's eyes squarely. There was a huge amount of hate in her eyes, a lot of reluctance in the tightness of her shoulders and so much regret in the way her hands clenched into fists.

This was going to be interesting.

"I need your help," Lady Etain said. "I need the Dana's help."

20. UNUSUAL REQUEST

Raelin raised an eyebrow.

It brought the anger back to Lady Etain's face, as familiar as the lap of waves against the Tourmaline Dreams' hull. As false as snow covering thin ice over a fast-moving river. Lady Etain raised her chin, hesitantly curled one lip as if to show disdain but it crumbled as Raelin crossed her arms over her chest and leaned back against the conference room table.

"Siobhan is... destroying Aingeal," Lady Etain said.

"And whose fault is that?" Mother snapped. "You put her on the throne. I know damned well that you forced Prince Toryn to marry her even after that bitch abused him!"

"Mother," Raelin said.

Just the one word but it snapped Mother back as Great-Uncle Jarmon froze halfway to sitting in one of the chairs. He slowly sat down, moving as quietly as a sixty-plus year old man with achy, crackling joints could. Mother, thankfully, only gritted her teeth before nodding to Raelin to go ahead.

"How do you do that?" Lady Etain asked slowly, warily.

She watched Raelin with that same puzzled frown. "We always believed that Anwyn was the future true ruler of the Dana. She's not, is she?"

"Goodness, no," Raelin said. She shook her head, chuckling. "The sheer idea of Anwyn in charge of anything. No, Annie's never been and never will be a leader of anything. Main instigator of trouble, sure, but lead? Nope. And neither am I. I'm the conscience. I'm the voice of reason. I'm the one saying 'no' and 'not now' and 'don't you have work to do?' Totally different thing."

Lady Etain, frowning, stared at the door for a long moment. Her lips moved as she whispered to herself. Names? Raelin was fairly certain that it was names flitting through her mind and over her lips.

"Gavin," Lady Etain breathed and then cursed viciously. "Damn it all to the Morrigan's waiting hands, I knew we needed him. He'll take over for Laoise."

"Gavin," Raelin agreed. "And Mari, of course. The true leader, however, isn't Mother. It's Great-Uncle Jarmon. He's been in charge since Great-Grandmother Anwyn disappeared and Great-Grandfather Tau died. Before that, even. And now I'm taking over Great-Grandfather Tau's place. If I died, if Gavin and Mari died, well, there are a handful of others who could take our places. We're not locked in like most Clans are."

Lady Etain's shoulders slumped. She licked her lips, not meeting any of their eyes. In fact, she stared at the door as if waiting for Mari to come back. Not very good at listening, was she? But then that was something Raelin had known since she was tiny. Reality rarely had much of an impact on Lady Etain.

At least until it blind-sided her. Then she raged at it until she figured it out, at which point she tried to exploit whatever it was. The key now would be keeping her from raging and exploiting the Dana the way she so clearly wanted to.

"What do you want?" Raelin asked. She smiled at Lady Etain's glower. "You'll get nothing out of anyone if you can't convince me. I told you. I'm the one who says no, and right now, anything you want or suggest is a hard no. Sell me. Try to, anyway."

"How do I need to sell you on this?" Lady Etain exclaimed. She flung a hand out towards the wall closest to the Royal Palace. "Siobhan is destroying everything Aingeal is built on. I don't hold with the worship of the Goddesses but everything else she's done is pure destruction."

"You're wrong there," Raelin said. She smiled harder even though she wasn't at all amused. "Siobhan is building the world she wants. The one she thinks will be best. Not for you or me or for the Clans. The best world for her. And frankly? You have no one to blame but yourself for that. You got rid of all the women standing at Siobhan's back with a knife. Sinead is dead. So is Danica. All the moderate Delbhana who could stand up to Siobhan are gone. Only the radical ones, the violent, angry, abusive ones are left. And they don't follow you. They never have."

"They follow Siobhan," Mother murmured. She groaned as she pulled out a chair and collapsed into it. "Rae, sometimes you're scary. I never know how you figure these things out and then stay calm about it."

"Oh, Mother, really," Raelin said. She rolled her eyes when Mother raised an eyebrow at her. "I told you about catching Sinead and Siobhan on the stairs when I was recuperating from the wood fragment poisoning my wound. Sinead outright said that she'd been assigned to stab Siobhan in the back if she crossed the line. Then she died and here we are, stuck with a mad, abusive bitch on the throne with no one who can tell her no."

Both Mother and Lady Etain flinched.

There truly was no one who could tell Siobhan no anymore. Granted, she was required to follow the rule of law. Queens had power but it wasn't absolute. The King had a say in how the country was ruled. So did the Royal Council, the various advisors and, always, there was the possibility of the people rising up.

Siobhan couldn't do everything she wanted. Yet. Given a chance, she would inevitably whittle away at the cultural, legal and social restraints holding her back. She was already doing that. But for now, she was limited.

"What we really need is a check against her power," Raelin mused.

"No one, not one single person, has ever been able to restrain her," Lady Etain grumbled. She crossed her arms over her chest like Raelin's little sister Erlina when she was told she couldn't have a treat. "Even as a tiny child, I could barely get her to behave. It's been a problem forever."

"And yet," Mother grumbled not at all quietly enough to not pick a fight, "you gave her the throne. And now we all have to deal with her abuse."

Raelin held up a hand to Lady Etain while slowly turning to Mother. "We all."

"Yes?" Mother said, staring at Raelin. After a second, she straightened up and peered closely at Raelin. She smiled grimly while nodding slowly. "What's going on in your head, Rae? Say it. Spell it out for us."

"I'm... we all," Raelin repeated while wagging a finger at Great-Uncle Jarmon. "Siobhan, all the queens, are responsible to the people. Siobhan swore oaths to protect us all. But she'd not. She's undermining that. Undermining everyone. But she's still, officially, responsible to us all."

Great-Uncle Jarmon nodded, watching Raelin just as closely as Mother was. "Yes. It's one of the base tenants of Aingealese society. The Queen rules but only with the consent and input of the people, provided by the Queen's advisors and by the Royal Council."

"Yes, and now Mother's on the Council," Raelin said. "So is Nolan's mother. And a bunch of other people who are not at all happy with Siobhan. All of you, I mean, Mother? The Councilor of Commerce has... not a small amount of power, right? And the Treasury? Tierney Yvon surely could stop a bunch of these new rules by saying that no, there is no budget for them. By killing any budget requests that Siobhan puts through."

Lady Etain had been glaring at them, perhaps for the digression, but as Raelin talked her eyes went wide. She shook her head and then threw up her hands in dismay. This time the cursing was varied, vicious and entirely focused on Lady Etain herself.

"How did we miss this?" Lady Etain finally demanded. "We've been plotting against the Dana and never realized that we can't win because every single one of you will take charge and lead the others without the slightest protest from the Clan. How can a Clan work like this?"

Raelin snorted. "We're a family. A disorganized, brawling, ill-tempered family. The Clan designation is just what's expected in Aingeal. It means less to us than it should. What matters is doing our best, taking care of each other and making alliances. So. You want orders? You want to fix this? Well, you need to go to your allies. You need to remind them that they have the power to say no. That they have the right and responsibility to protest, legally, against things that they don't like. We'll go to our allies and we'll all go blindside Siobhan with ten thousand complaints about her million and one changes."

Both Mother and Lady Etain shook their heads as if that was impossible. Ridiculous. Of course it wasn't impossible. It was the only logical path. Raelin glared at them both in turn before Great-Uncle Jarmon chuckled and patted Raelin's elbow.

His smile was fond, so gentle that Raelin's cheeks went hot. She frowned at him but it only made him chuckle.

"Rae," Great-Uncle Jarmon said as if she was tiny and on the verge of a tantrum. Or perhaps like she was a full-grown adult who he highly respected. It was hard to be sure when Great-Uncle Jarmon looked at her that way.

"What?" Raelin asked. "They're being idiots!"

"No, you just haven't sold them on the idea yet," Great-Uncle Jarmon said. "Just as Lady Etain needs to sell you, you need to sell them. This isn't an idea that is obvious to most."

Raelin stared at him for a long moment, mouth hanging open. "It's not? But it's so obvious? Gather the allies, whip them up and get them going. Throw them in mass as Siobhan and she'll be too busy dealing with that to cause too much trouble."

Great-Uncle Jarmon nodded as he patted her elbow again. Then he gestured towards Mother, who scowled, and Lady Etain, who looked as though she was on the verge of exploding with fury if Raelin said anything.

"You really don't see it?" Raelin asked Mother.

"No, Rae," Mother said. "I don't. I'm not going to make our people work with her. Or any of the Delbhana for that matter."

"My people barely work with me," Lady Etain snapped. "I cannot get them to work with you."

"No, no, not working together," Raelin said. She groaned and scrubbed one hand over the scars on her cheek. "Let me try to explain this. Because I guess it's not as obvious as I thought. Siobhan has power."

Both Mother and Lady Etain nodded impatiently.

"It's limited power," Raelin continued. How small of pieces did this need to be? "There are rules, laws, about what she can and cannot do. If she breaks those rules, there are people who are required to stop her. Lots and lots of people. Every single person on the Royal Council can stop some, if not all of her plans. There's the various Royal Advisors. There's the Royal clerks. There's the Clan Heads, and the Mistresses of all the disciplines. And, most importantly, there's the people."

"Yes, that's how the government used to work," Lady Etain said with obnoxious emphasis on 'used to'.

"It still does," Raelin said. "Siobhan thinks she can change everything but we've all been so stunned by grief that we've not come back at her. So no, your allies aren't working with us. They're working with you about the things you care about. And our allies won't work with you. They'll just work with us. And we don't tell the people that they need to protest. We just make a point of reminding everyone, publicly, loudly, of how the country works. A few riots from the people would knock Siobhan on her ass."

"No... comparing notes and working to maximum advantage?" Lady Etain asked far too warily.

"Nothing like that at all," Raelin said. "Because we don't agree on what the best place to start with is and frankly? If it's just one problem? Siobhan will do something, a token fix, while ruining everything else. No, we hit her everywhere. I care about this thing. Mother about that thing. You've got your thing. We hit her with all of them, all at once, as loudly and as frequently as possible. And we do not stop," Raelin stabbed a finger at Mother and then glowered at Lady Etain who took a step backwards in surprise.

Lady Etain nodded slowly as she glanced at the door again. Less like she was waiting for Mari to come back and more like she wanted to be out the door and out of the Dana Clanhouse. That was an improvement.

"How long do we keep this us?" Mother asked.

Raelin snorted. "We keep it up until either we're dead or Siobhan is dead. She's never, ever going to give in, Mother. She will always want to reshape the world in her own image. And we will never, ever accept that. So, it's a battle that will last for the rest of our lives. Or until the people of Aingeal rise up and overthrow her. That's possible, too."

"That cannot be allowed to happen!" Lady Etain shouted. Her face was bone-white, hands shaking with terror.

Raelin shrugged. "Well, get to work with your allies, then. Because, quite frankly? It's coming. Maybe not this month. Maybe not this year. But soon. People will get tired of her nonsense. If she's not checked somehow, there will be a revolt. An outright revolution, probably. And the instant that happens, all the countries around us and every ethnic group in Aingeal will decide that it's time for them to take back whatever they think was stolen from them. Work to curb Siobhan or watch Aingeal tear itself apart. Your choice."

Lady Etain stared at Raelin for a long, tense moment. She was still painfully pale, hands still shaking, but she didn't move. Didn't speak. Neither did Raelin.

When the moment stretched to the point that Mother shifted and grumbled under her breath, Lady Etain finally looked away. She nodded once before striding to the door, flinging it open so hard that it smacked into the wall, and then stomped up the hallway.

The doorknob left a dent in the plaster.

All Raelin could hope was that she'd managed to dent Lady Etain's determination to focus on the destruction of the Dana. Redirecting her towards Siobhan probably wouldn't work. After all, Lady Etain's plots had always been ridiculous, too complicated, and doomed to fail.

But it should, if they were lucky, distract Siobhan enough that Raelin could use the information Anwyn had gotten so painfully for them.

And that was worth everything right now.

21. SHIFTING WINDS

The apartment was dead quiet when Anwyn woke. Mid-morning by the slant of the light in the girls' bunk room. She stretched cautiously and hummed. Sat up and smiled. Hopped out of bed and grinned at the empty room.

No nausea. No foggy brain. Sure, her head still pounded but it wasn't half as bad as normal. The whole thing with feeling unstuck from her body just wasn't there and that, by itself, made it a great morning. Her head still felt like a little woman was sledgehammering in the back of her skull but hey, that was manageable. It was just pain.

"I might actually be able to get something done today," Anwyn murmured.

She laughed and tossed her night clothes on the bed. No one had set an outfit out for her. Normally she wouldn't have needed one until afternoon so that wasn't a surprise. Anwyn dug through her trunk and came up with comfortably worn Dana cloth pants, shirt and vest. A quick comb through her hair, her most comfortably worn boots, and Anwyn declared herself ready for the day.

No one was in the apartment. Kids would be down getting tutored right now. Mom was wherever dealing with the business, certainly. Dad was likely off getting groceries or dealing with paperwork for the Clan.

"Huh," Anwyn said as she headed down the stairs towards the warehouse, "it feels... quiet."

Amazingly quiet. Not so much because there weren't people around. There were. Anwyn could 'see' them. But their thoughts weren't quite as obnoxiously in her face as normal. Which...

Anwyn detoured to the guest quarters on the second floor, hunting through the dozen or so suites until she found Mistress Chie, a quiet storm of power that felt fragile and ancient. A quiet throbbing matched with terror told Anwyn that Danica was there, too.

"Hey, it's Anwyn," Anwyn called as she knocked and then opened the door. "Good, you're both here."

Mistress Chie had been given the Blue guest room, the one with Dana cloth curtains and carpet and two comfortably overstuffed chairs and one sofa all covered in Dana cloth. It was Anwyn's favorite out of all the guest rooms, warm, homey, nice big fireplace that wasn't lit at the moment, but it still gave the room a welcoming feeling.

Both Danica and Mistress Chie looked stiff at the interruption though Mistress Chie just shook her head and relaxed back into the sofa. She looked tiny next to its bulk, as though she was made of fine china and bits of aged spider silk about to fall apart at the least touch.

Danica's face was a swollen mass of bruises that completely hid her fine-boned features. Black eyes, both of them, a split lip, nose that looked like it might be broken. Maybe not. Could just be the black eyes.

"Should you be up?" Danica asked so sternly that Anwyn rolled her eyes. "I'm serious. You flattened yourself.

For no reason whatsoever, mind. I could have told them everything you said."

Anwyn shut the door and came in to flop on the couch next to Mistress Chie. "I'm fine. And I didn't do that for you. I did it for me. Everyone tries so hard to pretend that I don't have gifts that they disregard what I see when I use them. Had to make a point of it to get them to stop being stupid."

"Regardless, should you be up?" Danica asked. Her emotions shifted from quiet terror that seemed to just be part of her normal emotional... landscape for lack of a better term. Now she felt more of concern and wariness.

"That's the thing," Anwyn said with a grin at Mistress Chie that made both her eyebrows head for her hairline even as her lips twitched with amusement. "Poppy milk. Doctor Bernice always doses me up with poppy milk and the next day I feel terrible. Nausea, disconnected from myself like I'm about to float out of my body, can't think, can barely move. Rae convinced her to give me something else, a combination of willow and something that I can't remember because I was halfway passed out at the moment. Today I feel almost normal. Headache but that's it."

Mistress Chie nodded. "It happens. Poppy milk is from Chinwendu originally, a flower that the Goddesses were supposed to have stolen from the Morrigan. It's known that some people, especially those touched by the Ladies, have bad reactions to it. Didn't realize you'd been using it or I'd've said something years ago."

Anwyn wagged a finger at her, ignoring the way that Danica tried to smile and winced, as well as the way Mistress Chie chuckled. "I am telling Doctor Bernice that. And Mom. Dad, too. They all need to know so I don't get stuck with that stuff again. I hate what it does to me.

Which really wasn't my main reason for coming to pester you two. When are you leaving?"

The terror in Danica spiked. Mistress Chie scowled at the empty fireplace. Okay, so, there was a problem. Neither of them said anything so Anwyn shrugged and got back to her feet. Without any nausea or swaying or that weird feeling of her body staying in one spot while her soul kept on going.

"By the Goddesses' loins, I am never, ever taking poppy milk again. I can stand up without passing out today!" Anwyn declared. She swore just to get a new reaction from Danica. "This is wonderful. I might just have to make a point of doing stupid things with my gifts just to not feel so terrible afterwards."

Mistress Chie snarled for the profanity and threw a pillow at Anwyn who caught it, laughing. Danica just groaned and waved a hand at Anwyn.

"You're ridiculous and I'm not going to listen to you," Danica declared but she sounded amused, at least.

"Hah, got you to smile, sort of," Anwyn said. She grinned at them both. "I'll go see what's going on. We really should get you two out of the country quickly. Though I'm still not completely sure what the rush is besides older than dirt, Mistress Chie."

"I'm not that old!" Mistress Chie huffed. She shrugged, curling back into the couch like a spider going into its burrow. "I'm... worried if I'm here in the country when Queen Siobhan goes after immigrants it will affect Sunrise Shipyards. She can't claim that the Shipyards need to pay higher taxes or meet different regulations if I'm not in the country at all."

Anwyn stared at her for a long moment, then turned to Danica who sighed and nodded that Mistress Chie was justified in that worry. Well, there was a problem to investigate and fix. Maybe not fix. She could at least investigate and get the two of them out of Aingeal soon as possible. Probably.

"Well, I'll go check on that and then go tell Doctor Bernice that she's never, ever allowed to use poppy milk on me again," Anwyn said.

Danica laughed, shaking her head. There was amusement mixed with the terror so that was good. The joking didn't lighten Mistress Chie's mood as much but she did smile ever so slightly at Anwyn. It took Anwyn a moment to realize that Mistress Chie felt empty. That she was aching for something to do.

"Oh, I forgot," Anwyn said. She wagged a finger at Mistress Chie who raised that eyebrow of doom again. "Is there any possibility I could have you carve a little ship for Erlina before you leave? I keep meaning to buy one when I'm in Chinwendu but I forget while I'm there. Too much to do. It's kind of a tradition for me to get the kids something from the other side of the world but I think she'd like something from you just as much and a ship seems a good idea."

The fragile feeling snapped as Mistress Chie sat up and stared at Anwyn with interest. She felt alive for the first time which nearly made Anwyn grin at her. Yeah, she needed things to do. A lifetime of work wasn't something you could abandon, no matter what reasons you had for it.

Danica seemed to see it, too. She sat straighter, watching Mistress Chie and Anwyn through her puffy eyes. The amusement shifted to approval and a bit of surprise, as if Danica had only just then realized that Anwyn could and did use her gifts to help the people around her.

"I can do that," Mistress Chie said. "I'll need wood. Some tools. Make a mess, of course."

"Eh," Anwyn said, waving the concern away with dramatic casualness that had Danica groaning and Mistress Chie snorting a laugh. "Everything in here is Dana cloth. You'd have a hard time making a big enough mess to do any real damage. It'll be fine. Come on. We'll get you set up. I'm betting when people realize that you're willing to whittle toys, you'll have more people asking than you can handle."

That turned out to be marvelously true. Pretty much the instant Anwyn walked in with Mistress Chie, Danica at her elbow like a perfect shadow, and asked for wood and tools, women started asking if Mistress Chie would make them things, too. By the time Anwyn slipped away, having made sure that Erlina's ship would be first in the queue of toys to make, Mistress Chie was her old self, snapping orders, sending people running, vibrating with life and joy.

Finding Mother was impossible but Raelin and Great-Uncle Jarmon were both in his office, along with Doctor Bernice who came to her feet when Anwyn walked in. Anwyn grinned at her, flinging her arms out in so much joy that Doctor Bernice's flash of alarm went to the purest joy that Anwyn had ever felt from anyone.

Almost anyone. The last time Anwyn had sailed with Raelin, there'd been a moment when the sails boomed overhead, wind filling them after a tack, and Raelin's soul had sung with a bone-deep sort of joy that had left Anwyn breathless.

"You're better?" Doctor Bernice asked. She gripped Anwyn's wrist, checking her pulse, poking at her neck and peering into Anwyn's eyes. "No nausea?"

"No nausea, no disconnected feeling, still some pain but hey, I can handle it when I can think and move and not feel like a marionette with its strings half-cut," Anwyn said. "You are never, ever giving me poppy milk again. I went and asked Mistress Chie about it. Oh, Rae? I've set her to making carved toys. First one is a little ship for Erlina. But pretty much everyone jumped on board when she asked for wood and tools. She's in the warehouse now choosing wood and snapping orders while people run around doing her bidding."

"Really?" Raelin said and there was her joy, incandescent and relieved and so overpowering that Anwyn nearly stepped back.

"Back up," Great-Uncle Jarmon said to Anwyn. He put a hand on Raelin's arm, keeping her from getting up. "What did you ask Mistress Chie?"

"Oh, yeah," Anwyn said, grinning. "Sorry, I feel ridiculously good, all things considered, but I am a bit scatterbrained, I guess. Mistress Chie says that there are people in Chinwendu who simply don't tolerate poppy milk. Especially those who are touched by the Ladies which, frankly, is a large proportion of the Dana. I mean, not directly except me, but we're all Great-Grandmother Anwyn's descendants. So, whatever it was you used for me? That's amazing. I like it. I want to know what it is so that I can always use that in the future."

Doctor Bernice stared at Anwyn as she babbled. Maybe she wasn't quite as perfect as she felt. She was a bit... off. But it was still far better than Anwyn was used to, so she was happy. Very happy. Halfway to bouncing around singing and dancing a sea shanty, honestly.

"I'll write it down and make sure you get a copy," Doctor Bernice said after a moment. "Sit down. We were just talking about Mistress Chie. I have some concerns about her traveling so far at her age."

"She's old but she's got the right to decide where she lives," Raelin snapped.

"Eh, it's partially wanting to go home," Anwyn said with

one hand up to soothe Raelin, "but it's also that she's worried that Siobhan's going to put down rules that attack immigrants and immigrant-owned businesses. Mistress Chie wants to get out of Aingeal before they come down so that Sunrise Shipyards doesn't take the hit. It's why she retired, you know."

"Still, she's liable to die on the trip," Doctor Bernice said.

There was a worry, dark and painful, inside of her. It wrapped around Mistress Chie but it had very little to do with her. Anwyn looked at her for a long moment, teasing out the size and shape of the fear, the depth of it. Once she realized what it was, Anwyn sighed.

"You can't keep everyone alive," Anwyn told Doctor Bernice. "I know you want to. I mean, you're a doctor. But it's like ordering the tide to stay out when it's coming in. People will die. Mistress Chie is stupidly old. She's going to die. You can't change that."

Doctor Bernice winced.

Great-Uncle Jarmon nodded slowly, patting Raelin's arm. "Well said, Annie. We were just considering what ship to send her out on. And when you should head back out."

"Oh, soon!" Anwyn exclaimed. It made Raelin start laughing. "I want to go out as soon as possible. Frankly, I think I should go for much the same reasons that Mistress Chie should, but being at sea is always better than being on land. Can I go on a trip to Eastern Ntombi? We are still working on opening trade with the queen, aren't we?"

"Yes, we are," Great-Uncle Jarmon said with a snort of amusement. "Very well, I'll schedule that in. The Tourmaline is scheduled to head north to Atalya this time, so we'll have you on the Wave Dancer. Potentially with Mistress Chie and her... assistant."

Even though Anwyn could feel that Doctor Bernice

knew exactly who Danica was, Great-Uncle Jarmon didn't say Danica's name. Anwyn nodded, hummed at the though of it and then bounced back to her feet and grinned that she didn't sway or throw up or anything.

"No poppy milk," Anwyn declared with enough ferocity and a wide enough grin that Doctor Bernice started laughing. "Ever, ever, ever! I'm off to see what trouble I can get into."

"None!" Both Great-Uncle Jarmon and Raelin snapped that while Doctor Bernice laughed even harder.

"Oh, fine," Anwyn said. She threw up her hands and rolled her eyes. "I'll go see what work I can do. Is that better?"

"Much," Great-Uncle Jarmon said.

"Go ask Gavin for work," Raelin said. She shook her head, but she was smiling. Her soul was bright with relief and a thread of hope that was welcome after the gloom of the last few days. "He's sure to put you to work."

"Yes, ma'am!"

Anwyn strode on out, humming as she went. The whole Clanhouse felt better. When she carefully stretched outwards, amazed that she didn't immediately come unmoored from her body, Anwyn realized that there was a different energy to the city, too. People were thinking instead of cowering, acting instead of reacting. The women in the streets had purpose as they strode by.

Significantly, Anwyn felt far fewer spies lurking around the Clanhouse.

So maybe, if she was lucky, yesterday's stunt had done more good than Anwyn expected. At least it might have given Mother enough luck to ride the wave to a point where they weren't all in danger of crashing against the reefs of Siobhan's insanity.

22. EARLY COURT

Raelin grunted. She dropped her stack of records onto the table Mother had claimed for the early Royal Court meeting. Her bad arm ached from hefting them, but Mother'd had a stack twice as high so Raelin didn't complain. Not now. Not in front of the entire Royal Council.

It wasn't an official meeting. That wasn't for another three weeks, all thirty days of which promised to be filled with Mother and Dairine arguing over laws, paperwork and proper procedure.

No, this was the meeting that Tierney Yvon had called to address the Royal Treasury and what of Siobhan's orders could be implemented when.

And, because Lady Etain was brilliant at stirring up trouble, virtually every single Clan Head was sitting in the back of the room to listen in. The entire Royal Council was there when only five had to attend by tradition. Mother had brought a truly spine-threatening stack of law and records books, all filled with data on how much money Aingeal could expect to get at any point of time. Mother had also carried in the folio with her carefully prepared estimates of what all the new changes would do to those finances.

This promised to be either the moment when Aingeal returned to normal or when they all got their heads chopped off for impertinence.

"You don't need to attend this," Siobhan snapped as the door opened.

"I am the King," King Toryn snapped right back at her as he pushed past her in a whirl of black lace over dull grey kilts. "I want to see this. I know perfectly well that I have no say in how you run Aingeal, but I want to see this. Mother always allowed me to attend the interim meetings. I'm not giving that up."

His eyes were red, and he still wore the lace thing over his bun. When he glared at Siobhan, it wasn't defiance so much as it was regret mixed with a bone-deep sorrow that made Raelin glare at Siobhan.

"Let the boy watch," Mother said.

"Men have no place in this," Tierney Yvon said with enough shock that Mother rolled her eyes. "They don't. Nolan's an exception, but even he wouldn't have been allowed in this when he was still with me."

"Let him watch," Mother repeated. "It's a reminder of the past, of his family. Not like it makes a bit of difference in the end. Though, frankly? We didn't expect either of you, Your Majesties. This is just an attempt to sort through the budget before we figure out what happens first. There's no need for you to be here."

Siobhan stared at Mother, then at Yvon when she nodded marginally respectfully. She strode in, taking her spot at the head of the room with a sort of defiance that made Raelin wonder just how many people had been telling her that no, she couldn't do that, actually.

Interestingly, King Toryn smiled. It was a tiny smile, just the faintest curl of his lips, that disappeared nearly as soon as it appeared. But his eyes went dark and triumphant. Raelin wondered, abruptly, if this was what he'd planned all along.

Were they all tools in King Toryn's hands? Chisels and hammers to chip away at Siobhan's power until she was a figurehead with no ability to accomplish anything that she wanted?

He walked over, demure and controlled in his grieving clothes, to sit next to Siobhan with his hands folded politely in his lap. That, not Siobhan sitting, was what prompted everyone into starting the meeting. Lady Bethany cleared her throat before pulling out a sheet that proved to have the formal introduction to a Royal Council meeting on it. She read that off, frowning at the words as if she had a hard time sounding them out though she didn't hesitate or stumble as she spoke.

Siobhan glowered that no one looked her way. That no one paid her any attention. That King Toryn nodded approvingly once Lady Bethany was done and got a proper little half-bow from her in return. When Siobhan sat straighter and nodded too, no one bowed to her.

Yes, they were his tools. Raelin smiled as Mother gestured for the first book in the stack Raelin had hauled up the stairs for her. Good. This should be interesting. And, potentially, helpful.

"Right," Mother said. "This is an interim meeting of the Royal Council, first of this Council's. We're here to discuss the budget at Tierney Yvon's request. I've got a bunch of questions on the Royal Orders that have come out, mostly regarding legality and enforceability, but there're some issue on how they'll affect the taxes collected, too."

"They're legal because I say they're legal," Siobhan declared.

"Mmm, I am afraid that isn't quite true," Yvon said without meeting Siobhan's eyes. She was studying the paperwork in her very thick folio, sorting them out in front of her into the sort of particular order that Raelin had seen Gavin, Great-Uncle Jarmon and Nolan use. "You see, your decrees must be accepted by the Royal Council, at a formal meeting, and they must be properly funded to become effective."

"No, they also have to be ratified by all of the Clan Heads," Mother interrupted. "Well, not all. The Goddesses all know that the Dana and Delbhana have always voted against each other and laws still got passed. Need an eighty percent margin to pass and that's usually pretty easy to reach even with our clans at each other's throats. So, yeah, we've got a good bit to discuss here but it's all preliminary. Not a bit of it is binding at this point. It'll be a good two, three months before these orders become laws. Maybe a year for some of them. There're some serious, serious issues to address on a few of these."

Siobhan's cheeks went redder and redder as Yvon and Mother talked. Neither of them even glanced at her. They were too focused on their books and paperwork. Raelin did her best not to smile because old Lady Mab nodded so firmly that her head looked half a second away from falling off. The other Councilors didn't look Siobhan's way, either, pulling out paper and pen to take notes with, murmuring to their neighbors or over their shoulders to the closest Clan Heads listening in.

Frankly, Raelin was certain that the only ones in the whole room paying any attention to Siobhan were her and King Toryn.

"I'm the Queen!" Siobhan shouted. "You have to do what I say!"

"No, they don't," King Toryn said in a soft, respectful, absolutely implacable tone that dropped Siobhan's jaw. "I told you. The Queen rules through the people, for the people, with the people. It takes finesse to get things accomplished, not brute force."

As Siobhan spluttered, her face going so red it was nearly purple, Yvon started listing off each of the new rules Siobhan had issued in the same irritated tone that Nolan used when he found accounting errors in Raelin's ship logs and Minoo paperwork. She ended with closing the Temples. Mother wagged a finger at that one though she'd nodded several times as Yvon spoke.

"Got a major issue with that one," Mother said. "The entire port's structured around the temple bells that ring on the hour. Everything's running late or not running at all because no one knows what time it is. Add in that rule about men needing to have a woman in the shop when they're running a shop of their own? We're losing a good huge chunk of money already. Huge damned impact on commerce that I frankly didn't anticipate. Much bigger than I thought it'd be."

"Agreed," Lady Mab said before Yvon could open her mouth. "I've had to equip all my women in the Royal Guard with pocket watches and get clocks for every room in the Palace. It's a terrible expense just here, much less at my Clan, and there simply aren't enough shops in the city that sell them. Perhaps in the entire country. I can't imagine how much money we're losing on not having the bells."

"I can," Mother said, waving a piece of paper entirely covered with sums. "Already figured it out. We're dropping the gross tax revenues by three percent every day that the bells don't ring. We're losing about four percent for the shops that're shut because men run them alone. That's every single day. I can't recommend those rules stay in place, not with what they're costing us on commerce and taxes."

"Agreed," Yvon said so quickly that Raelin suspected that Mother'd stolen the words right out of her mouth. "My figures place it closer to six and eight percent, respectively."

"Eh, we went conservative on the figures," Mother said so calmly that it made Siobhan's spluttering all the more inappropriate.

Yvon nodded, flipping the comment away with a lazy wave of her hand. "Granted. Opinions on sustaining or sidelining those two rulings?"

As Siobhan spluttered, the vote was unanimous to overturn both rulings. Raelin didn't grin. King Toryn did for a brilliant, beautiful second that lit his face up like the sun coming through the clouds during a storm at sea where you hadn't seen land in weeks.

Siobhan didn't notice his smile. She was too furious, muttering and glaring, to pay attention to anything other than her fury.

Mother and Yvon ran through all the other rulings that Siobhan had issued. One by one, they were either struck down as costing too much or recommended for changes to make sure that they didn't disrupt people's lives too much. Of the one hundred and nine orders that Siobhan had given over the last week, they got through thirty-one of them over the course of an hour and a half.

Stunningly, Siobhan didn't explode until the they got to a new order requiring all immigrants to register and pay extra taxes.

"They don't belong in Aingeal!" Siobhan shouted as she leaped to her feet. "This is our country, not theirs. No immigrant belongs here. They should damned well pay for the privilege of being here!"

"Well, that's dumb," Mother said so casually that Raelin smacked her elbow. "Oh, shush, Rae. It is stupid. Aingeal is made of immigrants. Immigrants and conquering other, smaller countries couple of generations back. There's no one people with the right to be here because there's too many people mixed in here."

"As much as I hate to agree with you," Lady Bethany said with a grimace that looked absolutely heart-felt, "you're right. We cannot implement this rule without impacting every single clan and every single business in Aingeal."

"If you do this," Siobhan snarled, glaring down at them all, "I will have you executed! I am the Queen and you will obey me!"

"You can't execute them without a trial," King Toryn commented. He flinched when Siobhan whirled at him. "You can't. It's against the law, the oldest laws of Aingeal. The First Queen put them in place. You also can't decide their fate. Both are in the hands of the Clan Heads assembled here."

Lady Etain stood, glaring at Siobhan as if Siobhan wasn't her daughter. "We will never try or convict the Royal Council for doing their damned jobs."

Siobhan went bone white as every single Clan Head stood up and quietly or, in a couple of Dana ally cases, shouted their agreement with Lady Etain. Raelin snorted at the way Lady Etain jerked and stared at having Dana allies agree with here. It was close to the end of the world. She couldn't think of another time that it'd happened.

"I'm the Queen," Siobhan said, quiet, cold, furious in ways that made Raelin worry for King Toryn.

"That's basically Clan Head of all Clan Heads," Mother

said. She leaned her elbows on the table amid her papers and books, studying Siobhan with a sort of calm that was betrayed by the tension in her arms and shoulders. "Don't know what you were taught, but the Queen isn't absolute ruler. We're not in Ntombi. This is Aingeal. We're a bunch of argumentative, stubborn idiots who can't agree on much of anything, including how much power you should have at any given moment."

Yvon sighed and nodded. "I've had my daughter going through the records."

"So have I!" Lady Bethany laughed and grinned when Yvon snorted. "Neither of them are happy about it, I'm sure."

"Not in the slightest," Yvon agreed. "There's been Queens who were so loved that people did every single thing they asked. They hardly asked for a thing. And there have ben Queens who were so loathed that not one thing they ordered happened. It's all into how well the Queen works with the Royal Council and the Clan Heads. King Toryn's mother used to be very good, before she got sick."

"She tried very hard even after she fell ill," King Toryn said so sadly that Raelin's heart hurt for him. "There were days when she couldn't rise from her bed but she still had people bring her the news."

Silence fell for a few seconds. Raelin bowed her head, watching Siobhan from the corner of her eye. Where everyone else gave King Toryn the respect of not watching him carefully wipe his eyes with a simple grey handkerchief, Siobhan glared at him as if offended that he'd dared to speak.

"I want that ruling," Siobhan declared when they raised their heads.

"Gonna have to spend some time rewording it then," Mother said with a shrug that made her shoulders pop audibly. "It's too broad to be allowable now. Impact would be devastating."

"Agreed," Lady Bethany said. "I can put some work into rephrasing it if Your Majesty wishes. I should be able to have a new version that is passable within a week or so."

The only answer was the sound of Siobhan gritting her teeth.

"Might help to have an idea of why the ruling's so important," Mother said while shuffling her paperwork. "It's so short that there's no hint of the intent of the thing. With that, we could hammer it out. Maybe."

Siobhan snarled at them all and strode out of the room. The door slammed against the wall, then rebounded to shut with a bang. King Toryn hummed and nodded thoughtfully before smiling at them all in a way that made Raelin's spine snap erect. Clothing rustled all around the room as everyone else straightened, too.

"Please do continue, everyone," King Toryn said gently. "Let's take care of our beloved Aingeal."

Softly. Giving them an order that he officially couldn't that Raelin, that everyone, was more than happy to obey.

23. TEMPLE BELLS

The temple bells rang out over the port. Anwyn grinned from her spot in the crow's nest on the Tourmaline Dreams. Three days without the bells had been weird. Now, every time they rang people stopped and smiled back towards the Temple.

Anwyn included.

"Pay attention, Annie!" Rae shouted from the deck.

"I am!" Anwyn shouted back at her. "You pay attention to your own work."

"Like you're working up there."

Even from the crow's nest, Anwyn could see the way Raelin rolled her eyes. Truth be told, Anwyn wasn't working and she didn't care at all who knew it. Up in the crow's nest, Anwyn could see everything in the port. Dozens of ships were getting ready to sail out once the tide turned. A mid-morning tide shift always brought bunches of ships departing. It would be cautious, careful work for the tugs to get everyone out far enough that there wouldn't be any problems.

Anwyn had hoped that Mistress Chie and Danica

would be off to sea already but Mother had stomped on that idea. At least she'd managed to make sure that Mistress Chie kept busy with making toys and carving things. That'd brightened everyone's moods, especially Mistress Chie's.

Nice. A bit odd because Anwyn couldn't remember Mistress Chie ever being this cheerful before. Every time Rae saw it, she looked like she'd been decked. Then she grinned like Erlina getting a treat. So it was good, if strange.

Strangest thing, though, was being in the crow's nest and not feeling spies watching her every move. That'd been something that Anwyn had been aware of since she was, oh, little. A constant, there as long as she could remember.

No.

Not that long.

Anwyn shuddered and ducked down into the crow's nest because she really didn't want anyone to see her panic attack. Her heart pounded as Anwyn tried to breathe. Failed at it. Hard. Because her heart hammered away in her chest and her hands shook and she just about peed her pants from the sheer fear.

It'd started the day she went out to the City of the Ladies.

That was the day that Anwyn noticed the spies. Noticed people watching. Realized that there were people expecting things of her that she didn't understand. When she was little, Anwyn hadn't realized why. Hadn't understood.

The Ladies were just... people, really. Strange people with tentacles instead of arms and legs. With cities they'd built under the water the same as humans built on the land. It wasn't important that they were so different, not when they laughed at Anwyn's jokes and sang songs while Anwyn had played her panpipes.

Ten years.

Anwyn forced her lungs to breathe deeply, slowly, counting to eight, holding, exhaling for eight. It always worked for Caddie and it worked for her, too. After nineteen rounds of breathing slow and careful, the panic drained away.

She'd been watched for ten years and sudden they'd all gone away. Nice as it was, Anwyn was more than a little nervous about it now that she realized what'd happened. When Anwyn licked her lips, they tasted of salt. Her shirt was soaked but her jacket hid the worst of that.

No point in staying up above when the answers Anwyn wanted were down below. Anwyn swung out of the crow's nest and clambered down the rigging. Rae wasn't on deck anymore but Anwyn could feel her off in her cabin.

"Finally decided to help get some work done, did you?" Raelin asked when Anwyn opened her door. She raised an eyebrow at Anwyn. "What's got you sweating?"

"Panic attack," Anwyn said. She shut the door, leaned against it and slid down to the floor. "There's no spies watching me, Rae. Not one. They're out there but they're not watching me anymore. They've been there for ten years. And now they're not."

"Breathe," Raelin ordered. She stepped to Anwyn's side, knelt with a jerky lurch that reminded Anwyn, yet again, that Rae's scars went all down her body, right to the hip and thigh. "Breathe for me, Annie. Come one, in and hold, out and hold."

Rae breathed with Anwyn, gently prompting her to inhale, to exhale, to hold in the right places and the right times. Her good hand was firm around Anwyn's sweaty palm. Mind was just as steady, too. That helped as much as the breathing. It didn't take as long for the panic to drain away.

"Sorry," Anwyn whispered. Her mouth felt like sand, tongue like old shoe leather.

"Never a problem, Annie," Rae said. She settled on the floor in front of Anwyn. "I do know what happened, you know. It was after Mari punched Danica and you got carried off to bed."

"Really?" Anwyn asked. She stared but there was no lie in Rae's mind, heart or eyes. Just calm knowledge, acceptance. "What?"

"Lady Etain assumed that you were the next leader of the Dana," Raelin said.

The calmness shimmered with amusement for just long enough that Anwyn could only stare at her in shock. Laughter swept over Anwyn. Hard and fast as getting caught in a tsunami, the laughter sucked Anwyn under.

She laughed until tears rolled down her cheeks and coughs ripped at her throat. Through it all, Rae just grinned. She did get up, levering herself up on her good arm and leg, to get Anwyn a little flask of whiskey that she'd had stashed away in her desk. It was the cheap kind, barely good enough for getting falling-down drunk on. Definitely not for enjoying the process.

"Rank," Anwyn complained when she passed the flask back to Rae.

"Sinead gave it to me before she left." Rae sipped at the flash, shuddered and screwed the top on again. "Lady Etain's focused on Mari and Gavin now. They know it. So does Mother and Great-Uncle Jarmon. Should be fine, really. They are the ones who'll take over the clan when Mother finally decides to retire."

Anwyn nodded.

It still felt strange not to have that hovering awareness of people watching and wondering what she was up to in Rae's cabin. The finely carved walls that hid cabinets that would be full of trade goods that the crew had gathered looked strange. Even the scars on Rae's cheek, stretched and raw even two years later, seemed off.

"You'll get used to it, Annie," Raelin said. She leaned against her desk. "Besides, you can get into more trouble now that they're not watching your every move."

"They may not be but Mother still is," Anwyn said. She nodded her thanks to Rae who smiled and waved it away with a casual contentment that soothed the bubbling panic wonderfully.

"Just don't punch anyone who doesn't deserve it," Raelin said, amused. "Now go do something productive. I've got work to do."

Anwyn left her alone. Slipped right off the Tourmaline Dreams and headed back towards the Clanhouse. But no, not there. Not yet.

The temple was still closed though the priestesses had been allowed to come back and ring the bells as they always had. No point going that way. Market was just what it always was, crowded and busy, especially since men were allowed to run their own shops again. Their cousins has women guarding them, just in case, but most of the men shopkeepers hadn't bothered.

They wouldn't keep a shop if they had women in their lives who could do it, after all. Anwyn headed up Port Street, skirting past the stables and off into the worse neighborhoods of Aingeal City. Not the outright bad ones. Even a Dana woman had to be careful off in the slums that butted against the River Wall.

Didn't stop Anwyn from walking the streets and taking the feel of the city. She didn't know what she was looking for. If she was looking for something. All she knew was that her feet didn't want to stay still.

"We don't need your kind here!"

The shout was angry. Not angry-angry but afraid-angry. Anwyn went right for it. The fear-anger-resignation drew her. She couldn't have stopped herself from pushing straight into the crowd of women in their ragged Dana cloth, much of their clothes donations given to them by Caddie. She recognized Caddie's embroidery on nearly every jacket.

Center of the crowd was a Ntombi man, trembling as he clutched a bright yellow-green decorated bag to his chest. His skin of his hands was the golden-brown of a Western Ntombi woman's, sallow against the red brick wall he cowered in front of. He was covered, head to wrist to toe, in the enveloping veils that Ntombi men all wore. Like the bag, his veils were yellow background with huge green fern leaves dyed over them. There were small embroidered accents in red and white but from a distance he looked like a giant fern sprouting in the middle of the muddy red-brick street.

"Hey," Anwyn snapped as she pushed the lead woman away from him. "What's all this then?"

And, of course, Anwyn's luck was true to form because the woman she shoved aside was in a Delbhana red coat with bright, beautiful embroidery that couldn't be more than a few months old. Not a single snag on it that Anwyn could see.

"You stay out of it, Dana!" the Delbhana woman snarled. "His kind don't belong here."

"Pfft," Anwyn said, rolling her eyes. "You don't belong here. That coat'll get your throat cut soon, Delbhana. There's enough silk embroidered onto it to feed a family for a month if they pick it out careful."

The Delbhana's eyes went wide. She backed away from Anwyn and then went stiff as the women around her wouldn't meet her eyes. So, yeah, they'd been thinking it, too. Idiot didn't even have backup the way most Delbhana did.

"You wanna go stir up trouble," Anwyn said, placing herself between the Delbhana and the Ntombi man with her hands on her hips, "you should bring along some friends. I thought you Delbhana always traveled in packs. Never seen one with the guts to go around along. Gotta commend you for that, if not for your brains."

"You're here, too," the Delbhana said but she was edging away from Anwyn and the other women.

Anwyn waved and the other women opened a path away. The Delbhana glanced at the Ntobmi man with honest, true anger in her eyes. Then she ran away, quick-marching until she was past the crowd and then running like the coward she was.

"Idiot," Anwyn said, shaking her head. "Ready to stir up trouble until there's a chance she might get hurt."

"You're none too bright to be here, yourself," one of the biggest women commented. She was as wide as Mother at the shoulder and hip, as tall as Mari. Probably could lift two barrels at once if she wanted.

"Pfft. I'm Dana. You don't expect sense out of us." Anwyn rolled her eyes again. "You need work? You got the build for a dock worker. Seriously, built like a brick wall, there. You're like four of me."

The woman's jaw dropped. Then her eyes narrowed. "Don't joke about that."

"I'm not," Anwyn replied. She lifted her chin and stared the other woman down. "You got the build. You want the work? We're always looking for workers, especially strong ones. Sunrise Shipyards has a new owner. They're looking to expand. That's a ton of training but you master those skills and you'll never want for work. That matter, if you've got a delicate touch, I got a distant uncle who needs people to help make watches and clocks. He's looking for workers and not finding them. His backlog of orders is more than two years right now 'cause we all know the Queen's going to stop the bells again soon as she can."

By the point Anwyn was done, all of the women were staring at her with the sort of hunger that came not from an empty belly but from an empty wallet. Only took a few seconds before they all nodded and Anwyn was able to send them off after their new jobs.

Well, maybe new jobs. They'd have to apply and get the jobs and then keep them but the work was all real so it didn't take long before she was alone with the Ntombi man. Who trembled when Anwyn turned to him, terror of sexual assault high in his mind. The terror of robbery and death was much lower.

"Ugh," Anwyn groaned as she switched to Ntombian. She wrinkled her nose at him and instantly decided that his rank was as low as possible and that she really didn't care about him that much because she was not going to let him or anyone know that she could read his mind and see that he was very high-born. "Vloo-Jlaqudovyash-wu, I do not enjoy men. At all. Do stop cringing at me when I just saved you."

He jerked and then stared at her as his went wide for the 'vloo' and 'wu'. Or maybe for being 'jlaqudovyash'. After all, his life was meaningless to her. So far. Up to him to make her care for more than just stopping an attack against a man who didn't deserve it.

"I am most sorry to be disturbed by the violence offered to me, oh ish-Jlaquinugosi-she," the man said in the highest disrespect and most educated tone that Anwyn had heard since she visited Eastern Ntombi.

"Nice," Anwyn said in broad dockside drawl with a grin at him for combining the term used for those chosen for greatness by the Goddesses with the suffix of loathing. "You're out of place. Need an escort back to the embassy?"

He glowered but nodded reluctantly.

The walk back to the Ntombian embassy wasn't all that long. Port Alley led to Dana Street led to the Royal Road and there they were at the embassy where dozens of Ntombian warrior women clustered, talking urgently as she shook spears at once enough as if they were about to fight.

"Went out without your escort, did you vloo-Jlaqudovyash-wu?" Anwyn said to him from the side of her mouth.

"It should have been a simple errand to the Market to get presents for my nephews," the man replied. "I would not expect you to understand such menial things, oh ish-Jlaquinogoshi-she."

Anwyn burst out laughing, both at the idea that she wouldn't get presents for kids back home and the snide, sarcastic tone of his voice. He snorted and then laughed under his breath. Hands had relaxed dramatically so yeah, well done on her part and thank goodness she'd listened to her instincts.

The laughter caught the attention of the warriors who turned their way with glares, froze and then charged over chattering questions to the man. Every single one of them used the highest rank prefixes and suffixes for him. Anwyn watched and waited, grinning as he snapped at them until they stopped fussing.

"You will come and have tea," the man declared. "I am

Jinhai of the Second House of Ntombi and you are owed at least tea and polite conversation."

"Tea I'll take gladly," Anwyn said with a full-on proper Chinwenduese bow of lesser rank to highest rank. "Polite conversation isn't necessary though not being punched in the nose is always good. Can't stay too long. We've ships getting ready to go out and I really should've been helping load everything up."

Jinhai snorted at her, eyes laughing as he gestured for her to follow him inside despite the glares Anwyn got from the warrior women. The whole thing was a bit odd but Anwyn wasn't about to say no. Great-Grandmother Anwyn had destroyed their chances of every having a deal with Ntombi, way back when Great-Uncle Jarmon was younger than Anwyn was now. Might be nice to see if they could try and work their way back to a deal.

And if chancing on Jinhai in danger helped make that happen, well. Anwyn would take the luck of the Ladies and sail with it as far as she could.

24. QUIET REVOLUTION

"Anyone seen Annie?" Raelin asked.

The warehouse workers shook their heads. Most looked decidedly grateful about Anwyn's absence. Understandably. Annie was so often a distraction or a trouble-maker when they were staging supplies for ships going out. Raelin thought it was boredom, frustration in the limitations of her life, but Anwyn was far too often a problem instead of a help.

It was still odd that she wasn't around, though. Raelin would've sworn that Anwyn had headed into the warehouse ages ago but no one had seen her. She wasn't in the offices or Sean's school. Poking her head in got an avalanche of cheering and questions from the kids and a stern glare from Sean that sent Raelin running. Laughing, too, but still running. Sean had gotten quite fierce since he settled into his marriage to Eoghania.

Good to see that he had settled so well and that his daughters were so strong.

No Annie upstairs in the girls' bunk room or in their kitchen raiding for food. Raelin frowned. Downstairs again, Raelin didn't find her bothering Great-Uncle Jarmon who only shook his head and waved Raelin away.

"Why are you looking for her?" Mother asked when Raelin found her doing inventory of rope and barrels of pickled limes in the warehouse.

"She," Raelin paused, made sure no one was close, and then continued. "She had a panic attack because she realized that no one was spying on her anymore. Ten years of it, Mother. Ten years and suddenly they've switched focus. I wanted to ask her more questions now that I had a chance to think about it."

Mother nodded so grimly that Raelin peered at her. "I know. Got Doctor Bernice and some… other people investigating Danica's grandmother and mother. Annie was dead-right. They are the Delbhana spy mistresses. After your, heh, discussion with Lady Etain their focus has changed completely. They're on me, Gavin and Mari now. Bit of questioning on Great-Uncle Jarmon's work and attitudes but that's it. You and Annie aren't of interest at all."

"Huh." Raelin scowled. "Not sure I like that they're that easy to manipulate but I guess it's good for us. Maybe. They're not going to try and marry one of the men out of the Clan?"

"Nope," Mother said with a snort of amusement. She went back to her inventory, counting while talking and making no mistakes in her count. Raelin would've struggled with talking and counting at the same time. "According to our sources, marriage is now off the table. Uncle Jarmon and I already agreed that anyone wanting a Dana man, or woman for that matter, will be joining the Dana. We're not letting anyone go if we can help it. Especially Caddie. He's the next that they're going to focus on."

"Jewel of the Clan," Raelin said, nodding. "Right. Well, I'm heading off again, then. The Tourmaline is ready for loading, all ropes replaced and sails ready. She'll be set for sailing in three days, as long as we get the water barrels on board refilled in the next day or so."

Mother nodded, shooing Raelin away.

To Raelin's annoyance, Anwyn was apparently nowhere at all in the entire Clanhouse which meant that she'd gone off wandering through the city with no one to protect and escort her. Gavin and Mari both looked up when Raelin stalked into their office.

"What's got you scowling?" Gavin asked. He passed a stack of paperwork wrapped in color-coded waterproofed folios and log books over to Raelin, tapping them with one firm finger when she huffed at him. "These are yours. You'll want to stash them on the Tourmaline. Nice of you to come pick them up so quickly after I messaged you."

"I never got the message but fine," Raelin said. She set them back down on the corner of Gavin's desk. "I've been looking for Annie. I think she's off wandering in the city by herself."

"Oh, damn the girl to the Morrigan's hands," Mari groaned and laughed, hands pressing against her eyes as she tipped her chair backwards. "Gonna have to bail her out, aren't we?"

"Probably." Gavin sighed. He shook his head. "Well, neither of us can go hunting for her, Rae. We've too much work to get done here. Grab Eoghania and look for her. The last thing we want is Annie catching the Delbhana's attention again so soon after it switched over to us."

"So, you do know about that," Raelin commented.

"Hard not to." Gavin shrugged, mouth pursed as if he'd bitten into an underripe lemon. "They're not very good at hiding their interest in us. It does make sense of why Annie was always so jumpy."

"'Specially when she can hear 'em in her head," Mari

agreed with a shudder. "Don' think I could handle that. Go on, Rae. Find her. Bring her home. We'll give her a good scolding when she's back."

Raelin nodded, taking her paperwork out to the Tourmaline first. At this point, Anwyn had been gone for almost three hours. There wasn't much chance that Raelin would be able to track her. Might as well get one task done properly before starting the impossible job of finding Annie and bringing her home. Hopefully intact.

When Raelin emerged from her cabin, Eoghania was there, talking with Rae's best friend Bahb. The two of them snickered, heads together, so they had to be talking about men. Maybe Sean. Eoghania was completely smitten with Sean in ways that Raelin still found confusing.

But then she perpetually found that sort of thing confusing. Sex and romance, the two greatest mysteries in the world as far as Raelin was concerned. Even the Ladies made more sense than that.

"There you are," Eoghania said. She grinned and hooked at thumb towards the city. "Got news that Annie's off wandering. We're to go find her and bring her back."

"Yeah, I know." Raelin sighed. Then huffed as Bahb snorted and punched her in the shoulder. "What?"

"I was just saying that I'd know where to look if it were me or one of the crew members," Bahb said as she wagged her eyebrows suggestively. Though why wagging eyebrows was supposed to suggest sex Raelin had never understood. "For you, it'd be the Market or the Records office. Annie, not so sure."

"Well, it won't be a brothel with men in it," Raelin said and then snickered along with Eoghania and Bahb because Anwyn was as clear as anything not interested in men that way. "And frankly, I'd planned on going looking for brawls.

You hear a fight? Nine times out of ten it'll be Annie or Gwen in the middle of the fight."

Both Eoghania and Bahb nodded at that one. Bahb punched Raelin's shoulder again, always careful to only hit the good shoulder, then they were on their way. The bells rang the fourth hour of the afternoon as they headed up towards the Market. That was as likely as anywhere else after Anwyn had been gone for hours.

"What is your sister doing?"

Raelin stopped in her tracks, turned and then groaned as Lady Etain stormed at them with her hands in fists, her face so red it was nearly purple and a wild look in her eyes that didn't match the rage she tried to project.

"You know more than I do," Raelin said as soon as Lady Etain stopped in front of them. "We just realized that Annie wasn't in the Clanhouse. We've been sent to bring her home."

"She's off in the Ntombian embassy stirring up trouble!" Lady Etain exclaimed. "There's a rumor that she got in a fight with a Delbhana woman, no one knows who, and the father of the First House's heir was nearly killed in the battle."

Raelin stared at her. Turned to Eoghania whose jaw had dropped. She stared back at Raelin, horrified noises coming from her mouth. So, Raelin shook her head and turned back to Lady Etain who glowered at them as if it was their fault that Annie had gone off and found trouble. Again.

"Where's the embassy?" Raelin asked without trying to hide the 'I'm not old enough for this nonsense' misery in her voice.

It must be in her eyes, her face, her posture, too, because Lady Etain's fake fury cracked. She swallowed down laughter, pressed her lips together and gestured back towards the Royal Road that led to the Palace.

"They're borrowing a portion of the Nasrinian embassy for their visit," Lady Etain said. "Neither of you knew about his visit."

"No, most of Ntombi, especially the rulers, won't have a thing to do with us," Raelin said. "Great-Grandmother Anwyn stole the crown jewels and then lost them in a drinking match before she got home. Ntombi kind of hates the Dana for that."

This time Lady Etain didn't bother swallowing her laughter. She let it out in all its derisive glory before striding off with both her hands held up to say that she wasn't going to touch any of that. Raelin sighed. That was sure to be all over the city in hours but then it was a story that went around the city every few years.

While they never talked about Great-Grandmother Anwyn's piracy, her drinking, gambling and stupid decisions were fair game, especially when they needed to soften someone up. Or make a Delbhana feel good enough that they went away.

"Off to the embassy?" Eoghania asked.

"Yeah," Raelin agreed. "How does Annie do this?"

"Don't know," Eoghania said. "I'd be a wreck if I had so much stuff happen to me all the time. Not sure why she isn't."

Raelin nodded. They quick-marched it towards the Nasrinian embassy, a small brick building well away from the Palace and quite close to the Market. When they got there, it was quite obvious that there were Ntombian people visiting. The guards that stood in front of the stairs were Ntombian warrior women, tall and lean and strong in ways that made Eoghania looks slow and lumbering. Their spears weren't at the ready but Raelin had no doubt that they could be if she made the wrong move.

"I'm... looking for my little sister, Dana Anwyn," Raelin said to the guard who had the most battle jewelry on her collar and wrist gauntlets. "Apparently there was some sort of confrontation and she saved a Ntombian man? Lady Etain wasn't terribly clear when she yelled at us."

Despite having spoken slowly and clearly, it took several moments before the guard's head came up and her eyes went from blank incomprehension to understanding. She nodded, bowed once, slightly, and then marched right up into the building. Since she hadn't gestured for Raelin and Eoghania to follow, Rae stayed right where she was.

"Rae!" Anwyn shouted from a window on the second floor. "Hey, what're you doing here?"

"...Looking for you," Raelin called back up at her. "You're supposed to be working, not sitting around or getting in fights with people."

"Oh, nonsense," Anwyn said. "Hang on. I'll be right down. Jinhai and I were just talking about Chinwendu and Ntombi's trade. Super-interesting stuff."

She paused, looked over her shoulder into the room and then grinned before she turned back to Raelin. Without the slightest awareness, as far as Raelin could see, that the warrior women were tensing up. Or that Raelin was half a step away from charging into the building and dragging her out by her ear.

"Jinhai says that we should go visit," Anwyn said. "He's gonna write a quick letter inviting us and then tell the First and Second houses that we're welcome. Sort of. Anyway, I'll be right down."

Anwyn ducked back into the house, shutting the window so there was no point for Raelin to scream 'what?' up at her. Raelin certainly mouthed it. Then asked

Eoghania who was making the horrified noses while waving her hands again. The warriors, thankfully, had stopped looking like they were about to attack and now just grinned at them all.

Three very long minutes later, Anwyn emerged to bounce down the stairs with a properly folded and sealed letter in her hand. She patted Raelin's bad shoulder and then waved at the guards like she was seven instead of seventeen.

"Come on!" Anwyn exclaimed. "I want to tell Great-Uncle Jarmon and Mom all about this. Jinhai is actually Chinwenduese. He fell in love with the eldest daughter of the Second House and moved to Ntombi. Lovely guy. His daughter Ynes is a hoot. We laughed so hard while we talked and had tea."

She set off towards home, chattering and smiling like the Anwyn she'd been back before the visit to the City of the Ladies. Raelin followed, trying to find words beyond spluttering demands for Anwyn to slow down and explain things properly. Not that she really cared because Anwyn's chatter was clear enough, if calculated to make people look at her and smile at the young girl on her supposed first errand.

What really stuck in Raelin's mind was that Anwyn was happy. Free. Smiling and joking as she hadn't for so very long, unless she was at sea.

Anwyn flung open the formal entrance doors, beaming at the cousin who was on greeting duty, leaving him to close the doors because she kept right on going towards the offices on the other side of the building. "So yeah, it's pretty amazing. I got lucky to find him. Really, though, he was lucky that I was there. Whoever that Delbhana was, and I didn't recognize her, she obviously intended to incite a riot and get him attacked. At least beaten up and possibly killed. Terrible neighborhood for him to be in anyway, but hey, mixing up Port Street and Port Alley when you've never been in the city before is understandable."

"Annie," Raelin said, putting her hand on Anwyn's shoulder.

"What?" Anwyn asked. She blinked and then smiled quietly, happily. So very happily. "Yeah, I do feel better, Rae. It was weird to realize they weren't watching me. But then, as I wandered, I realized that they city's changed. The whole country, probably."

"What do you mean?" Raelin asked.

It was just the three of them in the hallway, one turn away from the formal entrance with its gold leaf and three turns away from the warehouse offices. Most of the time nobody came through this particular hallway because it was narrow and dark, no windows and few lamps to see by.

Anwyn looked back towards the formal entrance, her smile grimly satisfied. "Before the old Queen died, the Delbhana were our problem, Rae. We saw what they were up to. We fought them. Everyone let us take care of it. Now? Now they all know what's going on. They all see it. Everyone I passed in the city today was wary, watching. Aware that any moment the things they care about could be destroyed."

"The city's on the verge of riots?" Raelin asked as her throat went tight and her heart pounded.

"Oh no," Anwyn said. Her eyes went distant for a moment, as foggy as when she'd found Danica's mother and grandmother at the price of a migraine. "The city, the whole country, is on the verge of revolution, Rae. The Delbhana have their plots. They always do. But all they care about now is keeping power long enough to get

Siobhan off the throne and someone more... controllable onto it. We're not fighting alone anymore."

She grinned, wild and wicked, before striding off humming a sea shanty that was as obscene as anything in a brothel. Riding the luck. Raelin scrubbed her hands over her face. Eoghania groaned before patting Raelin's back. They followed Anwyn who started singing the sea shanty loudly enough that it echoed into the warehouse offices, carrying laughter back.

A revolution, just waiting to happen. Raelin pursed her lips as she shook her head. Anwyn might find that a welcome prospect but Raelin was far too aware of how many people could die in a revolution. How much damage it could do.

No, revolution wasn't what Raelin wanted for Aingeal but if it came to it, well. She'd fight for the Dana. For King Toryn. For Sinead off in Atalya, waiting for a chance to come home. And Danica, the common folk and the smaller clans and all their allies who relied on the Dana to pilot to the worst storms.

A revolution was a storm like no other.

Raelin nodded.

Well. If that's what was to come, she'd do everything in her power to make sure the Dana survived it intact. And she'd do her best to make sure Aingeal survived it, too.

25. SET SAIL

Anwyn stood at the end of the dock, bouncing on her toes as the Dancing Wave slowly raised her sails. The big mainsail boomed in the wind, catching and filling so quickly that it seemed like the Dana triple swirl in the center just flashed into existence. She cheered, much to the other sailors around her amusement.

Didn't care, not at all. Because Mistress Chie was standing on the deck, Danica by her side, waving back at them all.

When Anwyn started waving, the sailors waved, too. With amusement at first, then more earnestly because every single sailor on the Dancing Wave turned and cheered so loud that their voices echoed over the bay. Bounced off the steep, pine-covered hills, ricocheted back at them.

"I fail to see what's so important about this," Lady Etain said from behind Anwyn in a properly snide tone that didn't match the shuddery feeling inside her.

"Mistress Chie's sailing out," Anwyn exclaimed. "After half a century, more than that, she's sailing out again. It's huge! I wish I could go with her. I could learn half as much as Rae did when she fixed up the Tourmaline Dreams. But no, Mother has to stick me on the Shimmering Skies for a trip to Nasrin. Just plain not fair, I tell you."

She didn't look at Lady Etain. Didn't look at any of the sailors. Anwyn very firmly kept her eyes on the Dancing Wave and Mistress Chie who'd finally stopped waving. And that, as much as her words, had the other sailors feeling sympathetic for Anwyn.

"I doubt that she'll spend much time sharing her secrets of ship construction," Lady Etain said with a dismissive little sniff.

As the sailors moved off to get back to work, Lady Etain moved up to stand by Anwyn's side. She wanted something. Not just the normal needling and plotting, something more substantial. Not too good but hey, Anwyn could sail this route in her sleep. Lady Etain wasn't likely to surprise her, after all.

"As if that's what I want to know," Anwyn complained. She glanced sideways at Lady Etain's too pale, too tense face. "I wanna know about Great-Grandmother Anwyn. How's she set up trade with Atalya? Why'd she sail that far, the entire other end of the world? Was Great-Grandfather Tau actually that much like Rae? What, actually, is Great-Grandfather Tau's favorite tea and how do you make it because, wow, I'm telling you right now that if we could figure that out, we'd make thousands. On the spot. Somebody knows that secret and someday I'm gonna find out."

Anwyn wagged a finger at Lady Etain who'd lost the shuddery feeling and gone to fully amused by the end of it. It flipped again when Anwyn said she could make thousands, which was true, and then mixed in with the sort of plotting that Anwyn was used to from Lady Etain.

"Somehow I doubt that," Lady Etain said. "I'm surprised that your mother's not out here."

"Eh, she has way too much to do with that Royal Council post," Anwyn said. She shrugged. "I'm not part of it. I'm so glad I'm not. I swear, Mother worked almost every hour of the day already. Now she's working into the night and making Father cranky about it."

Predictably, though Anwyn hadn't thought about it before she said it, mentioning the Royal Council made Lady Etain grit her teeth. She'd expected to get the post. It hung there in her mind like a present that she'd bought for herself that had been stolen and sold to another person who clearly didn't deserve it.

And maybe, probably, Lady Etain did think she'd bought the seat. That she'd bought the throne. Stupid of her. No reason at all for Siobhan to trust her after she had the throne. In fact, there was every reason for Siobhan to make sure Lady Etain had no power at all, especially given that they were a daughter threatened by death by her own mother.

"I'm so sad for her," Lady Etain said through her clenched teeth.

"Lie," Anwyn said and raised an eyebrow when Lady Etain frowned at her. "That didn't even reach sarcasm. You can try to lie to yourself on that if you want. Just know it isn't at all believable."

Lady Etain's jaw worked. She turned and stared out at the Dancing Wave which was moving fast and smooth over the waves now. She always was a beautiful ship on the sea. Small and sleek, good for long journeys where you stopped every port or two. The Dancing Wave didn't have the width at beam that the Tourmaline did but she was just as sturdy and twice as pretty in Anwyn's opinion.

"One wonders what your future ships will look like,"

Lady Etain said. Interesting. That angled towards what she'd come to talk about.

"Much like they do now," Anwyn said and then grinned at the ferocious glower Lady Etain turned on her. "Rae knows all about our ships. We've been sending girls in to study under Mistress Chie ever since Rae's turn. We've got a very good idea of what we want and we pay to get it. Mistress Chie trained her crew well. They know what to do. So our ships'll be much the same. Yours could be, too. You just have to pay for all the reinforcement we get."

That got Anwyn the most ferocious growl yet. Anwyn laughed at Lady Etain and shrugged because she'd only said the absolute truth. You got what you paid for when it came to ship construction. Skimp on the reinforcement and your ships didn't survive as long or come through big storms as well.

Or at all.

"So nothing changes," Lady Etain said with a dramatic wave towards the Dancing Wave that was pure misdirection.

Anwyn studied her and nodded slowly. "For us? Not much at all, no. I know you think this feud is a big, important thing. The biggest deal of all deals. For us, it's not. I never even really hated any of you. Well, Siobhan. Excuse me, Queen Siobhan. But that's because she's a bully and she's mean to boys, not because she's Delbhana. Most of us have no issues with you, personally. It's the feud that we object to. You punch, we punch back and on it goes."

For some damned reason, that was the most startling thing Lady Etain had ever heard. She turned to stare at Anwyn, mouth dropped open, as a flood of emotions washed through her. Surprise, horror, dismay, regret, fury, joy and relief and resignation. Because yeah, the feud wasn't going to end.

It couldn't. Not with Siobhan on the throne and so many people outside their clans invested in it. Maybe a generation ago it could've ended easily but now? Nope. Not going to happen. Until something really dramatic happened, like the Delbhana or the Dana all getting killed, it would go on.

"Nothing is going to change," Lady Etain said, this time with a tired little snort-laugh.

"Eh, at least we're standing here arm's length from each other and not screaming," Anwyn said so brightly that Lady Etain started laughing and shaking her head. "And not hitting. This? Just so you know? Is real progress for me. I'm enjoying the lack of broken noses and black eyes right now. So, you know, you can not punch me as much as you want."

"I'm tempted to punch you on pure principles," Lady Etain declared. While grinning at Anwyn.

"You wouldn't be the only one," Anwyn replied in her gloomiest voice.

Lady Etain belly-laughed. Then threw up her hands and walked back up the dock. With a nice little bounce in her step and a better outlook on life. Not so much panic, a good bit more rational thought. She was still worried about Siobhan and angry about the loss of power and downright furious not to be Councilor of Commerce.

But better. Anwyn hummed. She waited until the Dancing Wave sailed out of sight before heading back towards home with a similar bounce in her step. Time to pass the latest onto Mother and Rae.

Both of whom turned out to be meeting with Great-Uncle Jaron, Gavin and Mari over tea and those incredible little tea cakes that Uncle Athol made. Anwyn poked her head into the conference room alongside Great-Uncle Jarmon's office, grinned, and promptly plopped her butt into one of the chairs so that she could raid the tray of as many tea cakes as possible before Gavin stole the tray right out from under her hands.

She got eight of them before Gavin grabbed the tray.

"Annie!" Gavin snapped. "We're having a meeting."

"Very important meeting," Anwyn agreed as she arranged the tea cakes in perfect lines in front of her, two sets of four. She took a bite of the right, back one and hummed happily. "So good. Want the good news or the bad news first? Can I have some tea, too?'

"No, you cannot have--!" Gavin started to say only to squawk when Great-Uncle Jarmon took a cup and poured Anwyn tea. "Fine. Let her invade our strategy meeting. I see how this works."

Anwyn grinned at him, took a sip of her tea and bowed proper thanks to Great-Uncle Jarmon. "Well, seriously, you need the news if this is strategy instead of meeting tea cakes."

Raelin started snickering. "Just start talking, Annie. Let us get back to work."

"Okay, fine," Anwyn said. "So, the Dancing Wave is off on her way and very happy for it. Got a huge cheer out of the crew when Mistress Chie waved back to shore. Which was, important for you lot, witnessed by Lady Etain."

Every single one of the others stiffened. They glared when Anwyn beamed at them. Though Rae did frown at Anwyn, too, scanning her for injuries that weren't there.

"Was there a dock supervisor standing with you?" Raelin asked. "I don't see any bruises."

"Not one punch was thrown," Anwyn said.

And then chortled as Great-Uncle Jarmon scrambled for paper and Gavin started cursing while Mari whistled in amazement. She explained the whole encounter, eating her cakes and then two more before Gavin looked up from his notes long enough to realize what she was doing.

"Leave the cakes alone, Annie," Gavin scolded her. He waved his pen at her when she tried for puppy eyes. "I don't believe a bit of that. Get on with it."

"Right," Anwyn said. She refreshed her tea and then settled back into her chair. "Mother, Lady Etain's still furious that you have 'her' post. She truly believed that she'd get it and I don't think that she cares at all that you're Prince Toryn's choice. She'll keep coming at you. Great-Uncle Jarmon, the feud continues. Not with the same ferocity, of course, now that Siobhan is queen, but it will go on. Which means that you two," Anwyn pointed at Gavin and Mari, "need to be at your best every time you write to someone, go out, or do any deals. Everything you do is going to be watched and the spies are fully focused on the two of you now."

"Lovely." Gavin sighed. "And the good news because that has to be the bad."

"Right you are," Anwyn agreed. She drank her tea in three quick gulps, setting the cup down with a firm click that got Raelin sitting up straight. "The good news is that Lady Etain is... not on our side, necessarily, but not against us. Outside of Mother's position, she'll back us when it makes sense for her side to do so. There won't be the same opposition just to oppose us. Though I do still think that you guys need to get me out of Aingeal as much as possible."

Mother sighed and nodded. She stole five of the remaining cakes, smacking Anwyn's hand away from them. Anwyn's news wasn't news, so much, as it was confirmation of what Mother already suspected. Regret and gratitude welled up, surprising Anwyn because the regret was for how Anwyn had been treated all her life. Gratitude, of course, was that Anwyn was willing to use her gifts for the family.

"We'll be sending you off to Ntombi after the mission to Nasrin," Mother said. "You'll take one of the boys with you to handle the men's side of the negotiation."

"Ravi!" Anwyn immediately declared, getting a hoot of laughter from Rae and a grin from Gavin. "I mean, Gavin can't go. Andros is too young. The cousins are all busy and not high enough rank. Has to be Caddie or Ravi and no way am I putting Caddie on a ship for a year or more, round drip. He'll cut my throat in my sleep if I try it."

Mother laughed and nodded that Anwyn had a point. "Fine. Go let Aravel know. The Nasrin trip should only take a week so he'll have plenty of time to pack his things. Oh. Do tell him that he's not to buy every single scrap of yarn he can find on the trip. If he has to knit constantly, he can knit socks and lace. Those won't take up so much space."

Anwyn bounced to her feet, reached for another tea cake and the laughed when Gavin smacked her hand away. "I'm on it. Rae, you should head out, too. You're not much of a focus but people know how important you are. They'll get more focused if you stay too long."

Raelin nodded. "I know. I'm heading north to Atalya a couple of days after you leave for Ntombi. It should be fine. Scoot and tell Ravi that I want socks when he starts knitting them. Those nice thick ones with the multicolor patterns he knits that all but stand up on their own."

"Yes, ma'am!" Anwyn snapped a salute Rae's way and then ran when Raelin tossed her napkin at Anwyn.

She hummed as she headed upstairs to give Caddie and Ravi the good news. Pretty soon she'd be back at sea, heading off to work deals. That was so much better than home. Much as she loved Aingeal, much as she loved the

Dana Clanhouse, Anwyn was always much happier when she was away.

Until she couldn't sail any longer, Anwyn was going to be at sea. Better than dealing with Siobhan and her nonsense, that was certain.

26. COUNCIL MEETING

Raelin settled next to Gavin, making sure he was securely bracketed between her and Mother. It was unexpected, extremely so, that Gavin would attend the meeting. But Yvon had specifically asked for figures on the Dana finances and taxes. That was Gavin's domain so here they were, facing down the whole Royal Council, Queen Siobhan's glowers and King Toryn's welcoming smile.

Narrowed eyes matched with a welcoming smile. Raelin wasn't sure which was the real emotion. If Anwyn hadn't already shipped out to Nasrin, she would have suggested very strongly that Anwyn attend the meeting with them. As it was, Raelin would just have to pay attention and pass paperwork to Mother and Gavin as needed. She'd been brought along purely for an extra body at the table.

"I still don't think men should be part of these meetings," Siobhan said, eyes sliding sideways to King Toryn.

King Toryn shrugged. "None of this is official. He can attend. And I will be attending all of the interim Royal Council Meetings. I find them quite fascinating."

He outright sneered at Siobhan, saying without words that she didn't have the brains or the training to see what he found interesting. Raelin kept her face blank as she patted Gavin's trembling arm. It wasn't fear making him shake. Gavin glared at Siobhan like he wanted to knock her head off.

"Breathe," Raelin murmured to him.

Gavin exhaled hard, not quite a snort and definitely not a sigh, before nodding once.

"If Your Majesties are ready," Yvon said in a brusque tone that said it didn't matter whether they were or not, "let's begin. Laoise, I asked for tax data. Did you bring it?"

"Gavin did," Mother replied. She shrugged at Yvon's frown and Lady Mab's grumbled complaint. "Taxes and paperwork are men's work in the Dana. We're too busy doing the physical labor."

"You're all dumb laborers, then?" Siobhan smirked.

"Traders, deal makers and builders," Mother countered with a grim little smile of her own that made Siobhan's cheeks go red. "Just like your mother was when she was Rae's age. Haven't heard her making many deals since then, of course, not that it matters. It's hard work running a Clan. Know she had plenty too much to do raising you and running the Delbhana for making trades or building things."

Siobhan's mouth opened, then snapped shut as Lady Etain lofted a quiet 'thank you' from the very back row of the room. The Royal Council room was just as full as the last meeting, packed with quietly watching Clan heads. This time there were a fair smattering of heirs, too, all of them wide-eyed as they watched the byplay.

"We haven't time for that nonsense," Yvon said. Her glare went all to Siobhan, none at all to Mother. "Fine, then, did you bring the tax data we wanted, Dana Gavin?"

"Of course," Gavin said in that firm, calm voice that he used whenever he wanted to look extra competent. "Rae can pass the copies out to you."

So, of course, Raelin had to run around passing copies to every single councilor, Siobhan and King Toryn, who smiled and took it to study it closely. She passed the stacks back to the waiting Clan Heads after Gavin nodded that it was okay.

"The full details of our taxes are proprietary," Gavin said as he nodded to Yvon who looked outright pleased with the information. "However, this is the high-level summary of our various businesses. The Clan has several and the individual members own quite a few more businesses which are taxed separately."

"Ah, that's what I was wondering," Yvon said. She tapped the sheet and looked to Lady Mab, Lady Fiora and the other councilors. "Is this structure common for your clans as well? The multiple businesses under the Clan banner with others associated with individual members?"

"Yes," Lady Mab said. She raised her chin when Siobhan snorted. "It's been that way in the Griogal since before I was born. Always been a tax benefit to it."

"Agreed," Lady Ciana said. "Virtually every Clan, baring those like yours, Tierney Yvon, which are too small for such things."

"Untrue," Yvon replied. "We have ten separate businesses despite being so small."

"What does that matter?" Siobhan demanded. "So there are businesses in each clan. Why does that matter to the Royal Council? You're not here to waste your time."

Yvon rolled her eyes. The surprise of that nearly knocked Raelin off her chair. Next to her, Gavin choked and then pressed his fingers firmly against his lips to keep from smiling. Mother, somehow, managed not to change expression in the slightest.

"I'm assuming that there's a new regulation that would affect the Treasury?" King Toryn asked. His eyes were so dark with pleasure that it wasn't really a question. He already knew exactly what had caught Yvon's attention.

Yvon nodded very respectfully to him. "Regulation four, issued on the first day that Queen Siobhan took the throne, required all the clans to be taxed on their businesses. Which is in direct contradiction to how taxes were assessed previously. Taxes were assessed against income, against property, and most importantly, every single business was required to pay taxes regardless of whether it was owned by an individual or a Clan. The way the regulation was worded makes businesses that are owned by individuals untaxable. We would, by my projections, lose approximately two-thirds of the annual tax income."

Shouting erupted instantly. Raelin shouted, too, mostly from the shock of that. She didn't expect an answer. As voices thundered around her, Raelin sank back into her chair to watch Yvon who pursed her lips in annoyance. And King Toryn who smirked at Siobhan.

"That's not what I said!" Siobhan bellowed loudly enough to cut everyone in the room off. The silence that fell echoed. Siobhan stood and glared at Yvon. "I didn't say that."

"The way the regulation is written," Yvon said as she held up a sheet of paper, "it specifies only Clan businesses. No other businesses are mentioned or even implied. If you wanted to confirm the old method of taxation with a higher or lower rate, then this will need to be completely reworked."

Siobhan stomped over, snatched the regulation out of

Yvon's hand, and scanned it. By the end of reading it, her face was purple-red. Her hands shook. She was breathing far too hard as she threw the sheet of paper back into Yvon's face. Then Siobhan stomped out of the Council room, slamming the door behind her.

"Hmm," King Toryn commented so mildly that Gavin smacked his hand over his mouth again, "I do wonder whether this will be a trend. That's the second time she's stomped off before a meeting was done."

Yvon grinned at him. "Quite so, Your Majesty. Now then. On to the real matters we need to address."

Raelin stared at her. Stared at King Toryn for long enough that he noticed and raised an eyebrow in her direction while smirking right at her. Laughter bubbled up so abruptly that Raelin spluttered and had to wave a hand when people glanced her way.

He'd planned this. King Toryn had set it all up so that Siobhan would be too enraged to actually rule Aingeal. Or, perhaps, he'd put the people he thought were best suited to make sure that she was infuriated in place and hoped for the best.

Either way, he'd brilliantly laid out his chess pieces and played his hand. Circumstances had trapped him in a largely ceremonial post but perhaps, if they all supported him and hampered Siobhan, King Toryn could keep Aingeal from falling apart.

She sat and listened as Mother and the other Councilors discussed the various revisions to the regulations Siobhan had issued. Every single one of them was voted to go forward to the Clan Heads in a form that neatly hamstrung Siobhan's intentions. It wouldn't give them what they wanted, freedom from Siobhan's demands, but it wouldn't give Siobhan what she wanted, either.

Good enough.

By the end of the meeting, King Toryn looked deeply satisfied with them all in his quietly determined sort of way. Gavin chattered with Mother as they gathered up the paperwork and notes. Around them, the Clan Heads were arguing about the regulations that had been recommended to pass the Council. From the sound of it, they were going to tear them apart a third time, bounce them back to the Royal Council and start what Raelin hoped was an endless cycle of revisions, comments and debate.

"You look pleased," King Toryn commented right at Raelin's elbow.

Raelin started and then bowed to him. "I am, Your Majesty. Good to see people taking all this ruling stuff seriously. I kind of didn't expect Mother to take to it but she's handling it well so far."

"They are doing well," King Toryn agreed. His smile was maliciously contented, so much so that Raelin grinned at him.

The room was emptying rapidly. Lady Mab stomped off, her cane thumping against the floor like she wanted to shove it straight through Siobhan's chest. Lady Fiora nodded to Mother while arguing animatedly with Yvon about the next set of regulations they'd be dealing with, well after Raelin was back on the sea.

"You're doing well," Raelin murmured. She shrugged when he frowned at her. "In a bad place. We all know that. But you're doing well with it."

"If this is your attempt to seduce me..." King Toryn started to say only to trail off when Raelin stared at him, aghast. "It's not."

"No," Raelin said. She shuddered. "I'm sorry, it's not that I don't respect you, your Majesty. It's just that I've never actually been in love with anyone. Or felt any need for sex. It makes no sense whatsoever to me. Seduction is something that I leave to Gwen. Seems as natural as breathing to her."

"You've... never been in love," King Toryn whispered. The idea seemed to stun him. He shook his head. "I thought I was the only one."

"Eh, no, there's a few like me that I know," Raelin said. "Not a common thing. Just something that happens sometimes. Though, frankly, with your wife? Not surprised."

King Toryn's jaw dropped open. He spluttered and then laughed, a delightful low chuckle that took him from too-serious and angry into delighted and just a little older than Raelin. She'd forgotten that he was her age, almost. Twenty to her nineteen. He always seemed so much older, every time she'd seen him.

"Thank you for that," King Toryn said with a huge grin. "I should be going, of course. She'll get angry if I don't dance attendance on her."

"Ick," Raelin said. "Good luck with that, then, your Majesty. Probably won't be at the next meeting. I'm headed back to sea, off to Atalya and parts north for a good two or three years. Be careful. And really? This was well done."

He nodded, perfectly controlled once more as he swept from the room. It was only Lady Etain, Mother, Gavin and Raelin left. Lady Etain glowered at Raelin and then snarled when Raelin shrugged.

"Don't deny it," Raelin told Lady Etain. "He's doing an amazing job managing Siobhan. Better than anyone else ever has. He's earned a bit of praise in his life."

Lady Etain winced. "I don't deny it. It's good you're leaving though. Siobhan is... jealous."

"Yeah, let's go home, Rae," Mother said. She patted Raelin's good shoulder in the way that always meant Raelin had missed something painfully obvious. "We've got to get your butt on a ship as soon as possible. Tomorrow, maybe."

"Soonest we can manage it is the day after tomorrow," Gavin said.

His look at Raelin was so fondly exasperated that Raelin held up her hands to Lady Etain, pointing at Mother and Gavin's backs to ask what she'd missed. Lady Etain shook her head and walked on past, muttering something about idiots.

"What?" Raelin asked. "Mother, what in the name of the Tripartate Goddesses am I missing? Gavin!"

Neither of them answered.

So, Raelin trailed along behind them, spluttering as she tried to see what, exactly, in her little conversation with King Toryn might be a problem. She didn't understand. She'd just told him he was doing well and, what? What had she said wrong?

There didn't seem to be an answer. No matter how ferociously Raelin demanded it. Maybe it didn't matter. She'd be back on the Tourmaline Dreams soon, back at sea. They'd sail back north to Atalya and Raelin would see how Sinead was doing.

That was more important than whatever it was she'd done with King Toryn. Nothing was as important as the Tourmaline Dreams. It was, after all, Raelin's future and her greatest joy. And if there was something she needed to figure out with King Toryn, well, Raelin would ask Bahb and then Sinead when Raelin saw her.

The most important thing was that Aingeal looked like it was in good hands while Raelin was gone. At one time, Raelin would've said that Aingeal could burn to the ground, other than the Dana Clanhouse. Not anymore. Maybe that was part of growing up. Maybe it was King Toryn himself.

Didn't matter. She'd be home on the Tourmaline soon and everything would be fine here. Come what may, Raelin's place was on the sea for as long as she could keep on sailing.

THE END

AUTHOR'S NOTE: FIGHTING THE MORRIGAN'S HAND

The plots that Raelin and Anwyn dealt with in this book are only the latest round of trouble the Delbhana have given them. Not that it only affects them personally, or the Dana Clan. Oh no, the Delbhana's plots extend across the entirety of Muirin and hit in all sorts of strange places in unexpected ways.

Including in Chinwendu, where Raelin's twin brother Aravel had to face down a battle against one of the Delbhana's worst with nothing but knitting, manners and a quick wit to protect him. Fighting the Morrigan's Hand takes place not too long before Fortune and Circumstance. The events in it are fresh in everyone's mind so I thought you'd enjoy a sample of the story.

Hope you enjoy!

1. COMING ASHORE

Aravel stood at the bow of the *Harmonious Song*, clinging to the railing. Two tug boats, six women in each, rowed hard as they pulled the *Song* into its berth. They ignored him. So did the *Song's* sailors. Even Captain Bryna paid him no mind. She was too busy shouting orders to reef the sails and get the *Song* ready to tie up.

Which was fine by Aravel. The twin cities of Yuzuki and Masumi on either side of the Strait of Rio were far more interesting than the work the women around him did to secure the *Harmonious Song*. Yuzuki City in Amadi was on the flat side of the Strait. Its buildings were low and broad, built on stilts that put the houses ten to twenty feet above the muddy ground with heavy roofs that reminded him of Idoya. Not surprising, really. They got much the same weather as Idoya, rain, more rain and still more rain with a brief dry season in the depths of winter where they got biting cold.

Masumi City on the right was on the steep hills of Chinwendu. The flat land of Yuzuki's flood plain gave way to hills and then cliffs and then mountains behind that.

The rain that put Yuzuki's streets under water half the time came from Masumi City's hills wringing the clouds dry before they wended their way into dry central Chinwendu where spider silk was harvested and woven into beautiful cloth.

Where Yuzuki City was built on stilts, Masumi City's building foundations were dug deep into the hillsides with deep gullies for gutters and more stairs than streets. Aravel closed his eyes and breathed deep. The smell of salt and sewage had faded the further up the Strait they went. Now the air smelled of rain and fragrant wood fires.

"Ravi!"

Aunt Colleen's shout startled Aravel. He turned and then sighed at Aunt Colleen's glower. Really, you'd think he was a baby the way she fussed over him. Every single port so far Aunt Collen had all but held his hand to keep him from exploring or talking to people. Aravel was fifteen and more than mature enough to handle handsy sailors, rude foreigners and the occasional fist-fight when someone didn't respect his no's. Either the laughing or the arch ones. The women who didn't take a no got a fist to the face and that always ended the problem.

"Yes, Aunt Colleen?" Ravi called back only to finch as her glare went five times as intense.

He sighed and trotted over, causally avoiding sailors, lines and the billowing sails as they were pulled up and reefed. Really, from the way she frowned you would have thought that it was his first time at sea. She caught his elbow and gave him a little shake.

"I thought I told you to stay in your cabin," Aunt Colleen snapped at him.

"And I thought you understood which of us has higher rank in the family and on this ship," Aravel snapped right back at her. "Aunt Colleen, no matter how good you are at the paperwork, and yes, you're amazing, I still outrank you. Mother said so. So did Uncle Jarmon. There's a reason I'm on this mission and you are not going to keep me from fulfilling it."

Her jaw clenched as her eyes went far too angry that he dared to reprimand her publicly. But really, she brought that on herself. She could have insisted on a private conversation. Oh no, let's scold the boy for daring to know his place.

"Mission," Aunt Colleen said so flatly that she called him a liar by implication. "You."

"Of course," Aravel said, smiling the 'you're Delbhana and I loathe you' smile that had gotten him in trouble a few dozen times before back home. And which might still get him slapped if he wasn't careful. "I'm to visit our relatives here and make sure that we still have allies here. Great-Uncle Jarmon has... worries... about things back home. And given the way Chinwendu politics work, it has to be me, not you. Rank, you know. You're not line direct. I'm the only one who is on the *Harmonious Song.*"

The anger transmuted into surprise and then worry. Aunt Colleen bit her lip and glanced over at Captain Bryna who had gone pale. Aravel watched them and then sighed. Lovely. Mother or Father or maybe Gavin had been meddlers and decided that he needed to be 'protected'. If it was Father then they'd been ordered to 'shelter' him from anything dangerous on the trip. Gavin would have just outright told them to keep Aravel from fathering any children along the way.

"Who?" Aravel asked. They both looked away and then blushed when he put his hands on his hips. "Who? Come now. You've gotten orders. Who from and what are the orders? I can't do my job if you're working against me."

"Laoise told me to keep you safe," Aunt Colleen said so

grudgingly that Aravel wondered if she'd started the journey with bruises from a fist fight between the two of them.

"Your brother Gavin instructed me to ensure that the crew treated you with all respect," Captain Bryna said a moment later, her ears bright red from the force of her blush. Given that he'd spent most of the trip 'entertaining' her instead of the crew Aravel supposed that she'd fulfilled that instruction quite well despite not following the intent of it.

"Well, you're fine," Aravel said to Captain Bryna with an airy little wave of his hand that made her snort a laugh. "I approve of your methodology there. You," he wagged a finger at Aunt Colleen, "are leaving things out. There are ways to keep a man safe that don't involve treating him like a toddler. Besides, you know I can hit as hard as you can."

That got him a grin from Captain Bryna while Aunt Colleen glowered at him. Ah. So she had left things out. Not that it really mattered, not with the gangplank going down and a group of Chinwenduese officials waiting at the end of the dock for them. Aravel bounced on his toes, kilts swishing around his ankles.

"We'll talk about this later," Aravel told Aunt Colleen. "Let's go say hello and do remember, this is primarily a family visit, not a business trip."

"We always do business in port," Aunt Colleen said, glaring at him.

"Of course we do," Aravel said and if he used his breeziest, most air-headed tone of voice, well, she'd brought that on himself with her attitude this trip. Months of this nonsense were long enough. "But that's not the point. That's just what Dana do along with breathing and getting into fights."

Finally, he got a bellowed laugh out of Aunt Collen.

Plus a huge grin from Captain Bryna that promptly relaxed the sailors quite a bit. Good. The two of them really did need to calm down. This wasn't that big of a deal. Aravel had been here a half dozen times before. He knew how to talk to his relatives and to the officials in Chinwendu.

He made sure that Aunt Colleen took the lead down the gangplank. She was older and female so that was appropriate. Captain Bryna stayed on board as was proper here. As soon as they were within three yards of the officials, Aunt Colleen stopped and let Aravel go first.

Dock Mistress with two attendants, one male and one non-gendered, both with clipboards and pens at the ready. They all wore the red and black of Great-Grandfather's clan so that made things easier. Aravel could address them as relatives rather than as strangers. The only fillip in the whole thing was the relative age differences between Aravel and the Dock Mistress.

She frowned at Aravel, trying to read his rank in his Dana blue plaid kilt, lack of petticoats and light shirt under a simple Dana blue vest. Every single thing he wore shouted a lack of respect for his family's power but he was on the other side of the world so he didn't have to hobble himself with petticoats and yards of lace if he didn't want to.

Aravel grinned and carefully pulled out the little insignia Great-Uncle Jarmon had given him, attaching it to his vest pocket. It was shaped like a pentagram divided in half. One half, the top, held the Dana triple-swirl done in lapis lazuli and gold. The bottom half held the Tamura family seal, a trio of hand scythes arranged in a bouquet effect, tied with rice straw where the handles crossed. That was done in onyx and silver, making the little insignia a beautiful but very pricy object.

The Dock Mistress let out a tiny sigh of relief,

nodding once nearly imperceptibly to Aravel. He nodded back, trying not to smile too broadly. Knowing what rank you held relative to another person was so desperately important in Chinwendu. They bowed at once, Aravel going slightly higher than the Dock Mistress who held the bow half a second longer than he did. Her attendants bowed far more deeply and held it until the Dock Mistress signaled them to stand up with a flick of her fingertips. Hopefully Aunt Colleen could manage herself. Aravel had to trust that she could. She'd taken up a post too far behind him for him to see if she was bowing properly.

"I wish you greetings, cousin of the Dana Family line of Aingeal of Aingeal City," the Dock Mistress said. "I am Damura Kamiko, Dock Mistress of the Trade Docks of Masumi City of Chinwendu, fourth daughter of the third son of the lady of the Damura."

"I thank you for your greetings, elder cousin Tamura Kamiko," Aravel replied. "I am Dana Aravel of the line direct of the Dana Family of Aingeal of Aingeal City, second son of the first daughter of the first daughter of the Dana Clan. This is Dana Colleen, my Grandmother's fourth daughter's second daughter who will be handling the trade and paperwork for Minoo while we are here. I would visit with our relatives at the bequest of my Great-Uncle Jarmon who was first son of Tamura Tau, who married my Great-Grandmother Anwyn and founded our Clan with her in Aingeal."

Kamiko's eyes went wide. She licked her lips and bowed very slightly, conveying her worry quite well without saying a word. Aravel pressed his lips together and let his eyes smile just as much as they wanted to while bowing back just a bit deeper to say that yes, of course she could ask.

"One would hope that the visit is not formal," Kamiko said.

"One would be quite right to worry about that," Aravel replied so brightly that Aunt Colleen snorted behind him and the two attendants shut their eyes and pressed their lips together so that they wouldn't visibly show amusement beyond what was appropriate to their rank. "If the visitor were of greater age. A visit of one below the age of maturity is, of course, never a matter of great formality. And this one," he gestured towards himself with a bright grin that made Kamiko swallow a laugh, "is not yet of age in either Chinwendu or Aingeal. Thus all formalness is avoided and pleasantness can abound for all."

That did get a laugh, not just from Kamiko but from a passing sailor who'd naturally eavesdropped on the conversation while carefully not meeting anyone's eyes. And from the Harbor Mistress, a stern eighty-some year old woman who was broad of shoulder, narrow of hip and flat of bust as most Chinwenduese chosen-women were. She shook her head, coming over to stare at first Aravel's insignia and then at his face for a long moment.

"It has been long since the Dana have sent a formal representative to the port," the Harbor Mistress said to Kamiko but she was really talking to Aravel.

Introductions would be required if they were to speak directly and since she was wearing green and brown, that would mean going through the whole rigmarole of determining exactly where the Dana ranked in Chinwenduese politics today. Versus yesterday or tomorrow or last year. Not worth the bother for anyone, honestly.

Kamiko hummed and nodded, staring thoughtfully into the distance while rocking on her heels. "One forgets how old the eldest son of Damura Tao is now."

"One could be very well excused for that," Aravel said as

if talking to the air while Aunt Colleen smothered a laugh in her fist. "Because Dana Jarmon, eldest son, has never admitted to being older than fifty-five even though he has seen seventy-nine summers."

That made both Kamiko and the Harbor Mistress splutter laughs as they pretended not to hear him. Kamiko nodded sagely, eyes sparkling with laughter before she managed to regain a properly formal expression.

"Age does tend to make long travel uncomfortable," Kamiko said as if offering a bit of wisdom from the ages.

"Quite so, quite so," the Harbor Mistress agreed.

She rubbed her back and then chuckled before bowing slightly towards Kamiko and then strolling on up the dock as if she'd merely stopped on her way to her destination. Nicely done, that. It allowed her to both find out what was going on and to leave quickly and efficiently instead of dealing with all the introductions, greetings and goodbyes required between non-family members.

Kamiko snorted, eyes a little hard as she stared at the Harbor Mistress' back. Hmm, perhaps more than just nosiness, then. "Will an escort be needed, eudi-Dana Aravel-duai?"

"Yes, I believe that would be appropriate, aeji-Tamura Kimiko-chu," Aravel replied. He shrugged at her frown. "Orders were given that I was to be kept 'safe'. As euji-Dana Colleen-chu has work here and the Captain and sailors have no link to any Chinwendu families, well, an escort would be necessary. Perhaps one of your attendants can run back and send a message? There is little need to rush. We should be in port for, oh, a time, I believe."

Kamiko looked over Aravel's shoulder to Aunt Colleen who gave him a hard look.

"We should be here for at least two weeks, twenty days, euji-Tamura Kimiko-chai," Aunt Collen said, giving

Kimiko the higher rank, unlike Aravel. He could get away with that because of his place in the bloodline. Her lower place in their genealogy meant she had to be properly polite and designate Kimiko as a younger woman with higher rank.

"Ah, my thanks, aeji-Dana Colleen-chu," Kimiko replied. "Our report will state as much. Eudi-Dana Aravel-duai, do please inform me or my staff if your visit will extend longer than that. It will influence the visas for your ship and crew."

"I will, aeji-Tamura Kimiko-chu, I promise," Aravel said with a flirty little bow that made her snort and her attendants grin. The neuter one raised a hand to keep from laughing out loud.

After that, it was a simple thing to get their visas for Captain Bryna and the crew. They were, after all, just slips of paper with the name of the individual, their rank on the ship and the duration of the ship's stay in port, meant to be kept in a pocket until needed for reference. So much easier than visiting Minoo with all their oppressive paperwork.

Of course, Aunt Colleen had to get the numbers of each visa, the names of Kimiko and her staff, and the exact date for the Minoo paperwork she would have to turn in on their way home but that was why she was there.

While she was at all of that, head together with Kimiko, the neuter attendant ran back up the dock and spoke to a young child who'd not yet chosen their gender. That child ran off into the city so his escort could come and collect him. Probably not what Aunt Colleen would want but she really did have a great many responsibilities with the ship and this was Aravel's task, not hers.

Only someone in the line direct from Tamura Tao could do this.

He rather hoped that Kimiko never found out that he'd

lied to her. There was so much more that he needed to accomplish than a simple informal visit. Great-Uncle Jarmon had been very firm about what Aravel had to do while they were in Masumi City. He even had a list of questions, long since memorized, that he needed to answer.

First and foremost, could the Dana relocate out of Aingeal to Chinwendu without losing their fortune and their ships to the regulations of the Chinwenduese government?

Because with the way things were going in Aingeal, there was every likelihood that they would be driven out in the next ten years.

2. CONFLICTING MANDATES

Watching Ravi walk away, blithely chatting with the little neuter the Tamura had sent to escort him, had made Colleen's teeth ache. Her jaw, too. Damn them, didn't they understand how important Aravel was? To send just a child, barely twelve, to walk him through the streets was an insult. It was almost a threat, not that Aravel seemed aware of it.

No, that boy was perfectly happy to take every scrap of freedom he could beg, bargain for or steal and then run with it. Laoise was going to break her neck if something happened to Ravi. She'd damned near done it before they left port back home.

"Breathe," Captain Bryna murmured. "The Harbor Mistress is coming our way. You don't want to give her cause to search us."

Colleen breathed, slow and deliberate, as she continued to mark off barrels as they were unloaded from the *Harmonious Song.* She watched the Harbor Mistress form the corner of her eye and yes, that was a woman who'd take anything she could get. You would have thought she was

Delbhana from the rolling, confident strut up the dock. That smirk was a dead ringer for... a Delbhana smirk.

Huh.

After this little encounter was over, Colleen was going to have to ask a few questions. Maybe grease a couple of palms. The Delbhana were working quite hard to steal the Dana markets from them. It would make sense for them to come after Chinwendu. Their cheap silk from other parts of the world wasn't ever going to compare to the real thing from Chinwendu and the Dana imported the best of the best. Everyone in Aingeal knew it.

Undercutting their position in Chinwendu by allying with one of the families here would do a lot for making that possible.

If, of course, the Delbhana allies managed to combine Delbhana bluff and plotting with Chinwendu politeness and politics. Colleen didn't think it was possible but who knew? Maybe the Delbhana had a genius hidden away somewhere who could do it.

And the Ladies might rise up out of the Strait to carry them all back to the Morrigan's arms where they'd all live in perfect peace and happiness.

Colleen snorted and then shook her head at Captain Bryna's curious look. "Sometimes my mind runs in circles."

"Everyone's does," Captain Byrna replied before switching to a low murmur. "She's definitely coming our way. Ito Aina, one of the Tamura's least favorite people. Watched her pretend not to interrogate Ravi before he left. She's a sly one."

"Reminds me of Lady Etain, actually," Colleen murmured back. "Too much confidence, not enough intelligence and flexibility to back it up."

Before Ito Aina had even introduced herself, she snapped her fingers at Colleen. Then pointed at the clipboard Colleen was using. Colleen stared back, making no move to pass the clipboard over.

"Papers," Aina demanded.

"You are?" Colleen asked in a similarly hostile though not quite so belligerent tone.

Aina's lips went thin as she glared. "Harbor Mistress. I require your paperwork, sailor."

"I am not a sailor," Colleen said, ignoring the out-thrust hand Aina pushed at her. "I am Dana Colleen, second daughter of the fourth daughter of the Dana Clan. I speak with for the leader of our clan Dana Laoise. You are?"

Speaking for Laoise gave Colleen higher rank that a mere Harbor Mistress and the truth of that made Aina's cheeks go blazingly red. She kept on glaring, kept her hand out as if just demanding the clipboard was going to work. So Colleen stared right back, trusting that eventually the sheer awkwardness of Aina breaking all the Chinwendu social protocols was going to take its toll on her.

"All foreign sailors are required to submit to inspection of their paperwork," Aina finally snarled. "Papers. Now."

Colleen shrugged, tucked the clipboard under her armpit, and then pulled out the Minoo paperwork that identified her as a member of the Dana Clan. Tucked into that little packet of seals and careful initials marked with double-checked dates was the single sheet that identified her as far as the Chinwendu government was concerned. If only the Minoo would be satisfied by something that simple.

"Here," Colleen said, passing the Chinwendu ID over. "My paperwork."

"The rest?" Aina said without looking at Colleen. When nothing happened her eyes snapped up to Colleen's face. "You risk arrest."

"No, I don't," Colleen replied with a little laugh despite

the fact that every single sailor in the area, every official, ever dock worker had stopped to watch their confrontation. "Minoo law requires that I do not ever pass that identification over to another person. You are breaking the law. In several ways. As well as being shockingly rude. I still do not know your name and rank, *Harbor Mistress.*"

The derisive tone that Colleen put on 'Harbor Mistress' made Aina's breath hiss between her teeth. Not that Colleen was wrong. She wasn't. Aina was completely in the wrong in this encounter and everyone knew it.

Strangely, it felt so much like being back at home on the dock by the Dana Clanhouse that Colleen almost expected to turn around and see Laoise strolling up the dock to see what the fuss was.

Probably closely followed by a Delbhana woman intent on making the trouble that much worse.

"I am Ito Aina, Harbor Mistress for Masumi City," Aina snarled at her. "I require all your papers and that clipboard be turned over to me. Now."

"On what authority?" Colleen asked.

She made sure that her voice projected. In a port, surrounded by water, that was an easy thing to accomplish. With the deeper tone Colleen had used, her voice boomed, drawing looks from everyone, even people up on the shore.

This area of the port went so quiet that Colleen could hear the crabs clicking their claws underneath the dock as they ate algae off the pylons. Aina's chin came up but her lips were too tight, too white, for her to be as confident as she was pretending to be. Her fingertips trembled, too. Colleen breathed slowly and caught the scent of fear-sweat coming off Aina.

Oh yes, this felt just like home.

Damn it.

"I am--"

"A Harbor Mistress does not have the unilateral authority to seize a sailor's papers unless they are guilty of the commission of a crime." Colleen cut Aina off before she could start spouting nonsense about her authority as the Harbor Mistress. She made sure to use the same booming tone of voice. "Guilty of a crime, not suspected of one. You are not the law, Ito Aina. You are not one of the Guard, charged with apprehending suspected criminals. You are not a Judge, assigned with the responsibility of determining guilt or innocence. And you most certainly are not a ruler, responsible for determining the fate of the guilty. You are a Harbor Mistress and you do not have the authority to take my papers or anyone else's!"

Colleen shouted the last bit while snatching her Chinwendu ID back from Aina.

Who gaped and backed off a step while going pale. Her hands came up to make the bow of extreme apology but then snapped back down to her sides as if someone had just poked her in the side with a very sharp knife.

"This is not over," Aina hissed, low and quiet so that her voice wouldn't carry.

"Excuse me," Colleen replied, loud and proud and glaring for all she was worth, "could you repeat that? I didn't hear you. Harbor Mistress."

The flinch was worth every bit of the snarl Aina gave her. Aina stomped up the dock, pushing past the dock workers who'd stood frozen through the entire confrontation. Strangely, she didn't accost anyone else. Not a single sailor or dock worker, not even the obvious foreigner from Ntombi with her ink-black skin and thick dreadlocks spiking off her head.

"Targeted," Colleen murmured to Captain Byrna.

"Oh yes," Captain Byrna agreed as she waved everyone

back to work. "Very much so. I find myself very curious what sort of gossip we'll get this evening in the taverns and bars."

"Me, too."

Not even eight months ago, Colleen's last visit to Masumi City had been a marvel of politeness and manners. She hadn't spoken to the Harbor Mistress but Colleen was fairly certain that Ito Aina wasn't the one who'd had that job before.

Something had changed. Something very major had changed. And she needed to find out what it was.

Unfortunately, Colleen also needed to keep Ravi safe if she wanted to keep from getting thrashing at Laoise's hands when they got home. Damn it. She should have fought Ravi about splitting up. If anything, she should be the one going up to Tamura Manor to talk to everyone there, not Ravi. He was just fifteen.

But then he couldn't do the paperwork that was her personal responsibility and Ravi apparently had a mission of his own.

Next time she shipped out she was going to insist on a sit-down meeting with everyone involved so that they could get all their stories straight before they left port. Since she hadn't gotten that, she'd have to sit Ravi's butt down and have him tell her what he was up to, too. Bring Captain Byrna in on it, get everything out in the open.

Yes, that's what she'd do.

Once she had all their cargo off-loaded. And then all the paperwork for Chinwendu filled out. Oh, and then submitted to Ito Aina who would poke every single hole she could in it just for sheer irritation's sake at this point.

So maybe tomorrow. Probably tomorrow, given Colleen's luck.

Damn it all.

She shook her head and focused back on what she had to do. Just like always. Take care of the little details and the big picture took care of itself. No matter what, Colleen would have to account for every single barrel and bale of silk to the Minoo authorities. Not to mention to Great-Uncle Jarmon.

So she'd get this done, all of it accurate as Colleen could make it. And then she'd fight her way through Ito Aina's obvious agenda. Fortunately, Colleen could read Chinwenduese as easily as Aingealese so there was no way for Aina to trip her up on misquoted law and regulation.

Yeah, she'd cope with this. But then she was nailing Ravi's twinkling toes down so that she could find out exactly what was going on. Only once she knew could she take steps to keep the situation from getting worse. And right now it looked like Ravi was the one who had all the real information.

He'd share it or so help her she was going to spank his bottom.

FIGHTING the Morrigan's Hand is now available at all major retailers in ebook and TPB format.

OTHER MATRIARCHIES OF MUIRIN STORIES:

In Reading Order:

The City of the Ladies
Fight Smarter
Hide and Seek
Stormy Arrival
Repair and Rebuild
Storm Over Archaelaos
Facing the Storm
Tea and Knives
Luck of the Dana
Homecoming
Delicate Introduction
Following the Beacon
Coming Together
The Solace of Her Clan
Running Before the Storm
Fighting the Morrigan's Hand
The Silk of the Guardian
Secrets in the Prayers

Fitting In

You can find these and many other books at www.MDR-Publishing.com. We are a small independent publisher focusing on LGBT content. Please sign up for our mailing list to get regular updates on the latest preorders and new releases and a free ebook!

AFTERWORD

Muirin remains one of my all-time favorite worlds to write in. There's so much complexity, so much history and culture that I want to get into the stories. I never feel like I've gotten enough onto the page. But that's part of why I keep writing--to get skilled enough that I can tell the stories I want the way I want to.

This one was a challenge for more than just the skill level reason. There are huge events coming for the Dana, especially for Raelin and Anwyn, and I absolutely had to tell this story to be able to get to the rest. As challenging as it was to write this, I'm happy with hout it turned out. Hopefully you enjoyed this one, too.

If you want more stories like these, please go sign up for my newsletter on www.MDR-Publishing.com. You'll get updates on whatever I've got coming up, special deals and you can get a free ebook or collection of my short stories. Or you can sign up at my Patreon and get even more amazing deals on my writing.

Thank you for reading!

Meyari McFarland
August, 2019
www.MDR-Publishing.com

AUTHOR BIO

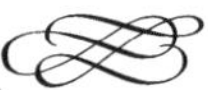

Meyari McFarland has been telling stories since she was a small child. Her stories range from adventures appropriate to children to erotica but they always feature strong characters who do what they think is right no matter what gets in their way.

Meyari has been married for twenty years and has no children or pets. She lives in the Puget Sound, WA and enjoys the fog, rain and cool weather that are typical here. When vacation times come, she and her husband usually go somewhere warm like Hawaii or they go on their own adventures to Japan and other far away countries.

Her life has included jobs ranging from cleaning motel rooms, food service, receptionist, building and editing digital maps, auditing and document control.

More from Meyari McFarland

Website:

. . .

www.MDR-Publishing.com

Social Media:

Facebook - https://www.facebook.com/meyari.mcfarland.5

Instagram - https://www.instagram.com/meyarimcfarland/

Twitter - https:// https://twitter.com/McMeyari

Pinterest - https://www.pinterest.com/meyarim/

Patreon - https://www.patreon.com/meyarimcfarland

If you enjoyed this story, please leave a comment on your favorite site. Also, please sign up for the newsletter so that you can hear about the latest preorders and new releases.